Change Her Mind

A Novel

Madeleine Mills

One

Every eye in the room turned to me. I stared straight ahead and tried to look unaffected, as though the psychiatrist was discussing some unfortunate stranger who had found her younger sister in bed with her fiancé.

"After Sophie walked in on Chloe and Nathan, there was an argument," continued Dr. Edwards. "Sophie told Chloe that she would never forgive her. Chloe stated that this fight was one of the triggers for her suicide attempt."

Silence fell in the conference room. Even the lawyers stopped tapping on their laptops. Aside from the Capacity Board adjudicators, everyone at the hearing had heard the story in advance, so this should not have been a surprise. But it still felt as though the room was holding its breath, watching to see how I would react.

I wished I hadn't come to this hearing, but Chloe had begged. She was desperate to get out of the psychiatry ward, but her psychiatrist thought she was still unfit to leave, so she had exercised her right to a Board hearing to settle the issue. Chloe thought that if the Capacity Board saw that I was willing to give her another chance, they might too. The problem was, I wasn't sure that I could forgive her.

Finally Dr. Edwards carried on. "After the fight with her sister, Chloe went home and took an overdose of quetiapine, which had been prescribed to help her sleep. She called 911 herself shortly after, and was brought to the hospital by ambulance. After a period of observation in the ER, the psychiatrist on call diagnosed her with bipolar mania. She was transferred to the psychiatry ward, where she has been for the past month. She has not consented to psychiatric treatment, but we have deemed her incapable of decision-making, and her parents have consented on her behalf."

He paused and flipped some papers in the binder in front of him. I was surprised that Chloe's lawyer hadn't interrupted to ask questions. I would have had several, including how much quetiapine Chloe had taken and whether she had needed any specific treatment for the overdose. Was it a serious attempt to end her life, or just a cry for attention? Based on my knowledge of my sister, I suspected it had been an attempt to distract from her recent behaviour.

I scribbled some notes. I started with 'Overdose – monitoring, treatment?, then 'attention seeking?' Dr. Edwards had a monotonous voice, and I started to doodle to help myself stay awake. I covered the left side of the page with a column of tulips, then the top with a row of hearts.

My pen ran out of ink. "Excuse me," I whispered to the man sitting next to me. He was one of my parents' lawyers; they had introduced him as Jack Delacroix. He looked up from his laptop with irritation.

"Can I borrow a pen?" I asked.

Jack glanced down at my page of notes and the corner of his mouth kicked up. He reached into his briefcase and handed me a ballpoint.

I smiled at him, but he had already turned back to his laptop. I put him at only a few years older than me, most likely early thirties, but he had a confidence that I envied and I doubted I would ever have. His looks probably helped with that, as he was one of the best looking men I had seen in my life.

Dr. Edwards continued. "Chloe has been treated with lithium, along with intensive psychotherapy. Unfortunately her progress has been slow. We learned that during the first week she was on lithium she was flushing it down the toilet, and she now receives her medications under direct supervision. She has been spreading delusions amongst some of the other clients.

For example, she told several clients that she was a long lost Russian princess, and convinced one young woman to act as her servant."

I wrote down 'CLIENTS' in big capital letters. This was in no way relevant to my sister's situation, but I found it amusing. In every other field, doctors called the people they treated 'patients'; only psychiatrists called them 'clients'. They liked to perpetuate the myth that people sought their services by choice, when the reality was that many patients were in hospital against their will.

"Chloe has told other clients that the food in the hospital is poisoned, and she frequently refuses to eat the meals."

My sister had never been delusional before. I thought it was far more likely that she was entertaining herself with one of the few means available to her in the hospital.

"She has been unwilling to engage in group therapy, and frequently performs stretching and ballet exercises through the therapy sessions. We are concerned that she has lost a significant amount of weight while in hospital. In addition, for the past week she has been consuming excessive quantities of water. We have tried to limit her access to fluids and only allow water at mealtimes, but she has found ways to get plastic cups from other clients, which she then refills at the bathroom sink. We are planning to involve the Eating Disorders team."

As though to illustrate this point, Chloe took a long sip from the large Styrofoam water jug in front of her. Her name was written in blue pen on the side of the cup, with a heart in place of the 'O'. Her fingernails were bitten ragged; her hands did not look like my sister's.

My mother spoke next. She described Chloe's erratic behaviour in the weeks leading up to the hospitalization, the poor sleep, reckless spending, and marijuana use. Chloe had declared that cooking was her new passion, and she spent over four thousand dollars on cooking supplies; chef's knives, fancy pots and pans, and special blenders. The majority of these items had been charged to my mother's credit card without her permission, because my sister's two cards were maxed out.

"My daughter is very smart and very talented," said my mother. "Prior to her first manic episode at the age of seventeen, she was an extraordinarily gifted ballet dancer, on track to become a professional ballerina. However, she has not been able to reach her potential due to poorly managed bipolar disorder."

In my opinion, this was a bit of revisionist history. It's true that Chloe had been an extraordinarily talented dancer, but she had lacked the dedication needed to make it professionally. She had entered the National Ballet School at age eleven, and for a few months there had been hope of a professional career. After two years, the administrators had met with my parents and suggested that she wasn't suited for the intensity of their program, and that she might be happier at a regular school. They encouraged her to continue her dancing, and promised that they would consider her for readmission should she 'rediscover her love of ballet', but everyone knew that she was being kicked out.

"Chloe's father and I want Chloe to come home, but we want her to come home well," my mother continued. "Right now, we fear that she is still mentally unstable and we strongly believe that discharge would be unsafe."

Chloe stared straight ahead and refused to look at my parents.

Chloe's lawyer, Jade Tomlinson, spoke next. Her anger with the health care system made it hard to take her seriously. "At its root, this case represents an attempt by a patriarchal system to take away a vulnerable young woman's right to make her own choices about her body and her life. She was seduced by an older man, her sister's fiancé, and yet her family blamed her for this."

I almost laughed at the description of Nathan as an older man. He was thirty-one to Chloe's twenty-eight; older, yes, but not nearly as much older as the lawyer had implied.

"She has been held in a mental institution and forced to take drugs against her will," continued Tomlinson. "She has been in forced proximity with people with severe mental illness, people with delusions and hallucinations, and it's not surprising that her health has worsened in this environment. Despite this, Chloe is forward thinking and she has goals. She was followed by a psychiatrist prior to this episode, and she knows she will need ongoing psychiatric care after her discharge. She wants to rebuild her life, and she is unable to do that while in the hospital."

Bill Goodwin, the chief adjudicator on the Capacity Board panel, latched onto the 'goal oriented' part of this little speech. He turned to my sister.

"Can you describe your goals for us, Ms. Ingram?"

Chloe had lost some of her lustre. Her skin had the gray pallor that comes from a lack of fresh air and exercise, and her baggy purple sweatsuit did her no favours. But she was still beautiful, with naturally blond hair and clear blue eyes, and when she opened her mouth it was clear that she hadn't lost her charisma.

"Well, my first goal is to get out of the hospital." Chloe smiled and laughed, and the Capacity Board members smiled back at her. She hadn't said anything particularly clever, but she had said it with such charm that it seemed witty.

"And after that?" The nurse on the panel asked encouragingly.

"I'd like to repair the relationships with the people I hurt while I was sick. My parents, my sister Sophie, and some of my friends. I'd like to get a part-time job, maybe in a clothing store because I've always liked fashion, or in a cooking store, which is another of my interests. And next year I'd like to go back to school to finish my marketing degree." It was a good answer. My sister had always been good at spinning a story.

"Okay. Is there anything else you'd like to tell us?" asked Goodwin.

"Only that I appreciate the opportunity to be heard by this board and I'm really sorry for the trouble that I've caused."

She was making a good impression. The psychiatry nurse

on the panel smiled at her sympathetically.

"Thank you, Ms. Ingram," said Goodwin.

"May I take another bathroom break, please, sir?" Chloe asked.

Goodwin decided to grant a twenty-minute break and asked everyone to clear the room to allow the board to discuss the case. Chloe and her lawyer rushed out together while everyone else packed up their laptops and papers. Somewhat surprisingly, Jade Tomlinson had left her ancient laptop closed on the table beside a pile of notes. There was big red sticker across the front of the laptop that stated: *This is what a feminist looks like.* I laughed. If a feminist looked like Jade Tomlinson's beat up laptop then the movement was in serious trouble.

"Are you okay, Sophie?" asked my mother.

I turned and saw my parents, their lawyers, and Dr. Edwards staring at me. I must have appeared to be laughing at absolutely nothing.

"I'm sorry," I said. "It's just that Ms. Tomlinson has a bumper sticker on her laptop, that says: *this is what a feminist looks like* . . ."

I trailed off as I realized that no one else found that amusing. My parents continued to look at me with concern. I declined their suggestion to get coffee with them and their lawyers, and walked until I found an empty classroom down the hall. The walls were covered with artwork and lists titled 'Reasons why I love myself' and 'Ten things I love about life.'

I set my notes and pen on the table and pulled out my phone. As I sat down, my arm hit the pen and sent it rolling onto the floor, and I crawled under the table to pick it up. I certainly didn't want to have to beg someone for another pen.

The door to the classroom opened and my parents' lawyers walked in. They were an attractive pair. Samantha was tall and beautifully put together, in a tailored navy pantsuit, subtle makeup, and stylish tortoiseshell eyeglasses that magnified big brown eyes. She appeared to be in her mid-twenties, and I guessed that she was the junior of the two.

"What do you think the board will decide?" she asked.

I was facing the door and could see them fairly well, but I quickly realized they couldn't see me.

"I don't have a clue," said Jack. "This whole situation is a farce. I have no experience with Health Law. And yet when Mark Sweetman called Tom Ingram this morning to say he had the flu and couldn't make this hearing, Ingram insisted I take over. And because I didn't have the balls to say no, I'm here babysitting a mental health hearing instead of working on something worthwhile."

I realized I should get up from under the table and announce myself, but felt irrationally ashamed to have been there in the first place.

Samantha giggled. "You're so modest, Jack. Ingram must really think highly of you to request you like this. I'm sure you know more than you think."

"No. I really don't know anything about Health Law." He shook his head. "All I've been able to do today is take notes in the hope that they'll be helpful to Mark if they decide to file an appeal. Oh, and I supplied the sister with a pen for her own notes. So I've added some value there."

Samantha giggled at his sarcasm. "Should I ask her for a copy of her notes? Maybe there will be something helpful."

He snorted. "She can barely dress herself, and I'm pretty sure she has toothpaste on her shirt."

I looked down at my T-shirt and sure enough, there was a smear of Colgate across my chest. I hadn't decided to attend the hearing until an hour before it started, when Chloe had called in a panic, so I had gotten ready in a rush.

"I doubt she does a lot of deep thinking," Jack continued. "But maybe she'll surprise us and come up with some brilliant insights that will decide this fascinating case."

Samantha laughed as though he had made the joke of the year.

"The interesting thing is that Ingram is actually a very competent executive," Jack continued. My father was CEO of the third largest bank in the country. "I've worked with him on a couple of deals for his bank. He gives clear direction, and he's fair. Doesn't change his mind every ten minutes." Jack shook his head again. "I guess it's not uncommon for daughters of a rich man to figure they'll never have to work for a living. It kills their ambition to achieve anything for themselves. They probably hope to marry rich, too."

Samantha laughed and then assumed a serious expression. An obviously insincere expression.

"We shouldn't laugh at them. It's actually rather pathetic," she said with fake sweetness.

They say eavesdroppers never hear anything good of themselves, and in this case it was proving to be true. I realized that there was nothing to be gained by remaining under the table, so I crawled out and walked swiftly from the room with as much dignity as I could manage. I didn't make eye contact with either of the lawyers, but I could see their stunned expressions as I walked by.

Two

When I got back to the conference room Chloe was talking to her lawyer, and my parents still hadn't returned. I carried my chair across the room and parked it next to Chloe's.

With her ill-fitting polyester pantsuit and poorly dyed red hair, Jade Tomlinson presented a very different appearance than Samantha. I stuck out my hand to her. "Nice to meet you, Ms. Tomlinson. I'm Chloe's sister Sophie. I have a couple of questions for Dr. Edwards that I think will help. Could you get permission for me to speak?"

She frowned, and appeared to be thinking hard. "I don't know, Sophie. It would have been nice to have discussed this in advance. Maybe you can tell me what the questions are, and if I think they're relevant I'll ask them."

I shook my head. "Thank you, but I'd rather ask them myself." Suddenly I was in the mood for confrontation.

I could tell she wanted to say no, but Chloe intervened. "Please let her, Jade. I trust Sophie."

Jade gave in with bad grace, and when the hearing resumed she asked if the board would permit me to ask Dr. Edwards a couple of questions.

Bill Goodwin frowned. "We were about to wrap up. This would be very irregular."

I gave him what I hoped was a winning smile.

"Please Mr. Goodwin. I'll be quick, and I think it will help everyone better understand Chloe's situation," I said.

I could see Samantha roll her eyes.

Goodwin relented. "Okay. But please be brief."

9

"Thank you." I jumped in before he could change his mind. "Dr. Edwards, when Chloe took her overdose of quetiapine, how much did she take?"

Dr. Edwards flipped through his binder of notes. "Uh, six tablets of 25 milligrams. So, 150 milligrams."

As I had thought, Chloe hadn't taken nearly enough to harm herself.

"Okay. And what is the recommended dose range for quetiapine? Say if she were taking it for bipolar disorder?"

"Well, I'd have to look it up to be sure."

"Okay. What's the highest dose you've seen prescribed?"

Now he looked uncomfortable. "Maybe 800 milligrams? But we always titrate it gradually. Chloe was only prescribed 25 milligrams as needed for sleep."

"I see. So she took less than a fifth of the maximum therapeutic dose." I paused and looked at the adjudicators to try to gauge how they were taking this. Goodwin was looking at me with more interest, and the nurse appeared to be taking notes. Encouraged, I pushed on.

"Dr. Edwards, I assume the Emergency doctor contacted the Poison Control Centre. What treatment did they recommend for the overdose? How long did they recommend she be monitored in the emergency room before she was referred to the psychiatry team?"

Samantha interrupted: "I'm sorry, I don't see how any of this is relevant to the questions we are trying to address, namely the need for ongoing psychiatric hospitalization and Chloe's capacity to make decisions."

Goodwin looked at her incredulously. "I find this very relevant, Ms. Albright. Dr. Edwards, can you tell us what treatment was needed?"

Edwards flipped a few more pages. "Well, I wasn't involved in her care at the time. It looks like she had some lab work done, and an ECG. From what I can see, she didn't need any specific treatment."

I nodded. "So the emergency doctor and poison control

team didn't think that the dose was enough to put her at risk of harm?"

"That's correct," said Edwards.

I turned to my sister. "Chloe, do you know where to look up information about drug doses and side effects?"

She looked as though I had asked an incredibly stupid question.

"Yeah, I Googled it."

"You Googled quetiapine before you took it?" I confirmed.

"Of course. I didn't want to take too much."

As I suspected, her 'overdose' was less an attempt to harm herself than an attempt to divert attention from the fact that she had slept with Nathan.

I smiled at the board again. "So, Chloe looked up quetiapine before she took it, and took less than a fifth of what Dr. Edwards estimates is the maximum therapeutic dose. An amount that didn't require any specific treatment or even a period of observation. This suggests that the overdose was more of a cry for help than a serious attempt to harm herself. Really, the most destructive thing she did was sleep with my fiancé, and since I no longer have a fiancé there is no risk that she will repeat that mistake."

Now my mother interrupted. "Sophie, I don't see how this is helpful."

I ignored her comment. "I have one more point," I continued.

Goodwin nodded. "Please go ahead."

"Dr. Edwards, you have told us that Chloe has been drinking large amounts of water while in the hospital. Is this new since she was hospitalized?"

He nodded. "As far as we know, yes."

"Could her excessive thirst be a side effect of her lithium therapy?" I asked.

He looked surprised. "No, we're fairly confident that this is deliberate behaviour, related to her mental illness. It seems to occur when she wants attention."

"But excessive thirst is a known side effect of lithium therapy, is it not? Caused by nephrogenic diabetes insipidus?"

The adjudicators all looked interested now. Samantha whispered something to Jack.

Dr. Edwards now looked harassed. "Yes, but it doesn't usually develop until someone has been on lithium for months. Years. Chloe has only been on lithium for several weeks."

"Right," I continued. "But it is possible for nephrogenic diabetes insipidus to develop in the short term?"

Dr. Edwards nodded. "I think so, yes. But not likely."

Goodwin interrupted. "Ms. Ingram, do you have a background in health care?"

I nodded. "Yes, I'm a physician. Right now I'm an Internal Medicine resident here in Toronto."

"Thank you," said Goodwin. "Can you explain a little about the condition you're describing?"

I nodded. "Nephrogenic diabetes insipidus is a condition in which the kidneys can't concentrate urine properly. It results in extreme thirst, as large amounts of fluid are needed to prevent dehydration. It's usually due to drugs, and lithium is one of the most common drugs to cause it."

As though to illustrate my point, Chloe took another long pull from her water jug.

"Is there a test for this?" Goodwin asked.

"Yes, it's quite simple," I answered. "You just test blood and urine chemistry first thing in the morning, before she's had anything to drink."

Goodwin nodded. "Dr. Edwards, has this been done?"

He looked uncomfortable. "I don't think so, no. As I said, this usually develops after long term lithium therapy."

Jade Tomlinson jumped in. "But if it's possible after short term use, it would be important to rule it out," she stated, as though she had made a brilliant connection. "This could be why she's thirsty all the time."

"Thank you, Ms. Tomlinson," said Goodwin dryly. He looked at me with growing respect. "Do you have anything else to add, Dr. Ingram?"

"No sir." I would quit while I was ahead.

"Okay. In that case, I'll ask my colleagues on the board to step out into the hall with me for a moment. I don't expect it will take long, so I would like you all to wait here." The three board members filed out.

"Sophie, that was amazing," said Chloe softly. "You should have been a lawyer."

"It's not always that easy," said Jade Tomlinson.

"Most things are easy for Sophie," said Chloe loyally. I almost laughed at that. I wondered if that was really how she saw my life. In my view, nothing I had achieved had come easily. I don't think I was unusual in this, and I suspect my path was common to many people trying to make it in a profession. Since high school, my life has been full of early mornings, late nights, self-doubt, and second-guessing myself. Staying polite when people were rude to me. Being unable to sleep the night before a big exam, or before the first day of a new rotation. And for the past month, being unable to sleep due to the knowledge that my medical error had caused serious harm to a young woman.

The board members returned and took their seats.

"We will provide you with a preliminary written decision tomorrow morning, and the full written decision within a week," began Goodwin. "But I will say now that we are troubled by some of the issues that have been raised. Most concerning is the fact that Chloe has developed excessive thirst while in hospital, and her treatment team did not consider the possibility that this was a side effect of her lithium therapy. In addition, it seems that the overdose Chloe took prior to admission was not nearly enough to put her at risk of harm. While she has demonstrated some challenging behaviours, we have not heard strong evidence that she is at risk of harming herself or anyone else. With respect to her social situation, we understand that she lives at home with her parents, so she has stable housing and family support."

Goodwin paused and cleared his throat. "So I would

expect a ruling against ongoing hospitalization, and I suggest you make plans for discharge tomorrow."

Dr. Edwards looked suitably chagrined. My parents looked stunned, as though they could not believe the Capacity Board could disagree with them. Jade Tomlinson looked equally shocked. I suspected she didn't win cases very often.

Goodwin continued. "Now, the second issue was that of Chloe's capacity to consent to treatment. Chloe, your lawyer has stated that you wish to continue to see your former psychiatrist, Dr. Jankovic, after your discharge. Is this true?"

Chloe nodded. "Yes sir."

"Very good," said Goodwin. "Dr. Edwards will come up with a treatment plan to bridge things until Dr. Jankovic can see you. I think we can all agree that lithium should be stopped." He looked at my sister. "Is this acceptable to you?"

Chloe looked at him as though he was her knight in shining armour. "Yes sir."

"Excellent. Expect our written decision tomorrow morning."

"Just a minute," said my father. "Can your decision be appealed?"

Goodwin looked irritated.

"Yes, the decision can be appealed to the provincial Superior Court. However, that would need to be done by a psychiatrist, not her parents. I expect the court would schedule a hearing within the next few months. Until then, our decision will stand. If you believe her condition deteriorates to the point that she is at imminent risk of harming herself, you can apply to a judge for an order to bring her back to the hospital. But that should only be done in an extreme situation. The courts frown upon the abuse of this power."

My father leaned over and whispered to his lawyers.

"So you're saying that we have to wait until she gets worse before she can be compelled to take treatment?" asked Samantha. "Who's responsible if she hurts herself again after she's discharged? Her next attempt could be much worse."

"What I'm saying is that this board, and the law, do not support the restriction of this young lady's freedom without good reason," said Goodwin. He reached for his briefcase and began to pack up his things.

I could tell my father was getting frustrated too. He wasn't used to people trying to leave a meeting before he, Tom Ingram, had decided it was over. He conferred with the lawyers again, then whispered to my mother, who nodded.

My mother spoke next, her voice clear and confident. "You mentioned that Chloe has a stable housing situation and supportive parents. We will continue to support her to the best of our ability, but we don't think that she is mentally well enough to be released from the hospital. We believe that the healthcare system has downloaded much of the responsibility for Chloe's mental illness to us, but we are not healthcare professionals, and we don't know how to manage her labile moods or erratic behaviour. We fear that by allowing her to live in our home, we have sheltered her from the consequences of her actions, and neither she nor her doctors have had to take responsibility for managing her illness. Chloe is an adult, and it seems that both she and this board believe that she is capable of making her own decisions. Consequently, her father and I believe that we can best support her with a tough love approach, and she will no longer be able to live at home with us."

There was a moment of tense silence. Chloe looked shocked, and I'm sure I did too. A tough love approach was the last thing I expected from my parents.

"I'm sorry to hear that," said Goodwin. "Chloe, do you have any ideas about where you could live if you are discharged tomorrow?"

Chloe still looked too stunned to speak. Jade Tomlinson laid a hand on her shoulder.

My mother spoke again. "Chloe, if you agree to stay in the hospital and cooperate with a treatment plan, we would be willing to reconsider this decision in several weeks."

My parents clearly thought they had played a trump card.

We had no other relatives in the city, and I assumed Chloe didn't have the money to rent her own place. I couldn't imagine her staying in a shelter. So she was effectively forced to choose between staying in the hospital and hoping my parents would relent, or throwing herself on the mercy of friends.

Samantha leaned over to whisper something in Jack's ear. He smiled.

I spoke without thinking.

"She can live with me."

Three

The walk home from the hearing took close to an hour, but it was an unseasonably warm fall evening, and it gave me time alone with my thoughts. Having Chloe live with me meant that Nathan wouldn't move back in, at least in the near future. I had told the Capacity Board that Nathan and I were no longer engaged, and while that was technically true, the situation was complicated. The night I found him with Chloe I had told him that the wedding was off, and I had asked him to leave our shared apartment. He had agreed to go on the condition that we kept the breakup secret for a few weeks, at least until the fellowship decisions were announced. Nathan was a final-year Cardiology resident and had applied for a highly competitive fellowship.

"You're like the girl next door, Sophie," he had said. "Everyone likes you, and everyone knows we're engaged. If people know we've broken up they'll assume it's my fault. The medical community is small, and gossip is vicious. Something like this could really hurt my chances."

I wasn't actually sure how true that was. From what I had observed, the most important predictor of success in academic medicine was the ability to get along with the administrators who ran the hospitals. It was also important to keep the residents and medical students happy by giving glowing evaluations that ranked each in the top 1% of his peer group (respect for statistics was not a requirement for success). Being a good doctor was helpful but not absolutely necessary. I had a growing suspicion that most of the bureaucrats couldn't tell the difference. And being faithful to one's fiancée? I doubted that anyone cared. The hospitals were full of doctors on their second or third marriages, and some had had really messy splits. My breakup with Nathan would be hot gossip for a week before people moved on to the next scandal.

But Nathan's fellowship application gave us a convenient reason to delay our scandal, and the vast majority of the guests who had received Save the Date cards for our May wedding had no idea that the wedding would not take place. Neither did the vineyard in Niagara that we had booked for the event, nor the caterer, nor the florist. I dreaded having to tell everyone that the wedding was off, and I had added this to my growing list of problems to deal with later. I suspected that Nathan was hoping that given enough time, I would forgive him and we could move past this. If I was honest, part of me hoped that Nathan was still hoping.

When I got home, I realized that my impulsive offer to let Chloe move in meant that I was going to have to deal with the problem of my apartment sooner instead of later. It was a one bedroom plus den, and from the moment Nathan and I had moved in five years ago we had had too much stuff for too little space. It certainly wasn't designed for two people who weren't sharing a bedroom and I would have to give Chloe the den, which Nathan and I had used as both a study and a storage room. Nathan's snowboard still leaned against one wall. I had nagged him to take it down to the storage locker for over six months, and refused to take it myself as a matter of principle. I suspect he had refused to move it on principle too.

The day after I kicked Nathan out, he had come back for most of his clothing and personal items, but a lot of his things remained. I had no idea if he had abandoned the rest of his stuff or had been just too busy to come back for it, as I hadn't been in contact with him for several weeks. For the first few days after our split he had called or texted me multiple times a day. Most of the messages were apologetic, but some tried to justify his behaviour. *It was a meaningless liaison. It was purely physical. Chloe seduced me.* After about a week, I had blocked his number.

Tonight, the sight of his snowboard leaning against the wall of the den made me wish I had kept the lines of communication open long enough to get him back his stuff.

I made a half-hearted attempt to clear out the den for Chloe, and moved most of the clutter out to the tiny living room to join the boxes of Nathan's things. I considered vacuuming the room, but decided that it would be character building for Chloe to do it herself, and retreated to the kitchen, which was the only clean area in the apartment. I had never been much of a cook, but in the month since Nathan left I had given up. I had cereal for breakfast, lunch at the hospital, and cereal again for dinner. There was a lot to be said for this approach, as it greatly simplified grocery shopping and generated very little mess.

I sat down at the kitchen counter with a bowl of Cheerios and a glass of white wine. On an impulse, I opened my laptop and looked up bipolar disorder, with the hope that reading about the condition would help me understand Chloe. The first review paper highlighted the fact that three-quarters of people with bipolar disorder had a close relative with either bipolar disorder or depression. I read further and learned that the major risks for 'bipolar mood episodes' were stress, insomnia, and drug and alcohol use.

I considered the possibility that I had an undiagnosed mood disorder and quickly rejected it. I was fairly certain I had never experienced a manic episode, but the euphoria and energy described in the paper seemed pretty appealing. The article went on to discuss that a significant percentage of people with a mood disorder were in denial about it. This was rather depressing. I took another sip of wine and closed the article.

The public library website had a long list of eBooks on bipolar disorder, with a book called *Breathing to Beat Bipolar* at the top of the list. The title was hardly inspiring, but it was their highest rated book on the subject, so I decided to try it. The author believed that imbalanced breathing was the root cause of imbalanced emotions, and the book described breathing techniques to 'bring your mood back to balance'.

Cleansing breaths were slow and deep. Calming breaths were in through the nose, out through the mouth. Energizing breaths were rapid and shallow. Subliminal breaths involved breathing without thinking about it. I realized that I had been practicing subliminal breaths for most of my life.

My mother called as I was reading about operatic breathing (deep and controlled, from the diaphragm). I considered not answering, but I knew there was going to be a confrontation sooner or later. I was actually surprised that I hadn't heard from her sooner.

"Sophie. You rushed out so quickly I didn't get a chance to talk to you."

"I had some things to do," I answered.

"Sophie, we need to talk about Chloe," she said briskly. "I'm sure your offer to take her in was well-intentioned, but I don't think you understand the severity of her mental illness."

I wasn't sure I did either. I had never been able to figure out how much of her behaviour was the result of her mental illness and how much was just bad behaviour. Chloe had been diagnosed with bipolar disorder after crashing her car into a tree at the age of seventeen. Fortunately she hadn't been injured and no one else had been involved. The bad news was that collision reconstruction evidence suggested that she had been going over twice the speed limit in a school zone, and she faced a dangerous driving charge and the possibility of a criminal record. My parents had hired a lawyer, who had in turn hired a psychiatrist, who had diagnosed her with a manic episode. All of a sudden she was a girl with a mental illness instead of a reckless driver, and the charge had been dropped.

I debated what to say to my mother. "She didn't seem to be getting better in the hospital," I began.

"She's not better! If anything, she's worse. That's why it's completely nonsensical for them to release her. She needs to stay in the hospital until the doctors can find the right combination of drugs."

"She doesn't need to be in the hospital for them to adjust

her medications," I countered.

"But Sophie, she doesn't take her medications reliably when she's at home. We've tried this. She needs to be in a supervised environment until she's stabilized."

"But as you said, she's not getting better in the hospital," I argued.

"She hasn't gotten better *yet*," said my mother. "They haven't found the right drugs yet."

"Dr. Jankovic has been treating her for years," I said. "Presumably she's been trying to find the right drugs, but she hasn't found a magic bullet. Probably because there isn't one."

People with no medical background (e.g. my parents) often thought there was some magic to being in a hospital, and that a hospital stay could 'fix' problems and send people home cured. More often than not, the problems were incurable, and all we could do was try to optimize things. I wondered if my parents had thought about the long-term plan. Did they hope that if Chloe stayed in the hospital long enough, she would emerge with a new personality and the ability to regulate her emotions? They couldn't be hoping she would live in the hospital indefinitely. I suspected they had seen the capacity hearing as a fight to be won, and it had caused them to lose sight of what was actually best for Chloe.

"All the more reason for her to stay in the hospital," said my mother. "I'm sure Dr. Jankovic has done her best, but she hasn't been able to find the right treatment. It's not too late to change your mind, Sophie. You can call the hospital tomorrow, tell them you've thought about things and decided that Chloe can't stay with you until she's mentally stabilized."

"Mom, the board told us they're going to release her tomorrow. At least if she lives with me I can keep an eye on her. Who knows where she'll go if I tell her she can't stay here?"

"Sophie, if she has nowhere to go she'll stay there. They're not trying to kick her out, she's pushing to leave. She has no money. Can you really imagine her going to a shelter?"

"I don't know, Mom. Not a shelter, no. But she probably

has friends and resources that we know nothing about."

My mother sighed. "At least promise me that if she seems to be getting worse, you'll get her back to the hospital."

"Of course I will."

"Our lawyer, Samantha, explained that if we have reason to believe that she's a danger to herself we can apply to a judge for a Form 2, to compel her to go to hospital for a psychiatric evaluation. I'll text you Samantha's contact, she can give you details about what kind of information a judge would need."

Hell would freeze over before I would contact Samantha Albright about this. "That won't be necessary, Mom, I'm sure I can figure it out."

"Well I'll send it along just in case. Sam's a lovely girl, she's been very helpful to us."

"Sure." I briefly considered telling my mother about the conversation I had overheard between Samantha and Jack, that had shown what that lovely girl truly thought about our family, but decided against it.

"Sophie, I'm concerned about you too, you know. I love Chloe, but the truth is, she's difficult to live with. You never know what kind of a mood she'll be in, or what she'll do next. It's hard to understand until you've lived with it."

"I guess I'll find out," I said.

"Have you considered that this will make it impossible for Nathan to move back in?"

"You don't think he would be interested in a ménage a trois?" I asked sarcastically.

"Sophie, that's not funny," said my mother. "I just want to be sure that you've considered the impact this may have on your relationship."

My mother had always liked Nathan, and I knew she thought I should forgive him for sleeping with Chloe.

"Mom, the relationship is done," I said firmly.

"Sophie, I just want to be sure you've thought this through. He made one mistake."

"That I know of."

There was a pause. "Do you have reason to believe he's cheated before?"

"No. But I wouldn't have believed he had cheated with Chloe if I hadn't walked in on them."

"I find it interesting that you seem willing to forgive Chloe but not Nathan."

"I haven't forgiven Chloe."

"You offered to let her move in with you!"

"She's my sister and she's in trouble. In addition, she's mentally ill. As far as I know, Nathan is not."

"I only hope that you can keep an open mind. You know the deposit for the vineyard is non-refundable. The wedding's not for six months; there's no need to make any hasty decisions."

"I'll compensate you for the deposit." I could add it to my line of credit.

"You know I'm not really worried about the money, sweetheart. But what if the two of you get back together?"

"Then we'll get married at City Hall. Or live in sin indefinitely."

"We sent Save the Date notices to three hundred people."

"Maybe Nathan could marry Chloe. The guest list would be pretty similar."

My mother sighed. "I just don't want you to make a mistake, darling. Most people your age are already in relationships, or have failed relationships, or children. It gets so complicated."

"You're right, Mom. It's complicated."

"Look after yourself. You didn't look like you've been sleeping well at all."

She was absolutely right. I hadn't been sleeping well for the past month. I stayed up for as long as I could keep my eyes open, reading trashy novels or watching trashy television, because I didn't have the energy to focus on anything meaningful. I had learned that the more exhausted I was when I finally fell asleep, the less likely I was to have the nightmare.

$$Four$$

The nightmare was always the same, a flashback to the worst night of my young medical career. I held Chloe indirectly responsible for the fact that my professional life fell apart shortly after my personal life did. The day after I found her and Nathan together I had to work an overnight call shift. The smart thing to do would have been to call in sick. The COVID pandemic had caused a major culture shift, and taking a sick day was now seen as a sign of responsibility rather than one of weakness. But I knew that Nathan would show up to work, so I resolved to do the same. It was a decision that would change the course of my career.

I was the Senior Internal Medicine resident on call. It was one of the worst call shifts in an Internal Medicine residency, with responsibility for admissions from the Emergency Department as well as coverage of urgent issues for the hundred-odd Medicine inpatients in the hospital. In theory I should have been done with this call after my third year, but because there weren't enough third year residents to cover the schedule, it had been decided that the fourth and fifth year Internal Medicine residents should fill the gaps. So during the months that I was supposed to have protected research time, I did at least one of these call shifts per week.

I was working with two medical students who were very quick to let me know that they weren't interested in Internal Medicine and expected to be sent to bed by eleven PM. I had no problem with that, as it was easier to do the work myself than to supervise students who didn't want to be there. I was also supervising a first year Internal Medicine resident, and a psychiatry resident, Benjamin Darling, who was doing his mandatory two-month rotation through Internal Medicine.

I could tell that patients loved Ben Darling because he took his time with them, and listened to all the irrelevant information they wanted to share. I had even heard one of them comment that 'Dr. Darling is a darling.' But Dr. Darling was driving me crazy by giving me a lot of useless data about how his patients felt about their illnesses. He hadn't grasped that his role as a junior resident was to sort through the story and distil it down to its key points. Overnight, we needed to identify which urgent problems needed to be addressed before the morning. If we got bogged down in trivia, other patients might suffer because we couldn't get to them in time.

So I had assigned Ben a case that I thought would be straightforward, a thirty-nine year old woman who had presented with abdominal pain and vomiting. The emergency doctor thought she had a bad urinary tract infection, and she had been referred for admission because she couldn't keep fluids or pills down. She would likely need a short hospitalization for IV fluids and antibiotics. But it was taking Ben a very long time to get to the point.

"Christine's medical history is significant for anxiety," he reported. "This was diagnosed about ten years ago, shortly after the birth of her first child. She has been on a small dose of an antidepressant, citalopram, for about three years. Lack of sleep and stress at work are common provoking factors for her depression. She works in IT but she doesn't get along well with her boss. She does, however, have excellent relationships with her husband Jeff and her sister Beth. She states that they're both key supports for her."

"How nice for her," I commented quietly.

"What?" asked Ben.

"Nothing," I answered. "Tell me about why she's here tonight."

Ben looked startled, and flipped a page on his clipboard. "Okay. Her pain started about 24 hours ago while she was walking her dog," he said. "She called her sister Beth, who is a nurse in Montreal. They talk every day. Anyway, she told Beth about it, and Beth thought she should come to the hospital -"

My pager beeped, and I pushed a button to silence it. It was the fourth page I had received since Ben began the story.

"Sorry Ben, I'm going to have to call those back soon." I glanced at his patient's lab work on the computer. Her urine test was abnormal and her white blood cell count was high, all in keeping with a urinary tract infection. "Why don't you jump to the bottom line? What do you think her diagnosis is, and what do you want to do for her?"

Ben's face fell. I felt like I had kicked a puppy. "Well, I don't think she has appendicitis," he began.

"Okay," I said to Ben. "The ER doctor thought she had a urinary tract infection and would need admission for IV antibiotics until she can keep pills down. Do you think her history fits with that?"

He nodded. "Yes, I think so. But -"

My pager beeped again. It was the third page I had received to the same number within a span of ten minutes, which suggested either a very urgent problem or a very impatient nurse.

"I'm sorry, Ben, I need to answer that. So finish your note, then go ahead and do admission orders. Continue the IV fluids and antibiotics. I'll pop in to see her and review your orders as soon as I've caught up on these pages from the ward."

Ben looked at me anxiously. "Okay Sophie, but -"

I had already picked up the phone to start answering pages. I gave Ben what I hoped was a reassuring smile. "I trust you, Ben."

When I returned the first page I was told that 'Bed 35-3 can't move his right leg.' I had no idea who was in Bed 35-3, but I rushed up to the ward to assess whether its occupant was having an acute stroke or other neurological catastrophe. I found his chart, and learned that his right leg had been paralyzed for years. I wasn't sure why the nurse had decided to call and inform me of this chronic finding at 1 AM, but I wrote a note and moved on to a patient with chest pain, and then to a patient in the ER with pancreatitis. Overall, two hours passed before I went to find Ben to finish reviewing his patient. I found him sitting in the cubicle in the corner of the ER that we used as an Internal Medicine office, patiently waiting for me.

"Okay Ben, where are we going?" I asked him.

"Pod A, Bed 8."

This surprised me. The ER was divided into three zones, organized by acuity. Pod A was for the sickest cases. Usually younger patients with urinary tract infections were triaged to Pod C.

"Is she pretty sick?" I asked him.

"Yes," he said simply.

As soon as I reached her room I could see that she was. She was hooked up to a cardiac monitor that showed that her heart rate was fast and her blood pressure was low. Her face was pale and she was breathing quickly. A man, who I assumed was her husband, sat at the bedside holding her hand.

I clearly hadn't appreciated the severity of her illness. She would need more IV fluids, strong antibiotics, and imaging to rule out a kidney stone. I introduced myself and explained that I had to put in a couple orders but would be back to talk to them soon.

I nodded to Ben and we walked out to the nursing station, where I pulled up her chart on the computer to enter the orders.

Ben looked over my shoulder anxiously.

"Was she this sick when you saw her?" I whispered to him.

"She was sick, but not this bad," he said. "I'm sorry Sophie, I should have told you."

"It's not your fault," I said quickly. In reality I thought he bore some responsibility for not opening with the fact that her vital signs were abnormal, or simply stating that she was very sick. But I should have asked him specifically what her vital signs were, and I hadn't. And consequently, she had received suboptimal treatment for several hours.

Ben shook his head. "I should have ordered more IV fluids," he said anxiously.

"It's not your fault, Ben," I said. "She's just sick."

The nurse came out to tell us that her blood pressure had dropped further, and that they had been unable to get a second IV line. She was going to need medication to try to raise her blood pressure, and a central line to run all the drips.

"Ben. Can you call the ICU resident? Explain that she's got severe sepsis and we're going to have to start pressors, so she'll need to go to the ICU."

Ben looked like he was about to vomit. "Okay."

I needed the ultrasound machine to do the central line, and had to search the entire department for it. Nothing was coming easily for me on this shift. I finally found the ultrasound in the corner of a supply room, which was probably where it was supposed to be stored but hardly ever was.

Ben found me as I was rolling the ultrasound down the hall to the room. It was kept on a cart with a wonky left wheel that caused it to veer to the left. I narrowly missed running over Ben's foot, and he jumped back against the wall.

"The ICU resident's in the middle of a procedure, but he'll come when he can," Ben explained. "They're getting a bed ready for her in the unit."

"Thanks Ben." It was a relief to know that there was an open ICU bed. If they were full we would have been told that she wasn't sick enough to go there.

I took a deep breath before walking back into Mrs. Gerard's room. I was stressed and sweating, but I tried to look confident and calm. I pushed the ultrasound machine slowly and carefully, with more pressure on the left side to compensate for the funny wheel.

"Hello again, Mrs. Gerard," I said. "As we discussed a few minutes ago, I'm concerned that you have a serious infection. We're giving you a dose of a strong antibiotic, and we're going to continue with IV fluids. Right now, I'd like to put a special IV line in your neck so that we can give you fluids and medicine more easily."

Mrs. Gerard had turned her head to look at me, but her eyes had the glazed look of serious illness, and I wasn't sure how much she was absorbing. Her husband gave me a panicked look.

"She's really sick, isn't she?" he asked.

I nodded. "Yes, she is very sick. But we're going to do everything we can to look after her. I'd like to explain the procedure for the central line and get your consent to go ahead with it."

"Do whatever you need to do," he said. "I trust you."

"Thank you," I said. "Let me explain what I'm going to do." I continued to talk to Mrs. Gerard, even though I wasn't sure how much she was processing. "I'm going to use the ultrasound to find a vein in your neck. I'll put in some freezing. Then I'll thread a wire into the vein through a needle, and then thread the IV tube over that. There may be a little discomfort, similar to going to the dentist, but most people find it doesn't hurt very much."

She gave a small nod. Her green eyes looked too big for her pale face.

"Okay. Every procedure has some risks," I continued. "The most common risks of this procedure are bleeding or infection, which are almost always treatable. Right now, I think the benefits of the central line outweigh the risks." I paused. "Do you have any questions?"

"No. Go ahead," she said in a small voice.

As I was getting my supplies organized, a young man in scrubs knocked on the door and walked in. He looked more energetic than anyone had a right to be at 3 AM.

"Dr. Ingram?" he asked. I nodded.

"I'm Alex Bowers," he said. "I'm a fourth year medical student doing an ICU rotation. I'm working with Dr. Wells. He's busy right now, but he sent me down to help you."

I mentally cursed Ryan Wells for burdening me with his medical student, but forced myself to smile at Alex Bowers. "Wonderful," I said. I must have successfully hidden my sarcasm, because he continued to smile at me.

"What do you need me to do?" he asked enthusiastically.

"Well, I'm getting ready to put in a central line," I explained.

"I've never done a central line, but I would love to try one," said Alex. He must have missed the lecture on things not to say in front of patients and their relatives.

I hadn't thought it was possible for Mr. Gerard to look more anxious, but now he did.

"Um, Dr. Ingram -" he began.

I cut him off quickly. "Mr. Gerard, this is Alex, a senior medical student. He's going to hold the freezing for me while I do this procedure."

Mr. Gerard let out a sigh of relief. Alex looked disappointed.

I was drawing up the freezing when Ryan Wells showed up. Ryan had been in Nathan's residency year, a year ahead of me, and I knew him relatively well. He and Nathan had been in the same study group, and they had met at our apartment occasionally. I was surprised that the study group had stuck together for as long as it did, because Ryan and Nathan had been rivals as well as friends. They had been considered the two best residents of their year, but Ryan had seemed to do everything just a little bit better and with a little less effort, and it had driven Nathan crazy.

"Hey Sophie," said Ryan. He took in the situation at a glance. "The ICU bed is ready, we can just take her up now and do the line there," Ryan said.

"That will delay it by over half an hour," I said. "I've already got everything set up here, I'll put it in quickly and then we can go." Throughout my residency I had frequently been told that I needed to be more assertive. One preceptor had told me to act like I deserved to be in charge.

Ryan shrugged. "Okay. Do you want any help?"

"No thanks, I got it."

And I should have had it. I had done central lines many

times, and she was a young, thin, and relatively cooperative patient. In theory it should have been easy. But of course it wasn't.

My sweaty hands stuck to the inside of the sterile gloves, and I couldn't get my fingers into them properly. The face shield of my mask fogged up, and because I was trying to keep my hands sterile I couldn't adjust it. The ultrasound gel spread all over my hands and all over my equipment, making everything slippery. When I finally got a flashback of blood in the syringe, indicating I had found the vein, I couldn't thread the wire down into it. Blood oozed out of the needle and pooled on the drape, but still the wire refused to thread through the needle.

"Is there usually so much blood?" Alex Bowers stood on a stepstool looking over my shoulder, and his voice sounded incredibly loud in the otherwise silent room.

We had parked Mr. Gerard on a chair in the corner of the room, where he would still be able to see his wife but wouldn't get in the way. He stood up and looked at me anxiously.

"There's usually some blood, yes," I said, trying to sound like I had control of the situation. "It looks like more than it is." Once I got through this procedure I was going to have a serious talk with Alex.

Fortunately Ryan returned from the nursing station, where he had been reading the chart. He must have sensed what was going on, because he walked up to Mr. Gerard, introduced himself, and explained what would happen when his wife went up to the ICU. I could see Mr. Gerard relax. Ryan had that effect on people. He fit the doctor stereotype perfectly; he was good-looking, athletic, confident but not cocky. He was male. Most people liked me, but I knew I didn't inspire confidence the way that Ryan did. Normally I would have resented that, but at the time I was just grateful that Mr. Gerard was distracted from what I was doing.

I pulled out my needle and took another look with the ultrasound, but it was hard to get good pictures. I was starting to feel shaky, and I couldn't remember when I had last eaten.

I thought about stopping, and asking Ryan to try to do a line on the other side. But that would take longer, and her blood pressure was still low. I put in more freezing and tried again.

This time I found the vein immediately, and the guidewire passed easily. I pulled out the needle and threaded the central line down over the wire.

"Almost done," I said confidently. I felt a great sense of satisfaction; despite the upheaval in my personal life I could still do some things well.

A jet of blood shot up from the line as soon as I pulled out the guidewire, and two more jets escaped before I could cover the opening with my thumb. I put a cap on the line with trembling fingers. The blood that had pooled on the blue drape was bright red, clearly brighter than it should have been.

The line was in the wrong place. I had missed the jugular vein and put a line in the carotid artery, a potentially catastrophic mistake. I had heard people talk about this complication, but I had never seen it happen.

I briefly considered pulling it out, with the wild hope that if I took it out and applied pressure, the hole in her artery would seal on its own and no one would ever know. But I had enough insight to know that it was a wild hope, and that the right thing to do was to leave the line in and consult vascular surgery to deal with it. And since Mrs. Gerard's blood pressure remained low, our first priority had to be to get a functional line into a vein, so that we could give her the fluids and drugs she urgently needed.

I called Ryan over and quietly explained the situation. To his credit, he stayed calm, as though he dealt with the accidental placement of central lines in carotid arteries all the time. He tactfully suggested that I hold my line in place while he put a central line in the other side of her neck. I watched him do it quickly, dexterously, without spilling a drop of blood on the fresh drape he had laid down. He worked with the nurse to get norepinephrine running through his line, which brought Mrs. Gerard's blood pressure up within minutes, and then called the vascular surgery resident to ask for an urgent consult.

I kept my hands glued to the line in her carotid as we wheeled her up to the ICU, as though holding it in position could somehow prevent disaster.

"You can let go of the line now." The vascular surgery resident was brusque and dismissive. He took a look with the ultrasound, then motioned to Ryan to come and see the images. I stepped out of the way.

"Yep. It goes straight through the jugular vein and into the artery," he said to Ryan, shaking his head. "Best to secure it with tape and leave it until morning. I'll talk to the staff surgeon. We'll need a CT angiogram. It'll probably need a stent, hopefully not open surgery." He shook his head. "I've read about this happening but never seen it. Whoever did this really screwed it up."

I don't think he knew that I was the person who had really screwed it up. Or maybe he did but he just didn't care. He certainly didn't seem to care that Mrs. Gerard was awake and could hear every word. The sterile drapes had been removed, and she looked more alert now that we had gotten her blood pressure up. I could see her panicked face as she listened to his blunt summary of the situation.

Ryan Wells gave me a sympathetic look, and all of a sudden it was too much. I sank down to the floor, buried my face in my knees, and cried. One of the nurses came and helped me to a chair in the nursing station, which was smack in the middle of the ICU, in full view of all the staff working there. Someone draped a blanket over my shoulders and handed me a tissue and a can of Ginger Ale, as though I were a shock victim. Through a haze of tears, I could see the nursing staff whispering among themselves.

Nathan was right that the medical community was small, and gossip was vicious. In my experience, stories of professional errors spread far more quickly and were far more damaging than stories of personal ones. Before the end of the week, everyone would have heard about my failed central line, and about my emotional breakdown in the ICU. I was unlikely to ever get a job in the city.

In little more than twenty-four hours I had been betrayed by my fiancé, broken my engagement, and ruined my chance of getting a job in my hometown. I had also potentially caused serious harm to a young woman who had trusted me to look after her.

Thanks to the electronic medical record, I could follow Mrs. Gerard's progress without having to return to the ICU. The next day the vascular surgery team stented her carotid artery and removed my misplaced line. Her kidney infection improved quickly with antibiotics. The ICU doctors were hopeful that she would make a full recovery.

The day after that she suffered a stroke, and a CT scan showed that the stent in her carotid artery had clotted. The radiologists were able to extract the clot, but not before significant damage was done. She was left with weakness in the left side of her face, arm, and leg.

And I was left with nightmares.

Five

C hloe was discharged the day after the hearing, and I took an Uber to the hospital to meet her. She was waiting outside when I arrived, wearing the same sweatsuit she had worn for the hearing but already looking brighter.

"Sophie, my saviour!" she exclaimed when she saw me. "Seriously, you saved my life."

"How are you feeling?" I asked.

"A million times better," she said. "That place is a nightmare. I would have died if they hadn't let me out. I'm not exaggerating."

"Well, I'm glad you're feeling better," I said cautiously. "I thought we could stop by Mom and Dad's so you can get your stuff. I can help you pack."

Chloe looked shocked. "Sophie, I can't go to Mom and Dad's. You saw what they tried to do to me yesterday. If it were up to them I would still be in that hellhole of a hospital."

"I guess we can go straight to my place," I said. I changed the destination on the Uber app and told the driver about the change of plans. "I can go pick up some of your clothes and things later. But you're going to have to talk to Mom and Dad eventually."

"Sophie, Mom and Dad have paid for almost everything I own. I can't wear any of those clothes without being reminded that I'm in their debt. And I don't need to talk to them again. Ever."

"What are you planning to wear?" I asked practically.

"I was hoping we could stop at the mall. I'll need all new

35

clothes, makeup, everything. Can you believe they wouldn't even let me have my electric toothbrush in the hospital? Apparently they were concerned I would try to electrocute myself," she said, rolling her eyes. "If I'd been in there much longer I would have considered it."

"Buying all new things will be pretty expensive, Chloe," I said, choosing to ignore her attempt at dark humour. "Replacing all your clothes could cost a few thousand dollars."

She nodded. "Oh, at least. But I need to do this, Sophie. I need a fresh start. This is the beginning of my new, independent self." She paused. "I figured you could lend me some money."

"Chloe, I don't have that kind of money to lend," I protested. "I asked Nathan to move out, so I've taken over his share of the rent."

"But you work as a doctor, Sophie," she pointed out. "Surely you could afford a little money to help me make a fresh start?"

I was disturbed that she considered a few thousand dollars 'a little money.'

"I work as a resident doctor, Chloe," I explained. "I gross less than six thousand dollars per month. The government takes income tax. Then I pay for rent, utilities, and food. If I have any money left, I pay down my line of credit."

"You know Mom and Dad would pay off your line of credit if you asked," she said. "They're very proud of their successful daughter."

"I'm trying to be independent," I told her. "And they're proud of you too, Chloe."

She rolled her eyes. "Don't lie to me, Sophie. I've had more than enough of it over the past month." She spoke in a singsong voice. "You are capable and strong. You are valued. You are loved." Her voice changed. "So capable and strong that we are going to force you to take drugs to blunt your personality, and keep you locked in the hospital against your will. So loved that your parents will fight to keep you in the psych ward and refuse to let you return to their home."

"I think they really believed it was for the best."

"Are they angry at you for interfering?"

"I don't know," I said truthfully. "They're disappointed in the outcome. I think they understand that I pushed for what I thought was best for you." I didn't mention that my decision to help her at the hearing had been motivated by the need to prove something to a certain lawyer. In truth, yesterday I would have argued any position that opposed that of Jack Delacroix.

"I'm not sure our parents understand anything," said Chloe. "I'll never forgive them."

"Well, regardless, I won't be able to lend you money for new clothes," I said, in an effort to change the subject. "I'll go to Mom and Dad's later to pick up your stuff."

"I don't understand why you still work as a resident," she said. "I thought you passed your exams? Shouldn't you be earning real money now?"

She made an excellent point. I had passed my Internal Medicine licensing exams and was actually qualified to practice independently. Historically, a Canadian Internal Medicine residency ended after four years of training, and doctors who didn't want to subspecialize started independent practice. But about ten years ago it was decided that more training would be better, and the specialty of General Internal Medicine was born. It wasn't entirely clear to me how this differed from regular Internal Medicine, except that the residency took five years instead of four. This was ostensibly to give us better training, but I had come to suspect it was to keep a group of senior trainees around in the hospitals for an extra year, to do front line work and free up the staff physicians to do research and attend meetings.

"Yes, I passed my exams," I said.

"So why can't you work independently?" Chloe asked.

"I could, actually." I had applied for an independent licence earlier this year and had planned to do some locum work on weekends, but I had been so busy with residency and the research project that I hadn't picked up any shifts.

"So why do you still work as a resident?" she asked.

"It's just the expectation now. No one gets an Internal Medicine job in an academic centre without a five year residency," I answered.

"So you'll be done after this year?" she asked.

"Well, I'll be done residency," I explained. "I would still need to do a Masters before I could get an academic position. And probably a fellowship." I had been preparing an application for a Masters of Education at the time of the Central Line Incident.

Chloe looked confused. "But you could work as a doctor without a Masters, right?"

I nodded. "Yeah, I could probably get a job at a suburban hospital, or in a smaller town."

"So why would you want an academic position?" Chloe asked. She seemed genuinely puzzled by this.

"Well, I could do research, and teach medical students and residents," I answered.

"I didn't think you liked teaching the medical students," Chloe said. "You're always complaining that they're entitled and lazy."

That did sound like something I had said.

"Not all of them," I protested. "Some of them are keen and hard-working, and it's satisfying to teach them. Also, it's a way to give back."

"Do you get paid to teach?" Chloe asked, circling back to the financial aspect.

"Not while I'm still a resident," I explained. "If I get a staff job then yes, there would be a small stipend for teaching."

"Sophie, this sounds like some sort of scam," said Chloe, looking personally offended. "Like a pyramid scheme. How do they convince people to continue as residents when they could work independently for real money?"

"It's not quite that simple, Chloe," I tried to explain.

"They must have brainwashed you all. I bet they put hallucinogenic drugs in the hospital water supply," she joked. "Don't worry, Sophie, if you end up on the Psych ward, I'll support you at your capacity hearing."

"Thank you," I said dryly.

"But seriously Sophie, why would anyone sign up for that?"

"Well, a lot of people have partners to consider. Nathan wants to be an interventional cardiologist, so he'll need to work in a big centre, and the job market will be tough. So if we wanted to find a job together, I would have needed the qualifications to work in an academic centre.

Chloe's face fell at the mention of Nathan.

"Sophie. I'm so sorry about Nathan," she said. "If it makes you feel better, it was lust, nothing more."

That didn't really make me feel better.

"And you really shouldn't blame him. I initiated it," Chloe continued. "He was too much of a gentleman to turn me down."

I burst out laughing. "Funny, Chloe, he said almost exactly the same thing. He was such a gentleman that he didn't hesitate to blame you."

She looked downcast. "Sophie, I feel so incredibly guilty. The psychiatrists explained that I was manic, that I didn't know what I was doing and therefore it wasn't my fault. But I still feel responsible. It haunts me."

"Yeah, me too, Chloe," I said. I knew what she wanted me to say, but I couldn't say it. It was probably unfair, but I resented the way she used her mental illness as an excuse. I would have respected her more if she had just acknowledged that she had made a mistake and apologized.

"Do you think there's any chance that you and Nathan will get back together?" she asked hopefully.

"No," I said.

"Mom said that you've kept the break-up secret and you haven't cancelled the wedding," she said.

"That's true, but it's only because Nathan thinks that it could affect his chances for a fellowship. Once the fellowship decisions are announced, we'll let everyone know that the wedding is off."

"So I'll have to live my whole life with the knowledge that I've ruined yours," she said dramatically.

"Guess so," I said, and almost laughed at her look of surprise. She clearly expected me to reassure her that she wasn't responsible for ruining my life, but I couldn't do it. I wouldn't have phrased it so dramatically, but her actions truly had turned my life upside down. I hadn't even told her about the Central Line Incident, which I attributed at least in part to my emotional distress after finding her and Nathan together. I had the fleeting thought that if I wouldn't accept her bipolar disorder as an excuse for sleeping with my fiancé then I shouldn't use 'emotional distress' as an excuse for my medical error, but I didn't care.

"Home sweet home," Chloe said as I turned the key in the lock. "Sophie, your apartment is a mess."

She wrinkled her nose at the sight of the boxes piled in the living room. It was clear she wasn't impressed, but I was too tired to care.

***

Shortly after I showed Chloe how to set up the pull-out couch, I got a text from a number I didn't recognize:

Sophie, it's Nathan. I'd like to come pick up some things from our apartment.

Sophie: You changed your number?

Nathan: I borrowed my med student's phone. I assume you blocked my number.

Sophie: I blocked your number because I didn't want to talk to you.

Nathan: Any news from the REB on Moppet?

Although his last question wasn't as nonsensical as it seemed, I didn't reply. The REB was the Research Ethics Board, and MoPPET was our research project, the Mobility

Preservation Program in the Elderly Trial. At one time Nathan and I had hoped that the project would set us on the path to academic stardom, and more importantly, to jobs as Attending Staff. There was a precedent for this; several years ago a fifth year resident named Chris Gardner had published a project on preventing falls in the hospitalized elderly that earned him an Attending Staff job straight out of residency. Falls put patients at risk of awful things, including fractures, head injuries, and cognitive impairment. Of primary importance to the hospital administrators was that patients who fell were admitted to hospital more frequently than those who didn't, and once in hospital, they stayed longer. Which translated to more stress on our frail health-care system.

So Chris Gardner started the Hospital Inpatient Program for Prevention Of Falls, better known as HIPPO-Falls, in which a Falls Prevention Consultant (otherwise known as an Occupational Therapist) developed a personalized plan to decrease the falls risk for every patient. Many of the recommendations were the same for each patient: Ensure the room is well lit! Clear the room of trip hazards like cords and loose carpets! Make sure the patient is wearing glasses! Whenever a patient had a fall, every nurse on the ward had to take part in a 'debriefing huddle' to discuss what had gone wrong.

Unfortunately, most of the big risk factors for falls, like age, frailty, and cognitive impairment, were not modifiable. The nurses quickly learned that the most important modifiable risk factor was the frequency with which a patient got out of bed, and so patients were discouraged from getting up. The number of falls fell by half, and Chris Gardner won a national award.

Several months later, the administrators realized that the average length of stay for Internal Medicine patients had increased by a full day, resulting in more patients in hallways waiting for beds. Complaints from patients and families doubled. Head-scratching and hand-wringing ensued in the administrative offices. Finally, a bright young intern compared lengths-of-stay by ward, and realized that the first ward to see an increased length-of-stay was the ward that had piloted HIPPO-Falls. Because the HIPPO-Falls program discouraged patients from getting up, they got so deconditioned that they were unable to go home. The number of patients referred to rehab doubled.

According to Nathan, the Chief of Medicine had wanted to scrap HIPPO-Falls altogether, but the CEO was concerned with the optics of such a move. After all, everyone knew that falls were bad. Families were angry when their relatives fell in hospital, even though many were admitted because they were falling at home. HIPPO-Falls had launched with great fanfare, and the hospital leadership had boasted of having the first Falls Prevention Consultants in the world. So HIPPO-Falls continued, and the MoPPET project was born.

MoPPET would involve a Mobility Consultant (otherwise known as a Physiotherapist) who would design an individual Mobility Preservation Plan for every patient. Three years ago Nathan had been handpicked to lead the project under the supervision of Dr. Erika Hastings, one of the department's star researchers and the head of the General Internal Medicine division. Nathan was incredibly happy to be chosen. It was a high profile project under a high profile researcher, with the potential for publication in a high impact journal. There was good evidence that poor mobility put people at risk for all kinds of awful things, like falls, cognitive decline, and longer hospital stays. Nathan already knew that he wanted to subspecialize in Cardiology, but with the right spin, MoPPET could be made relevant to that too (movement is good for the heart).

Nathan spent almost a year writing a grant application and eventually secured funding for the project. Shortly after the grant came through Nathan decided he was too busy with Cardiology to lead the project, and had suggested that I take it over. Initially I had been thrilled, as we were strongly encouraged to do a research project during our residency, and I didn't have any brilliant research ideas of my own. Although

Nathan would be first author on the paper, it would still be impressive on my CV.

Unfortunately we couldn't move forward without approval from the Research Ethics Board, and I had spent the past year going back and forth with them over concerns that a mobility program could put patients at risk of falls. I had submitted a fourth revision of the study protocol two months ago and was still waiting for their response. But for some reason, Nathan thought that the delay in getting Research Ethics Board approval was my fault.

Chloe wandered into the kitchen, and I welcomed the distraction.

"Do you have anything to eat?" she asked, opening the door to one of the cupboards.

"Yes, actually," I said proudly. I had gone grocery shopping that morning for the first time in over a month, with the rationale that healthy eating would be important for Chloe's mental and physical recovery. "I bought ingredients for a chicken casserole." I paused, remembering that cooking had been one of her recent passions. "Do you want to help cook?"

Chloe pulled a bag of salted peanuts from the back of the cupboard.

"No thanks, I'm good with this," she said flatly, and turned to go back to her room.

"Okay, maybe we could make it tomorrow," I suggested.

"Maybe," she said. "What's your Wi-Fi password?"

"Crazylikeafox," I answered. "All one word." Nathan's last name was Fox.

Chloe burst out laughing.

"That's so Nathan," she said when she recovered her breath.

"Yeah, it wasn't my choice," I said dryly. I would have to change the password.

Six

The day after Chloe came home from the hospital I had to start a two-month rotation on the General Internal Medicine ward. My official title was that of Junior Attending Physician, meaning that I was supposed to run things as though I was the Attending Physician. The actual Attending Physician, Dr. Erika Hastings, would have her name on the charts and bill the government for looking after the patients; I would do everything else. Coincidentally, Dr. Hastings was also the Staff supervisor for our MoPPET project. MoPPET was only one of many projects she was involved with, and I suspected I had been assigned to run her team so she would have more time for research. I had never worked with her clinically, but she had a reputation for being pretty hands-off.

My team was composed of two other residents: Lucas Everson, who was in his third year of Internal Medicine, and Benjamin Darling, the first year psychiatry resident. There was supposed to be a first year Internal Medicine resident, but she was off on stress leave. In addition, we were assigned three third year medical students. For reasons that no one understood, the students rotated on a different schedule than we did, and they were beginning their second week of the rotation. Unfortunately it was only their second week doing clinical work in the hospital, so I expected them to be pretty green.

The five of them were already there when I arrived at our team's office. An awkward silence fell when I walked in the door, and I blushed. Either they were giving me the respect they would give a true Attending Physician or they had been talking about the Central Line Incident.

Shortly after we completed introductions and exchanged phone numbers Nathan walked into the room and set a cardboard coffee cup in front of me. It was the first time I had seen him since the night I broke up with him, and I was momentarily paralyzed. I thought about handing it back to him on principle, but by the time I regained the powers of speech and movement he had turned and walked out. My name was written in black marker on the cardboard sleeve. Beneath it, in Nathan's distinctive handwriting, were the words 'I'm sorry.'

Another awkward silence fell.

"I apologize, Ellis, please continue," I said to the medical student who had been about to present the patients he had seen on call the previous night. I had already identified him as one of the incredibly keen medical students who liked to demonstrate their keenness by asking obscure and irrelevant questions to try to stump their supervisors.

Ellis flipped through his notes. "Mr. Warner is a forty-eight year old man who came to the emergency room with joint pain. He has previously been diagnosed with rheumatoid arthritis but he believes that his arthritis was caused by a spider bite that he suffered on a vacation to Mexico three years ago. He noticed a bite on his right lower leg after sunbathing. He put some calamine lotion on it but it still swelled up. The next day he saw a local doctor there who prescribed him some sort of anti-inflammatory. He has noticed that his arthritis is always worse in his right leg."

A lot of medical students suffered from the delusion that more information was always better. They were wrong.

I scrolled through his labs and X-rays on the computer. Everything pointed to rheumatoid arthritis.

"He's been treating his arthritis with nutritional therapy," said Ellis. "He follows a special diet to keep his body in the proper pH balance to prevent his arthritis from flaring."

"So why did he come here?" I asked. "He doesn't need to be in the hospital for nutritional therapy. In fact, it's probably easier for him to follow a specialized diet at home."

"His pain became too severe for him to treat naturally," Ellis explained.

"So how are we treating it?"

"Morphine," said Ellis.

"And steroids for the inflammation?" I asked.

"No, just morphine," explained Ellis. "He doesn't want anything synthetic or unnatural."

"Okay," I said. I was pretty sure the morphine he was getting wasn't natural either, unless the drug companies were still extracting it from poppies. "Let's just go see him together."

But Ellis wasn't done. "He asked if we knew of any other natural therapies that might help him."

"Well, I've been reading about holistic breathing techniques," I said, hoping to lighten the mood. "Healing breaths, calming breaths, energizing breaths, that sort of thing."

"That's a good idea," said Ellis seriously. I could tell that Lucas was trying not to laugh, and I felt guilty.

"He's sensitive to air pollution and has requested a room with a HEPA filter," Ellis continued.

Lucas nodded. "One of the lasting adverse effects of the COVID pandemic," he commented.

Ellis looked confused. "Sensitivity to pollution?"

"No, public knowledge of HEPA filters," said Lucas. "I think the hospital only has two. If he wants to wait for one he'll probably never make it off his hallway stretcher."

"Um, okay," said Ellis. "He also needs to know what kind of laundry detergent the hospital uses, as he has multiple chemical sensitivities. I promised I would ask you."

"That's a good question, Ellis," I said. "Unfortunately, I have no idea."

Ellis's face fell. "Oh. How would I find out?"

"You'd have to ask someone in housekeeping, I guess," I said.

"I can do that," said Ellis. He pulled out his phone. "Do you think they're on social media?"

Lucas turned his face away and made a strange noise that

sounded like a cross between a laugh and a cough. "I think we should start seeing patients and look into this later," I said diplomatically.

"What should we tell him about the detergent?" Ellis asked.

"You could say you'll look into it. Or if he's really concerned, he could ask his family to bring in his own sheets."

"He says he's incredibly sensitive. Even his roommate's sheets could be a problem for him."

"Well if he's that sensitive, Ellis, he would probably have had a reaction already."

"He said it could happen at any time."

"I see. Well, what do the sheets smell like to you?"

Ellis looked anxious. "I don't know."

"I think they smell like Tide," said Lucas, who was already halfway out the door.

"I agree," I said. "Ellis, you can tell him we think it's Tide."

We trooped down to the emergency room to see the new patients together. Although it was only their second week in the hospital, the medical students seemed to have mastered the essential skill of walking with their eyes fixed on the floor straight ahead of them, and avoiding eye contact with anyone they passed. An elderly lady parked in a wheelchair by the nursing station called out "Help me, what does it mean?" in an endless loop, and we marched past without slowing down. Ellis led us to a stretcher in the hallway and pointed out Mr. Greenfield, a middle-aged man with pneumonia.

"Nice to meet you, Mr. Greenfield," I said. "I'm Dr. Ingram, the senior resident on the Medicine team." I glanced at Ellis's ID badge to remind myself of his last name. Under an incredibly blurry photo it read 'Mr. E Stanford.' "Mr. Stanford is one of our senior medical students and he's told me all about you," I said.

"It's Mr. Archer, actually," said Ellis.

I wasn't even aware that there was a Mr. Archer under our care. I looked down at my patient list, but didn't see the name.

"I'm sorry, Mr. Archer," I said to the man on the stretcher.

He looked at me in confusion.

"I'm Mr. Greenfield."

"Of course, Mr. Greenfield," I said smoothly, trying to give the impression that I was capable of leading an Internal Medicine team at what was supposed to be one of the top teaching hospitals in the country. "Patients get moved around so often in this hospital that we have to double check."

"My name is Ellis Archer," said Ellis. "But this is my first rotation at this hospital, and the security office gave me a defective ID badge. It didn't work on any of the locks. So I've borrowed my classmate Elliott's. He's currently on elective in Montreal."

Mr. Greenfield bore the confused look of a man who thought he had come to a hospital for medical care and had instead found himself in the middle of a bad stand-up routine. "Okay," he said.

"As I was saying, I'm Dr. Ingram," I said. "Ellis has told me your story," I said. "Are you feeling any better after some antibiotics?"

***

From: Cindy.McArthurCEO@torontohealthalliance.ca
To: Alldoctors@torontohealthalliance.ca
Subject: Bed Capacity Crisis

Dear Colleagues:

As you know, our institution continues to face critical capacity challenges. Bed occupancy is currently at 116%. There are currently 62 patients in the Emergency Department waiting for a bed on the ward. This makes it very difficult to provide the high standard of care that we take pride in at Toronto Health Alliance.

We ask you to do everything possible to ensure your patients are discharged in a timely way. Please aim to write at least one discharge order by 10 AM. We encourage you to escalate any barriers to discharge to the Senior Leadership Team.

Sincerely,

Cindy McArthur BA, MBA
CEO, Toronto Health Alliance
An Alliance of Care

One of the most common barriers to discharge was that the patient did not want to leave.   The hospital provided three meals a day and twenty-four hour nursing care, which was considerably more care than most would receive at home. Telling a patient or her relatives that she was being kicked out was one of my least favourite parts of my job. The flipside was that if I didn't stand firm, I would accumulate a large group of patients who no longer needed to be there, and the number of patients under my care would swell to an unmanageable number. I might even start getting personal emails from the Senior Leadership Team asking if I needed support with the discharge process.

So one of my goals for my second day on rotation was to set a discharge date for Winnie Campbell. Winnie was an 87-year-old lady with advanced dementia, who had been bedbound for several years and was unable to speak or swallow. All of her nutrition was provided through a feeding tube in her stomach. When she wasn't in the hospital she lived with her daughter Elaine, who had resisted numerous suggestions to put her on a list for a nursing home. Unfortunately Elaine had also resisted numerous suggestions that her mother be discharged home. Winnie had been admitted ten days ago with pneumonia, but she had finished her antibiotics and no longer needed oxygen, so she no longer needed to be in hospital.

I had met Elaine Campbell three years ago, during one of Winnie's previous hospitalizations. I was a second year resident then, leading a team for the first time. Winnie Campbell was known as a difficult discharge, and her daughter was famous for putting up one roadblock after another to prevent her mother from leaving hospital. At first I was confident that it would not be a problem for me; I would be fair but firm, explain that Winnie was medically stable to go, write a discharge order, and that would be that. Unfortunately it hadn't worked out that way. Elaine had first failed to return my phone calls, then she had involved the Ombudsperson, and finally she had threatened to sue me if her mother had a medical complication post discharge. For poor Winnie, the question of future medical complications was more of a when than an if, and I had backed down. When my rotation ended I had handed the problem over to a colleague.

I was determined that this time would be different. I had called Elaine yesterday to give her a medical update and lay the groundwork. Today I had to close the deal.

"Good morning, Ms. Campbell," I said. "It's Dr. Ingram. I wanted to follow-up on our conversation from yesterday."

"Hello Dr. Ingram, I'm glad you called," she said. "And please call me Elaine." She spoke incredibly slowly. I wasn't sure if it was her natural tempo or if she did it deliberately to irritate me.

"Well, Elaine, as we've discussed, your mother has been medically stable for several days now. She will need ongoing support at home, and I'd like to put in a request for home care services to start Friday -"

"This Friday? She can't go home this Friday. The new Bond movie doesn't open for a month."

I tried not to laugh at this non-sequitur.

"I don't see how that affects our discharge plan, Elaine."

Elaine tittered. "My mother hasn't missed a Bond premiere for as long as she can remember. She always goes on opening day. Most recently we've been going to the matinee, because it's not as busy as the evening show. Sean Connery is still her favourite Bond, but she's very excited to see the new one. She can't miss this movie."

"I see," I said politely, as though this was interesting and relevant information. "And we will aim to have her discharged well before the new movie premieres."

"But she can't walk. If you send her home on Friday, how am I going to get her to the theatre when the movie opens?"

I tried and failed to imagine Winnie Campbell in a movie theatre. I had never seen her out of bed.

 "Won't transport to theatre be an issue regardless of when she goes home?" I asked.

"I assumed that the transport team could take her directly to the theater on the day of her discharge. I don't know if it would be best for the paramedics to wait while she watches the movie, or whether we could just book another pickup afterward?"

I bit my lip to stifle a laugh.

"I think that's something that you'll need to organize on your own, Elaine. Have you considered taking her yourself in a wheelchair taxi?"

"Too expensive. She's on a fixed income."

There were a lot of things that I wanted to say to that. *And your solution is that we keep her in the acute care hospital for another month so that she can be discharged directly to a movie theatre? This is why our healthcare system is broke! This is why our healthcare workers are broken! Clearly talking to you is a waste of my time.*

I took a cleansing breath. "I'm sorry Elaine, but I don't have any other suggestions."

***

From: Stacey.Sullivan@torontohealthalliance.ca
To: Sophie.Ingram@torontohealthalliance.ca
Subject: Discharge plan

Hi Sophie!

I received a phone call from Elaine, the daughter of Winnie Campbell, who is currently admitted to your service. I

understand that you have discussed her discharge plan. Elaine
has requested that her mother's discharge be delayed for a
couple of weeks to allow her to attend the premiere of the new
James Bond movie. I advised her that I would liaise with you to
see how we can make this happen.

Thank you in advance for your help with this issue!

Warm regards,

Stacey Sullivan, BA, MA
Office of the Ombudsperson, Toronto Health Alliance
Committed to Equity and Excellence

***

From: Sophie.Ingram@torontohealthalliance.ca
To: Stacey.Sullivan@torontohealthalliance.ca
Re: Discharge plan
Dear Ms. Sullivan:

Thank you for your email!

I'm a little confused.   Are there concerns that Mrs. Campbell is
not medically stable for discharge?

If her medical stability is not in question, are you suggesting
her discharge should be delayed simply because her daughter
requests it? If so, should I extend this courtesy to all of the
patients under my care, or only if the request is related to the
opening of a movie? I am deeply committed to equity and I
wish to be consistent in my approach. I am, however, aware
that our institution is facing critical capacity challenges, and the
Senior Leadership Team has asked to be notified of any barriers
to discharge. Do you think we should liaise with the Senior
Leadership Team about this concern? Perhaps they could liaise
with the theatre about an advance screening of the movie?

Warm Regards,

Dr. Ingram

***

53

From: Stacey.Sullivan@torontohealthalliance.ca
To: Sophie.Ingram@torontohealthalliance.ca
Re: Re: Discharge Plan

Hi Dr. Ingram,

Discharge decisions rest with the medical team. I would never try to interfere with your medical decision-making. My role is to support you, the patient and the family through this process. Please let me know if I can be of further assistance!

Warm Regards,
Stacey Sullivan, BA, MA

<h1 style="text-align:center">Seven</h1>

The hospital was bursting at the seams. Due to the shortage of traditional beds, more and more patients were placed in 'unconventional spaces', like hallways and closets. I had heard that the administrators had recently tried to take over the tiny office that we used to review cases with the junior trainees. The Chief of Medicine had intervened, and told the administrators that if they took away our teaching space they would also need to take away the medical students. As the administrators prided themselves on running an Educational Centre of Excellence they had backed down.

But the patients kept coming through the doors, and we received daily emails telling us to discharge patients as quickly as we could, without sacrificing quality medical care or patient satisfaction. This was always difficult and sometimes impossible, and I spent my days scrambling to deal with sick patients and unhappy families. My evenings were spent struggling to support my unhappy sister, who in turn spent her time drinking Diet Coke, watching reality TV, and complaining about our parents. I tried to provide nourishing food and a sympathetic ear, but it was physically and emotionally exhausting. I felt like the only time I had to myself was the ten minutes I spent in the shower every morning.

So I wasn't thrilled at the prospect of wasting an hour at a special All-Staff meeting to hear a Very Exciting Announcement from the hospital CEO, Cindy McArthur. It would mean a longer day at work, and if I hadn't been supervising junior trainees I probably would have skipped it, but I thought I should set a good example. So after we reviewed the patients who were admitted overnight I led my team down to the auditorium. Prior to COVID there would have been coffee and stale bagels available, but the free food had ended with the pandemic.

The auditorium was only half full. I spotted Nathan in the second row, tapping on his cellphone and I grabbed a seat about halfway back. Although there were plenty of empty seats next to me, the rest of my team chose to sit in the very back of the room. I tried not to feel insulted. There could be an awkward dynamic between senior residents and the junior trainees, and maybe they thought I wouldn't want to sit with them.

I pulled out my phone to give myself something to do. At the top of my inbox was an email from Nathan. The subject line read MoPPET Mobility Consultant, and he had cc'd both Dr. Hastings and someone named Jessica Scott.

Hi Sophie,

I wanted to connect you with Jessica Scott, who will be working as our Mobility Consultant for the MoPPET trial. She is a recent physio grad and is really excited to be joining this project. The department of Medicine has agreed to fund half of her salary, and the remainder will come from our grant funding. She will be on this project full time, beginning next week.

I have suggested that she set up a meeting with you in the near future to discuss the vision for the project.

Cheers,
Nathan

I took a calming breath. As we couldn't start the trial until we got Research Ethics Board approval it seemed like a criminal waste of grant money to start paying a physiotherapist next week.

My friend Lucy Zhang slipped into the seat next to me. We had gone to medical school together, and she was now a fifth-year resident in orthopedics. As a petite female she didn't fit the stereotypical appearance of an ortho resident, but she had the classic no-nonsense personality. I hadn't seen her in a few weeks, and I hadn't told her about my break-up with Nathan, or that Chloe had moved in with me.

"What do you think this is about?" she asked.

I rolled my eyes. "No idea. Except that our CEO thinks it's going to be Very Exciting."

Lucy snorted. "Unfortunately I think that Cindy McArthur's idea of excitement is different from mine. She has great hair, though." And she did, loose blond waves that always looked perfect.

Cindy McArthur stood near the front of the stage, surrounded by six other executive types. As usual, she was immaculately dressed, in a magenta pantsuit and high heels. An outfit like that wouldn't survive an hour on a hospital ward. Cindy tapped the microphone. "Thank you for coming, everyone. We're just waiting while the videoconferencing is set up." A couple of IT guys fiddled with the computer under the podium.

"I'm surprised you even came to this," I said to Lucy. "I would have thought you'd be in the operating room."

Lucy looked aggrieved. "My Attending sent me down. They're doing a really interesting case too. And they let Peter stay." Peter was another resident in her year, and they had never really gotten along. "Figures they'd send the only female resident in the year. " She scanned the room. "I think I'm the only person here from the entire division."

Cindy McArthur tapped her microphone again.

"This is a historic day for our institution," she began. "This announcement reflects weeks of brainstorming, hard-work, planning, and consultation with internal and community stakeholders." She spoke slowly and deliberately, as though she wanted to give her audience time to reflect upon her words.

Lucy leaned over to whisper in my ear. "Do you think any of the underlings standing behind her will talk, or are they just up there for moral support?"

I bit my lip to keep from laughing. "Maybe the one with the briefcase is her stylist and that's why she always looks so well put together," I replied.

"As you all know, the COVID pandemic has brought destructive change to the healthcare field," Cindy continued. "Whenever we're faced with change, we try to see not only the challenge, but also the opportunity, and the pandemic has forced us to examine everything we do. We have questioned why we do things the way that we do them, and asked ourselves if there is a way to do things better. My friends, we are entering a new era of health-care. The old system will not be good enough."

"Never was, really," muttered Lucy.

Onstage, Cindy continued. "And so, I am here today to announce that to better reflect this new reality, we are going to be renaming the hospital. The Toronto Health Alliance group of hospitals will become Toronto Health Teams. This will be an acknowledgment of the critical importance of teamwork in everything that we do."

Lucy looked at me incredulously. "Is this for real?" she whispered.

"You can all expect to receive an email later today outlining the details of this change. The name will officially change on October 27th, and we will have a ribbon cutting ceremony in the main atrium. Unfortunately we will be unable to have a cake due to infection control regulations, but we have engaged a local bakery to create a pyramid of individually packaged cupcakes. The mayor will make a speech. All staff will receive new email addresses with the new institutional name. You will be asked to sign up for an online training session to review the process for transitioning to the new addresses. You will also receive instructions about where and when to get your picture taken for a new ID badge bearing the new name."

"I hope there's online training for the ID photos too," I whispered to Lucy.

"Do you think Cindy gives hair advice?" she asked.

"This brings me to the second major part of this announcement," said Cindy. "We are going to be choosing a new slogan for the hospital. I think of this as more than a slogan. It is our commitment to ourselves and to the community we serve." She nodded to one of the people standing behind her, and a slide flashed up on the screen.

"Our executive subcommittee has come up with five possible slogans for the hospital rebranding, and I am very proud to share them with you today." She read off the slogans as they appeared on the screen behind her head. *In it together. Teamwork makes the dream work. It's About Team. Team For Care. Leveraging Liaisons.*

At *Leveraging Liaisons*, Lucy made a strange choking sound and doubled forward, shaking. After about a minute she straightened in the chair, taking slow, deliberate breaths. A man in the row in front of us turned and glared.

"I take it back," she whispered. "The surgeons will be sorry they missed this. They won't believe me when I tell them about the slogans."

"We want your feedback on which slogan to choose," said Cindy McArthur. "So we will be holding a vote, and you will be emailed a link to a poll. We encourage everyone to participate. Everyone who submits a vote will be entered in a draw for a T-shirt bearing our new name."

"Now, the difficult part," she continued. "We always expect a certain amount of resistance to change. We are asking you all to be ambassadors, to help promote the new name within our organization and within the community. We will now take a five minute break to reflect upon what this new name will mean for you. Please feel free to discuss it amongst yourselves."

Chatter broke out through the room. A young woman beside Lucy turned toward us with an earnest expression. I recognized her as one of the pharmacy residents.

"I kind of like 'Teamwork makes the dream work,'" she said timidly. "You know, for the slogan?"

"I'm afraid I can't comment," said Lucy seriously. "My residency program has a strict rule against slogans. I could be kicked out."

The pharmacy resident looked confused, but Lucy's expression must have sent a clear message, because she turned away from us to talk to the man on her other side.

"It's hardly her fault, Lucy," I said.

"Sophie, we all must bear some responsibility for sitting silently and listening to this assault on our time and our society's resources. No one has the courage to call this BS."

Nathan walked quickly down the aisle with his phone glued to his ear. "I'm surprised Nathan came to this," said Lucy. "I would have thought he would have been busy, treating heart attacks and saving lives. He's probably off to do that now." Lucy had always thought Nathan had an inflated sense of his own importance.

"Well, the heart's pretty important," I said.

She nodded. "Yep. Pumps blood to the bone," she said. "Do you know, I had to call him last week about a patient. He knew it was me, and he still introduced himself as Dr. Fox. So I introduced myself as Dr. Zhang. You'd never know we socialize outside of work."

"I'm sure he just wasn't thinking," I said. I hadn't told Lucy that Nathan and I had broken up."

"Maybe," she said. "Do you call him Dr. Fox in bed?"

I blushed. "No." I must have looked uncomfortable, because Lucy apologized.

"I'm sorry, Sophie. Not the time or the place. Do you want to come for dinner tomorrow?" she asked. "You can bring Dr. Fox if you want."

I really wanted to say yes, but there was no way I could sit through an entire evening with Lucy and not disclose the fact that Nathan and I were no longer a couple, or that Chloe was living with me.

"I wish I could, Lucy, but I have to work this weekend. I'm on call tonight and Sunday." In theory, this kind of call just meant I had to be available to the residents by phone, but in reality I would likely end up at the hospital. "And tomorrow I have to clean my apartment, because it's a disaster."

Lucy raised an eyebrow. "I'll try not to be offended that you would rather clean your apartment than have dinner with me. Can't you make Nathan do it?"

I was so tired of keeping secrets. I'd known Lucy longer than I had known Nathan and I needed to unburden myself.

"Actually Nathan and I broke up," I said quickly. Lucy's eyes widened.

"Sophie! When was this?"

"Just over a month ago," I said. "It's a long story. And my sister Chloe's living with me now." Lucy had never met Chloe, but she had heard a lot about her.

"So the wedding is off?" She asked.

"Yep," I said. "We haven't actually cancelled all the plans yet. But I told him it's over, and he moved out."

"Wow." Lucy shook her head. "I'm sorry, Sophie." She paused. "I can't say that I'm sorry you're not marrying him," she clarified. Lucy had always been honest to a fault. "But I'm sorry you're going through it."

I nodded. "Thank you."

"So we'll expect you for dinner at six on Saturday," she said.

***

I returned home that evening to find Chloe parked in front of the TV, watching a cooking show. There was a box of doughnuts on the table, and it appeared that three had been eaten. My spirits lifted; maybe Chloe had left the apartment to buy doughnuts. This seemed like a step in the right direction.

"Hey, Chloe," I said. I tried a bite of something that looked like a blueberry fritter. "This is delicious. Where did you get them?"

"Samantha brought them," she answered.

"You had a friend over?" I asked.

"No, the lawyer? From my hearing?" she clarified. "She apparently had a meeting with Mom this afternoon, and she offered to drop off my cooking stuff."

I looked at my small kitchen, which now contained four cardboard boxes full of kitchen equipment. They blocked access to the fridge and most of the cupboards.

"Why was she meeting with Mom?" I asked. I didn't understand why Chloe had refused to see or speak to our parents since the capacity hearing but had allowed Samantha Albright to waltz into our apartment. I didn't like the idea of Samantha seeing my living space.

"I don't know. Maybe Mom needed to pay her?" Chloe guessed.

My phone beeped twice. I opened a text from my mom to find pictures of my apartment. Most were of the den that I had quickly converted to a bedroom for Chloe. Two empty cans of Diet Coke lay on top of the unmade sofabed, and three suitcases were open beside the bed with clothes spilling out of them. I had intended to move Nathan's snowboard but hadn't gotten around to it, and it still leaned against the wall beside a jumble of shoes. There were shots of the overflowing garbage can in the bathroom, and of the boxes of Nathan's things that were still stacked in my living room. Ironically, there were also pictures of the kitchen, rendered unusable by boxes of cooking supplies that Samantha had delivered that very day.

Another text came through from my mother.

"She needs to go back to the hospital. This is grounds for a Form 2 application. Lack of competence to care for herself."

I flushed with anger. The state of my apartment was as much my fault as Chloe's, and it was none of my mother's business.

My phone rang. It was, of course, my mother,

"I'm worried about Chloe," she said. "How is she doing?"

"Fine. She's asked me not to talk to you about her," I answered.

"Sophie, I know you're caught in the middle, but you must see -"

"Have you applied for a Form 2 yet?" I cut in. I had a vision of police showing up at my apartment to take Chloe to the hospital. I briefly considered getting her a room in a hotel somewhere to hide from the authorities but I realized that wasn't a long-term solution.

"Not yet. Samantha is researching the legal position and preparing a case. We plan to take it to a Justice of the Peace next week. Apparently they don't like hearing something like this on a weekend unless it's truly an emergency."

"You're not supposed to apply for a Form 2 in the first place unless it's truly an emergency."

"This is an emergency, Sophie."

"Are you going to apply to have me hospitalized too?" I asked sarcastically. "Since Chloe and I are sharing the same living space?"

"Don't be ridiculous, Sophie, you never lived like that before Chloe moved in."

That was not entirely true, but I was too tired to argue.

"Okay," I said.

"Would you be willing to help us prepare the application? Since you're living with Chloe you'll have a lot more information about how she's doing."

"No."

"*Sophie*. Think about it. As her family, we can't stand by and watch her self-destruct."

"I still think that going back to the hospital would cause her more harm than good. She spent a month there and I don't think it helped."

"Do you think she's improving with you?" My mother sounded both skeptical and hopeful.

"I don't know," I said honestly.

Eight

I spent Saturday morning cleaning my apartment and moving Nathan's things from the living room down to the storage locker. By lunchtime, the kitchen was still cluttered with Chloe's stuff, but the boxes were off the floor and there was a clear path to the fridge.

I decided to walk to Canadian Tire to pick up some things for Chloe. My latest library book, called *How to Beat Bipolar*, recommended a 'Goals Calendar.' It seemed pretty lame, but I didn't have any better ideas, so I bought a monthly dry erase calendar for the fridge to help Chloe track her goals. While I was there I bought her an aloe plant (because plants help combat depression), and a yoga mat.

When I got home I found Chloe flopped on the couch in our newly decluttered living room, drinking Diet Coke. "I bought a couple things for you," I told her. "This is an aloe plant. It's a succulent, so you only have to water it once a week." She rolled her eyes.

"I also got a yoga mat," I continued. "I thought you might want to do some dance exercises or something."

"I don't dance anymore, Sophie," she said flatly.

"And this is a goals calendar," I explained. I pulled it out of the bag and handed it to her. "We'll stick it on the fridge. You can write down your goals. They can be small things, like taking a walk or cooking a meal. Maybe write a résumé. I read a book that said no goal is too small.

Wordlessly, Chloe picked up a pink dry erase marker and wrote TAKE A SHOWER in big block letters diagonally across three squares, then walked over and stuck the calendar on the fridge with a magnet.

"How did you sleep?" I asked her.

"Fine."

"At the hearing you mentioned getting a part-time job. Have you given any more thought to that?"

"No. Have you given any thought to moonlighting so you can earn some real money?"

"Yes, I've thought about it, but Chloe, I'd like to talk about your plans, not mine."

"One of the therapists in the hospital suggested that if a conversation made me feel challenged or uncomfortable, I should turn the conversation around on the questioner." She smiled. "So have you made any plans to moonlight? Because I'm concerned you're not working to your full potential."

"No. Have you thought about going back to school?"

"With my record, I wouldn't get accepted to anything worthwhile."

"Have you seen Dr. Jankovic this week?" So far Chloe had refused to tell me anything about her mental health plan. I didn't know if she had seen her psychiatrist since her discharge, or if she was taking medication.

"No."

"Chloe, you have to work with me," I said in frustration. I could hardly believe that this was the same girl who had charismatically told the Capacity Board about her goals for the future. "It's been over a week. I understand you're down, but you're not going to feel better if you just mope around my apartment and watch TV."

"I don't choose to be depressed, Sophie." It was as though she had read my mind.

"Chloe, do you believe you have a mental illness?" I had noticed that Chloe only raised the subject of her mental illness when she needed an excuse for bad behaviour.

It was a blunt question, and when she fell silent I was concerned that I had offended her, but she appeared to be giving it serious thought.

"Do you know, you're the first person who has ever asked me that?"

"None of the psychiatrists?"

She rolled her eyes. "Of course not. They're too busy telling me what they think. And how I should think."

"And what do you think?" I persisted.

"Right now I just don't see the point. I'm not qualified for anything other than a minimum wage job. There's no way I'd be able to afford rent in the city. But living with Mom and Dad is getting pathetic, and I don't want to be dependent on them for the rest of my life. It gives them control of me."

"You could go back to school. I'm sure Mom and Dad would support you if you had a plan."

"I'm too old."

"You're twenty-eight!" I protested.

"Yeah. And I'd be starting where most people start when they graduate high school. I don't think I could do it."

"Of course you could."

"You could. I couldn't. I'm not strong like you."

She looked young and vulnerable, curled on my couch in a set of frayed pink flannel pyjamas that were several sizes too big for her and emphasized her thinness. I thought about my parents' plan for a Form 2 application, and imagined the police coming to the apartment to take her back to hospital. Nothing was likely to happen over the weekend, but I had a decision to make by Monday. I could explain the situation to Chloe and try to persuade her to go back to the hospital voluntarily, which might be less traumatic for her than being taken there against her will. I could beg my parents to reconsider. Or I could ignore the situation and let the chips fall where they may.

"I'm going to a friend's for dinner tonight, you should come," I said impulsively. Bringing Chloe would mean that I couldn't tell Lucy the full story about what happened with Nathan, but it wouldn't matter. The idea of Chloe spending the evening alone in her pyjamas, drinking Diet Coke in front of the television, wasn't pleasant.

"No. Thank you, but no."

***

Lucy and her husband Ben lived in a semi-detached in East York that they had bought when they moved to Toronto for her residency. At the time many of our friends had thought they were crazy to buy a house, as the housing market was incredibly high and they would likely have to move again for Lucy's fellowship. Four years later the market was, incredibly, far higher, and if they decided to sell they would make a nice profit.

We ordered Thai from a place down the street and ate it outside on the back deck. Ben told stories about the kindergarten kids he taught and Lucy told us about her fellowship interviews. I contributed very little to the conversation, but I had known them long enough that there was no awkwardness. There was something therapeutic about sitting on the deck with friends, enjoying the smell of the fall leaves.

After dinner Ben went inside to watch a baseball game, leaving Lucy and me on the deck.

"So you ended things with Nathan?" she asked bluntly.

"Yep. We're trying to keep it quiet, though. He's worried it will affect his fellowship prospects."

Lucy snorted. "Yeah, I can see how that would be his biggest fear."

"I really wish we hadn't sent out Save the Date cards," I said. "I'm not sure of the etiquette in this situation. Do I email everyone to say the wedding's off? Or send another round of cards in the mail?" Rationally I knew that this was the least of my problems, but I dreaded making the announcement.

"I would just email," said Lucy. "Don't waste any more time and money. I'll take care of the emails for you if you like," she offered.

"What would you write?" I asked cautiously.

"Sophie Ingram has come to her senses, and will no longer be marrying Nathan Fox," she suggested. "Clear and concise."

I laughed. "I'll let you know."

Lucy took a sip of her wine. "So what happened?" she asked.

"I found him in bed with Chloe," I said. I told her about Chloe's overdose attempt and hospitalization, and the miserable capacity hearing. When I explained that Chloe was now living with me, Lucy whistled.

"You're a far better person than I am. If my sister pulled a stunt like that I'd never speak to her again. She sure as hell wouldn't be living with me."

"It may not be for long, though." I told her about my parents' plan to apply for a Form 2 to try to get Chloe readmitted to the hospital, and the photographs Samantha had taken of our apartment.

Lucy shook her head. "I can't believe the lawyers snuck in like that," she said. "There must be rules against that. What did you say their names were?"

"Samantha Albright," I said. "And Jack Delacroix. To be fair, only Samantha broke in, but -"

I broke off when I realized Lucy was staring at me.

"I've heard of Jack Delacroix," she said. "Sophie, he's a pretty big deal."

"And he knows it," I said.

"No seriously, he was, like, the youngest person to make partner at his firm in ages. Maybe in the history of the firm."

"How do you know this?" I asked curiously.

"My cousin Mel's a paralegal, and she goes for drinks with a group of other paralegals every few weeks. I went once. They talked about Jack Delacroix for over half an hour. Apparently he had just fired an associate, and the girl left in tears.

"That doesn't surprise me," I said, remembering the cutting words I had overheard at Chloe's hearing.

"Yeah, they say he doesn't suffer fools," Lucy continued. "Can't blame him for that. Anyway, not a warm and fuzzy personality. Despite that, all the junior lawyers want to work with him, and all the women at the firm want to date him. So far no one has managed a date; they say he only dates models and movie stars."

I rolled my eyes. "That must be inconvenient for him, given how few movie stars live in Toronto." The gossip sounded highly exaggerated, and I was surprised to hear it from Lucy.

"Google him," said Lucy. "He was at a film festival with someone famous a couple of years ago."

I obediently typed his name into the search bar on my phone. The first hit was his profile at his firm's website which showed a very serious looking photo and a description of his areas of expertise. The second result was an article from the *Toronto Times*, a free online news site. It was dated two years ago and used the same photo as his firm's website. It seemed that he had made their list of *Ten To Watch in Toronto*. There was a short blurb beneath his photo.

Jack Delacroix has had a good year. Although only thirty-two, he's already made a name for himself in the competitive world of corporate law. Earlier this year he was made a full partner at Reynolds Reilly. Then, in the spring, he was lead counsel for Bennett Hodges's acquisition of Icarus Industries, rumoured to be a multibillion-dollar deal. Outside of the office, he was seen accompanying the lovely Lily Lawson to the Toronto International Film Festival in the fall. Mr. Delacroix is known for his punishing work ethic, cutting wit, and dreamy dimples. He's also a man of mystery, and was the only one of our Ten To Watch in Toronto who declined to be interviewed for this feature. Apparently he had too much work to do. Will all work and no play make Jack a dull boy? Sources say: Not likely.

I handed Lucy my phone to show her the article.

"Lily Lawson," Lucy said triumphantly. "I knew it." Lily

Lawson was a Canadian actress who was currently a big name in Hollywood.

Lucy tapped the screen a few times before handing my phone back to me. She had found a photo of Jack and Lily Lawson standing outside a restaurant. Lily wore a floor-length blue ball gown that probably cost more than I earned in a year as a resident, and was looking adoringly at Jack, who was smiling down at her.

I set my phone aside. "Well. Proof that he looks good in a tuxedo and has at least one famous friend. Doesn't change the fact that his legal tactics are ethically questionable."

"Didn't you say your sister had a lawyer for the hearing?" Lucy asked. "What did she say about the photos?"

I hadn't even thought of Jade Tomlinson.

"Yeah, there was a lawyer but she was pretty underwhelming," I explained.

"Still, she might be able to advise you," Lucy suggested.

"Maybe," I said. But I knew I wouldn't call Jade Tomlinson. Samantha and Jack had violated my personal space, and I wanted to deal with this myself.

Nine

From: Stacey.Sullivan@torontohealthalliance.ca
To: Sophie.Ingram@torontohealthalliance.ca
Subject: Nutritional Therapy

Hi Sophie,

I received an email from Mr. Philip Warner. He is currently admitted under your care, being treated for arthritis from a spider bite. He has been seeing a holistic nutritionist and is concerned that the hospital has been unable to accommodate his nutritional therapy plan. He has sent me a document outlining what he can eat. He prefers locally sourced, seasonally inspired food. I reassured him that I would pass this information along to you so that you could act on it appropriately.

Stacey Sullivan, BA, MA
Office of the Ombudsperson, Toronto Health Alliance (soon to be Toronto Health Teams)
Committed to Equity and Excellence

A month ago I would have sent Stacey Sullivan a diplomatic reply, but today I didn't have time. I debated whether to forward her email to the dietitian or the trash can, and ultimately decided on the dietitian. It was Monday morning, and I needed to arrange a meeting with my parents' lawyers before they applied for a Form 2. I rushed the trainees through their review of the new cases and told Lucas I was leaving him in charge. I knew he wanted more autonomy, and today he would get it.

I reached an automated directory at the law firm and tried Samantha's extension first. It went directly to voicemail. I recognized her voice on the recording, so she probably wasn't senior enough to have a secretary. I hung up and tried Jack, and his extension was answered after the first ring.

"Good morning, Mr. Delacroix's office, Mary speaking. How may I help you?" The voice was brisk and slightly condescending.

"Yes, good morning," I tried to sound confident. I had never liked talking to strangers on the phone. "I need an appointment to see Mr. Delacroix and his colleague, Samantha Albright. Today if possible."

She laughed. "My dear, Mr. Delacroix is in meetings all day. His next available appointment is in two weeks. Are you currently a client with us?"

"Not exactly, but my parents are clients," I began. This woman was making me nervous.

"Then perhaps your parents should be calling for an appointment?" Definitely condescending now.

"But it's in regard to the unauthorized entry to my apartment - "

I was quickly cut off. "Mr. Delacroix does not practice criminal law."

"It's not exactly a criminal matter -"

"He doesn't deal with landlord-tenant disputes either."

"It's not a landlord-tenant issue. The unauthorized entry was by Mr. Delacroix. Well, his associate, Ms. Albright. Most likely working under his direction."

Mary laughed again. "You're saying Samantha Albright broke into your apartment?"

"Well it's complicated -"

"Miss, I don't have time for jokes. If you would like to leave your name, I will let Mr. Delacroix know that you called."

"Sophie Ingram."

"Thank you Miss Ingram. Have a nice day."

***

I remembered that Samantha had texted my sister to coordinate their doughnut date, so I got her cell number from Chloe. She answered on the first ring.

"Samantha Albright," she answered. Her voice was also condescending and confident. I guess shrinking violets weren't drawn to the legal field.

"Samantha, it's Sophie Ingram. Chloe's sister. I'd like to meet with you to discuss the photos you took of my apartment."

"Sophie! Nice to hear from you. I'm sorry, I don't think it would be appropriate for me to meet with you. My clients are your parents, not you, and any details of your sister's case are privileged -"

Anger gave me confidence. "Then my next call will be to the Law Society, Samantha, to file a complaint about your conduct. You convinced my sister, whom you and your clients have argued is incapable of making decisions, to let you into my apartment. My home. Under the preteens that it was a social visit."

A note of panic crept into her voice. "It was a social visit. We have a mutual friend on social media. I'm surprised we've never met in person before."

"Right. Surprising that you never sought to meet in person before my parents hired you. Tell me, Samantha, did you get Chloe's phone number from your mutual friend? Or from my mother?"

There was a beat of silence. "I was trying to help -"

"Well Samantha, I had hoped to discuss it with you. In person. Today. But, as you don't think that would be appropriate, I'll discuss it with the Law Society instead."

"I'll meet you."

I smiled. "I appreciate it. Can you be free in half an hour?"

"I have meetings all morning." She sounded truly

panicked now. "I have half an hour blocked off for lunch. But I don't have an office, just a cubicle. There won't be enough space, and I won't be able to book a conference room last minute. Can I meet you in the lobby of our building?"

I wondered if she was trying to ensure the meeting was brief by not allowing me to sit down, but her explanation sounded plausible. I didn't have an office either.

"Okay, I'll meet you in the lobby."

It was a really posh office tower, with a bright lobby with a fountain in the centre. Well-dressed people streamed off the elevators, likely heading out for lunch. I spotted Samantha standing by the fountain, dressed in a pencil skirt and high heels. I felt underdressed and conspicuous in a long sleeved T-shirt, scrub pants and sneakers.

I had rehearsed what I wanted to say on the walk to her office, and I jumped right into it.

"Samantha, regardless of your social media connection, you are not friends with Chloe, and no one would believe otherwise. By coming to our apartment like you did, you took advantage of a woman whom you claim is mentally ill, and -"

I broke off when I saw Jack walking through the lobby with three other men in suits. He spotted us right away, and by his look of surprise I guessed that Samantha had not told him about our meeting. He said something to his colleagues then turned and walked toward us.

"Hello, Dr. Ingram. Can I call you Sophie?" He gave me a warm smile that lit his dark eyes, and some of my anger evaporated.

"If I can call you Jack," I said.

"Of course. It's nice to see you." He turned to Samantha, clearly waiting for an explanation for why we were chatting in the lobby, but she just stared at her shoes.

"So what brings you here, Sophie?" asked Jack. "I hope Chloe is well?"

"Oh, she's quite well, thanks," I said. "But I think you know why I'm here."

He looked confused.

"I don't, actually. But I'm glad you are. I wanted to apologize. We acted disrespectfully and I'm sorry. I know Samantha feels the same."

"So you do know why I'm here," I said.

He still looked confused. "You came for an apology?"

"Not exactly. I came for a discussion of boundaries. I wanted to clarify whether Ms. Albright is a personal friend of my sister's. If so, I don't think it's appropriate for her to act as my parents' lawyer for matters concerning my sister's health."

Jack looked surprised. "Personal friends? Sam, I didn't know you knew Chloe?"

Samantha turned red. "We have a mutual friend on Instagram."

"Okay, but a mutual acquaintance on social media hardly makes you personal friends," said Jack. "Had you ever met her prior to the hearing? Even had any online communication?"

"No." Samantha's voice was soft.

There was a beat of silence while I waited to see if she was going to bring up their meeting after the hearing. It quickly became clear that she was not.

"So when you came to my apartment to visit her, that was in your capacity as my parents' lawyer," I said. "And investigator, I guess, since you took pictures of my home and sent them to my mother."

"What are you talking about?" Jack asked. Either he was an excellent actor or he really hadn't known.

"Samantha came to visit Chloe Friday afternoon while I was at work. They chatted over doughnuts. Sometime during the visit Samantha took the opportunity to take pictures of my home, which she then sent to my mother. My mother has told me that my housekeeping doesn't meet her standards."

Samantha was staring at her shoes.

"Sam?" asked Jack.

"Well, as I mentioned, Chloe and I have a mutual friend," she said defensively. "I was at her parents' house for a meeting, and I noticed some boxes of Chloe's things packed up by the door. I thought I could do Chloe a favour by dropping them off. So I sent her a message and offered to stop by with her stuff, and she invited me in."

"And the photos?" I asked. "Do you frequently take pictures of your friends' apartments and forward them to other people?"

"I was concerned about her living situation," she said primly. "I wanted to help, and I thought it was in everyone's best interests that I notify her mother."

Jack raised his eyebrows at that explanation, then turned to me. "Sophie, I understand why you're upset. Why don't we go up to my office to discuss this further?"

"I have to get back to work." I turned toward Samantha, who was once again looking at the floor. "But I wanted to make it clear that you can't be both Chloe's friend and my parents' lawyer. It's an obvious conflict of interest, and I'm confident that the Law Society would agree with me. If you, or any of your colleagues, want to communicate with Chloe, you contact her lawyer. If you pull this kind of stunt again I'll file a complaint. I expect you to delete the photos. I've kept notes on how you obtained them, and if they feature in any future hearings I'll make sure everyone knows the story. I'll also explain that the majority of the mess was mine, and in no way related to Chloe or her mental state."

"Sophie -" Jack tried to interrupt, but I was on a roll.

"I've had a lot going on in the past month, in addition to working full time," I continued. "But that's really none of your business. My apartment isn't a fire hazard, and -"

"Sophie -" Jack tried again.

"Having a messy apartment is not a symptom of mental illness. But if you think it is, you can try to get me certified. If you succeed, maybe I'll be able to quit my job and collect disability insurance. You may be doing me a favour."

I stopped and took a deep breath. Samantha was still staring at her shoes. They were wonderfully impractical shoes, almost three inches tall with stiletto heels.

"Sophie you're right," said Jack. "On all points. It was inappropriate. I can speak for Sam when I say that the photos will be deleted. Immediately. We will ensure that any further communication with your sister goes through Ms. Tomlinson. Sam?"

She looked up. "Yes, of course. I'll delete them right away."

"And you'll advise my parents against filing a Form 2 application? Or at least explain why the apartment photos can't be used for any application, as they were inappropriately obtained."

Samantha looked at Jack, who nodded. "Yes," she answered.

"And we owe an apology to Chloe and to you," continued Jack. "It was an invasion of your privacy and it was wrong."

My anger only diminished slightly. I was pretty sure he would say anything to get me to shut up and go away. The security guard was looking over at us.

Sam looked at her watch. "Sophie, Jack, I'm so sorry, I'm supposed to be at a client meeting in ten minutes. I have to run. But you have my word about the photos." She turned and walked back towards the elevator, her high heels clicking on the polished floor.

To my surprise, Jack made no move to leave. "Sophie. Will you let me buy you lunch so we can talk about this?"

"I don't think there's much more to discuss."

"Well, coffee then," he said.

I shook my head. "I only drink coffee first thing in the morning. Thank you though." This was an outright lie, as I routinely drank several cups of coffee per day. More, since Nathan had started buying me morning lattes.

Jack looked amused. "Then you can do me a favour and sit across the table from me so I don't have to drink alone."

I unsuccessfully fought a smile. "I have to get back to work."

"Ten minutes, Sophie."

"Did they teach you this in Negotiation 101?"

He raised an eyebrow. "No, this is upper-year stuff."

I wasn't quite sure how it happened, but I found myself following him to the Starbucks across the lobby. The barista greeted Jack with a big smile.

"We'd like a venti chocolate chip frappuccino and a tall black coffee," he said.

"Whipped cream and chocolate shavings on the frappuccino?"

"Yes please." He tapped his credit card.

I was irritated that he hadn't bothered to ask what I wanted. It seemed that men thought that buying expensive caffeinated drinks would atone for any sin.

"Do you think that buying me a ten dollar frappuccino is going to somehow make up for the little stunt you and Samantha pulled?"

He feigned confusion. "The frappuccino is for me. You said you didn't want anything. I ordered a coffee in case you changed your mind."

Wordlessly, I grabbed the black coffee off the bar. He picked up the frappuccino, thanked the barista, and steered me towards one of the small tables along the wall.

"Sophie, I want to apologize for what I said on the day of the hearing. It was unprofessional, but more importantly, it wasn't true." He paused. "It's been on my mind, actually, and I had been thinking of a way to apologize to you."

I didn't believe that, and I didn't say anything. After a beat of silence, he continued.

"I've already informed your parents that I will no longer be working with them on this. I know they were unhappy with our performance at the hearing, and I suggested that their best option might be to find a new lawyer at a different firm. I had no idea that Samantha had met with your mother, or that she was planning to visit your apartment."

"Did Samantha know that you had given up the case?" I asked.

He nodded. "I told her the day after the hearing." He took a sip from his frappuccino. I was impressed that he managed to drink it without looking ridiculous.

"So why would she photograph my apartment?"

Jack shook his head. "I don't know, Sophie. Maybe she hoped your father would send some other work her way. I intend to sit down with her and try to get a better explanation. But we both know that what she did was inappropriate and that you could make a very valid complaint to the Law Society."

There was something satisfying about his acknowledgment that she had crossed a line.

I noticed he was staring at my left hand, which was wrapped around my coffee cup.

"You're still wearing your engagement ring," he commented.

I looked down at the ring and nodded. It was a round diamond in a halo setting on a simple yellow gold band. Nathan had taken me to Tiffany's where I had chosen it myself, and part of me would be sorry to give it up. We had agreed that I would continue to wear it until his fellowship decision was announced.

Jack looked thoughtful. "I thought you told the Capacity Board that your engagement was off?"

"It is. But I still find the ring convenient. It decreases the number of men who pressure me to drink coffee with them."

He smiled. "I can see how you would find that annoying. Especially as you don't drink coffee."

I set down my cup. It would have been better with cream and sugar, but even black it was pretty good. "Exactly," I answered. "But we were talking about Samantha."

"Right. Sophie, I'm asking you to cut her a break. She's working her ass off as an associate in the hope that she'll make partner in a few years, but so is every single one of her colleagues. The competition is fierce and she's looking for any advantage she can find. I imagine Medicine is pretty similar. She knows she made a mistake and she's sorry."

I was softening. It was a good apology, but it would

have been better coming from Samantha herself. I suspected Samantha wasn't sorry she had done it, only sorry she'd been caught.

"If you didn't know about it, why are you apologizing for her?"

"I was the senior lawyer on the case, so I bear some responsibility for her actions."

My phone rang. It was Lucas, my senior resident. I mouthed an apology to Jack and answered it.

"Hi Sophie, I'm sorry to bother you." I had never heard Lucas sound so frustrated. "Mrs. Campbell's daughter just showed up at the nursing station and she's very upset. She says you left a voicemail saying that her mother would be discharged on Wednesday and she insists that won't be possible."

"Did she give a reason?"

"Yeah, her dog is sick."

"Her dog is sick? Lucas, that's a really lame excuse. And something of a disappointment, after her attempt to convince us that her mother needed to be discharged directly to a movie theater. Which was at least original." I took a deep breath. "Did you ask her what she would have done if her dog had gotten sick while her mom was at home?"

"Yep. She would have brought her mom to the hospital. She has to look after the dog."

"So instead of taking her sick dog to an animal hospital she would have dropped her mother off at the ER."

"Pretty much, yeah. Her priority is to look after the dog." Lucas now sounded like he was enjoying this.

"Lucas, I don't care if her dog is *dead*!" I paused. Jack was looking at me with amusement, and a man at the next table had turned his head. I lowered my voice.

"I mean I *care*. But I don't care in respect to the discharge decision."

"Right. You want me to tell her that?"

"Yes please. And if you really must, you can delay her discharge until Thursday."

I tucked my phone back into my pocket.

Jack grinned. "People don't want to leave?"

I rolled my eyes. "You have no idea. People come up with one excuse after another to explain why they can't go home. So I usually start with an optimistically early date to leave room for negotiation. If I can get this patient home by Friday I'll count it a win."

He laughed. "So what happens if she doesn't want to go home Friday?"

I shrugged. "Every case is different. It depends on what reasons they give and how many people are stuck on stretchers in hallways waiting for beds. We hear some pretty crazy excuses."

"Like what?" He actually seemed interested.

"Well, I once had a patient's sister show up and tell me that the patient's husband was having an affair with the neighbour. Apparently the patient didn't know but most of the neighbourhood did. The sister argued that if the patient found out, it would sabotage her recovery, and told me I had a professional obligation to stage some sort of intervention. She thought I should meet with the husband and neighbour to explain that their cheating was putting the patient's health at risk."

Jack burst out laughing, loudly and uncontrollably, and it somehow made him seem more human. His elbow knocked over my coffee cup, spilling coffee across the small table, and some splashed onto my sleeve. I stood up to get out of the way.

He stopped laughing and jumped to his feet. "Sophie, I'm so sorry." He grabbed some napkins from the counter and tried to mop up the mess.

I smiled. "It's okay. It was meant to be a funny story."

I dabbed at my sleeve and he noticed the stain.

"Oh, Sophie, I'm sorry. I'll pay for dry cleaning, of course, or to replace the shirt."

"It's okay, it's just a t-shirt. No one trusts a well-dressed doctor, anyway."

Jack looked confused. "What do you mean?"

"Well, most doctors doing front-line work give up on flashy dressing pretty quickly. It's a lot of unpredictable hours and it can be messy. The only well-dressed doctors are the really junior trainees who know they contribute so little to the medical team that they have to dress to impress. Or the doctors who have crossed over to administration and only do a few weeks of clinical work a year to keep their license. Style over substance."

I could see Jack looking down at his tailored suit.

"I'm sure it's different for lawyers," I said, flushing.

"It's okay, I often prioritize style over substance. In my line of work most people can't tell the difference." He smiled. "Seriously, though, if you come up to my office I'm sure I can find someone to lend you a shirt. Actually, my secretary probably has one, I'm sure she'd be happy to lend it to you and I'll get yours dry cleaned."

I gave him a skeptical look. "I've spoken to your secretary on the phone . . ."

I let the sentence trail off, but my expression must have been telling, because Jack smiled. "Yeah, she scares me too. But she's the fifth secretary I've had in the past three months, so I can't get rid of her without raising some eyebrows at Human Resources."

"You've had five secretaries in three months? What do you do to them?"

He looked a little sheepish. "It's a long story. Mary's the fifth. When did you talk to Mary?"

"This morning. I wanted to book an appointment to discuss the apartment photos. I was informed that you are very busy and important but that she would get back to me when she had nothing better to do."

"I'm sorry Sophie. Mary's still pretty new to my office, she wouldn't have known. I'll talk to her, make sure she puts you through next time you call."

I felt irrationally flattered, until I remembered that I would have no reason to call his office. "Um, but I probably won't call. Seeing as you're no longer working on my sister's case."

Was it my imagination, or did Jack Delacroix look disappointed?

"Unless you and Samantha have pulled some other ethically questionable trick that I haven't found out about yet?" I asked.

He laughed. "If Samantha has, I haven't found out about it either."

He reached inside his pocket and pulled out a business card. "Here. My email and cell number. If you need to reach me, just call me directly. I owe you a favour for not pursuing a complaint against Sam. Call me if you ever need legal advice."

I didn't remember agreeing not to pursue a complaint against Sam. He was altogether too smooth, and I remembered all the reasons I had to be angry with him.

"Thank you. But I would have to be desperate." On that exit line, I turned and walked out of the building.

$$\mathcal{T}en$$

Nathan brought me vanilla lattes every morning for a week, and every day there was a different message written on the cardboard sleeve. The initial I'm sorry was followed by I miss you, you're beautiful, I adore you and Je t'aime. I realized that since the Cardiology team usually started their day at seven-thirty AM and I started at eight, delivering hot lattes in the morning must have been inconvenient for him. On the fifth day Lucas jokingly suggested to Nathan that it would be even more impressive if he brought coffee for my entire team, and the following day Nathan showed up with one of the group coffee carafes and a stack of cups. There was still an individual latte for me, with the message you complete me. It was corny but I was touched. So when the following day's message was please call me, I did.

Against my better judgment, the phone call led to dinner plans, which was how I came to be rummaging through my overstuffed closet for something appropriate to wear to an upscale restaurant in Yorkville. One of the few good things to come out of the COVID pandemic was an acceptance of scrubs as appropriate work attire for all healthcare workers, regardless of whether we ever saw an operating room. Unfortunately I doubted that latitude extended to upscale restaurants. I finally chose a long-sleeved navy dress and black tights. I brushed my hair and put on some eyeliner, and was about to head out the door when Chloe wandered over to inspect my outfit. She had been very excited to hear about my dinner plans with Nathan, and I knew she thought that if we got back together she would be absolved of her sin.

She looked me up and down and wrinkled her nose.

"Sophie, you can't go to dinner like that, you look like a librarian," she said decisively. "Let me help." She grabbed me by the shoulders and steered me into her tiny bathroom.

I protested that I was happy with how I looked, and that she would make me late, but she ignored me and fluttered around with a straightening iron and makeup brushes. Ten minutes later, I barely recognized myself. She had used the straightening iron to coax my auburn hair into loose curls, and made up my eyes so that I looked fresh instead of exhausted. I thanked her and ran out the door.

The restaurant was only a few blocks from our apartment. Nathan had wanted to pick me up, but I wanted to prevent an awkward encounter with Chloe, so I insisted on meeting him there. Thanks to Chloe's style intervention I arrived ten minutes late and flustered, and the smiling blonde hostess informed me that Dr. Fox had already arrived. She must have noticed that I was sweating, because she winked at me. "First date?" she asked.

"No." I said simply.

Her face fell. "Oh. Well welcome to Mario's. Let me show you to your table."

Nathan stood as I approached the table. He must have changed after work, because he was impeccably dressed in a black suit that was far too formal for clinical medicine. He had clearly made an effort, and he looked good. I was suddenly glad I had let Chloe do my hair. My traitorous heart sped up.

"You look beautiful, Sophie." To my surprise, he looked almost as anxious as I did. He reached out his arms for a hug, which I stiffly reciprocated. He handed me a bouquet of flowers that had been resting on the table in front of him, still wrapped in florist's paper.

"Thank you." The hostess had pulled out my chair, but I stood there awkwardly holding the bundle of flowers. I wasn't sure of the etiquette; did I leave them wrapped and set them back on the table? Ask for a vase? The tables were stylishly small, and if I put the flowers in front of me there would be no room for my food. I wondered if Nathan had done this deliberately, to punish me for not allowing him to pick me up at the apartment.

"Can I put those in water for you?" chirped the hostess.

"Please." At last I sat down.

Nathan broke the ice.

"How was your day at work?"

"Okay."

"I've already ordered a bottle of Pinot Grigio, I hope that's okay."

"Great."

There was a beat of silence while he waited for me to throw the conversational ball back, but I didn't. At one time I would have made an effort to fill the silence, to entertain him, but the balance of power had shifted and I enjoyed making him do the work.

But he gave me a wounded look.

"Is this how it's going to be, Sophie?" he asked quietly. "You know I want to get back together, and I was really looking forward to tonight. But I'm beginning to wonder if it was a mistake."

All of a sudden I felt petty.

"I'm sorry Nathan. I've had a rough week and I'm tired."

He took my hand in his. I had held hands with Nathan hundreds of times before, but it felt as awkward as the first time. Far more awkward, actually. I remembered the first time I had held his hand, on our first date as medical students in Kingston. We had gone for a walk along the lake and bought dinner from a French fry truck.

So much has changed since then. I don't think Nathan has eaten a French fry since starting his Cardiology fellowship.

"You look exhausted." Nathan's sympathetic voice brought me back to the present.

"That about sums it up." Apparently the makeup wasn't as effective as I thought.

The hostess returned with a dozen red roses in a mason jar, which she set down on the table. "What beautiful flowers," she commented. I wondered if they kept a supply of mason jars for just this situation.

"Thank you for the roses, Nathan," I said.

We sat in silence for a moment, and were searching for a safe topic of conversation when the waiter mercifully showed up to take our orders.

"I'll have the chicken parmesan," I said.

Nathan smiled. "You haven't changed," he said. "I don't think you've ever ordered anything else here."

I smiled at the waiter. "Actually, I've changed my mind. I'll have the lamb ravioli."

"It won't go with the pinot grigio," Nathan pointed out. "Would you like to order a red?"

"It will be fine." Silence fell again.

"So how is our research project going?" Nathan asked.

"Still waiting on the Research Ethics Board," I replied.

Nathan shook his head. "What's the problem?"

I rolled my eyes. "Apparently they're concerned that patients will be harmed by attempts to help them to get out of bed and walk around."

"But didn't you point out all the potential consequences of immobility?"

"Of course I did." Nathan had been copied on all of my correspondence with the Research Ethics Board.

He looked thoughtful. "Do you think there's any way we could reframe this project through an equity lens?"

"What do you mean?" The fact that Nathan could use a term like *equity lens* in a sentence ensured him a bright future in academia.

"Just that projects involving equity seem to get faster ethics approval. We should look into whether women and patients from disadvantaged communities have higher rates of immobility and associated complications."

I laughed. "I doubt it. Women are more likely to be running around looking after their men," I joked.

"I'm serious, Sophie. People from marginalized groups

probably live farther from recreation centres, and are less likely to be able to afford things like physio and proper assistive devices. They're less likely to have good nutrition. The hypothesis could be that patients from lower socioeconomic backgrounds are more likely to have poor mobility. We could do mobility assessments of patients on admission and correlate it with their demographic data. It would be a slam dunk publication."

"But what would this achieve?" I failed to see how this would help anyone.

"The second part of the project would be the MoPPET mobility intervention, but instead of including all elderly patients we would only include those from marginalized populations. It would be an attempt to improve mobility equity. The ethics board would love it."

"Couldn't we just say that all elderly patients are marginalized because they're elderly?" I asked.

"But then we would lose the equity angle."

"It seems like this would make things needlessly complicated," I said. I wasn't sure why we needed an angle at all. "I think that all elderly patients would benefit from a mobility program, and I don't want to discriminate on the grounds of socioeconomic status."

Nathan looked frustrated. "Yes, but if we don't get Ethics approval there will be no program and no one will benefit." He paused. "Do you think your parents know any of the members of the Research Ethics Board? I mean, most of the board members aren't even in health care, they're businesspeople, lawyers, that sort of thing."

"Maybe."

"You could probably get a list of the board members. It might be worth reviewing it with your parents. If they know someone, you might be able to arrange an informal meeting to pitch the project."

I laughed. "You think I should try to corrupt the Research Ethics Board? That would be ironic, don't you think?"

He looked surprised. "No! It wouldn't be like that."

"Trying to use my parents' contacts to arrange a meeting with a board member outside of the usual channels? What would you call that?"

He took a sip of his wine as he thought about it. "I would say that's how things get done. People use their contacts, it's nothing to be ashamed of. Besides, this is to benefit patients, not to benefit you or the board members, so there's nothing corrupt about it."

"Nathan, all researchers think that their work will benefit humanity."

"Yes, Sophie, but this actually will." He looked at me so earnestly that I was almost convinced.

"So you're not motivated by the prospect of publication?" I asked.

"Well, publication is a big part of it. We have to think big, Sophie. As it stands, this project can only help patients in Toronto. If we publish, this research could benefit people all over the world."

"Right."

"So think about it. I bet your dad knows someone on the board, and I'm sure he wouldn't mind making an introduction."

"I'll think about it," I said. I realized I didn't care if this project resulted in a publication or not. The Central Line Incident had ruined any hope I had of a future in academic medicine, so I no longer needed to publish to advance my career. In a way it was liberating. So there was no way in hell that I would take advantage of my father's connections to try to sway the Research Ethics Board, but it wasn't an argument I wanted to have tonight.

The waiter brought our food, which provided a welcome distraction. It was delicious, and we ate in silence for several minutes.

"How is work?" I asked, in an effort to introduce a safe subject. Nathan loved to talk about his job.

"Busy. Since we've started sixth year residency, a lot of

the staff have us handle the CritiCalls for them, in addition to all the usual work. Often the small town docs just need advice." CritiCall was the provincial phone system that coordinated patient transfers between small hospitals and tertiary centres.

I nodded. "It must be stressful to work in a small centre, though."

"I guess," he said. "So there's a lot of virtual hand-holding there." He rolled his eyes. "And you may have noticed that some genius programmed our electronic medical record to give a pop-up alert every time a troponin is positive?" A troponin was a blood test that indicated stress on the heart.

I nodded. "Yeah, I've seen that. There's a message that *a positive troponin may indicate a heart attack, consider Cardiology consultation.*"

He rolled his eyes. "Well, we get that same message. Even though we're the Cardiology team, the computer still suggests we consult Cardiology, on average once or twice per day, per patient." He sighed. "But the bigger issue is that we now get consulted for almost every positive troponin in the hospital. Even if the problem is actually an infection, or end-stage cancer, the computer thinks that Cardiology should weigh in. We ran the numbers, and we're actually seeing about 30% more consults compared to before this stupid pop-up message. We usually say that the high troponin is the result of another illness causing stress on the heart, not a primary cardiac problem. So we suggest treating the underlying condition, and say thank you for involving us in the care of this lovely patient, etc. The Attending Staff love it, of course, because they're billing for all of it. But for those of us actually doing the work, it's a huge waste of time."

"I can see that," I sympathized. "Who decided to put in the alert?"

"I heard that it was done on the advice of risk management." Nathan lowered his voice, as though he was about to share a big secret. "About six months ago a surgery patient had a post-operative heart attack that didn't get picked up for almost twenty-four hours. The patient had all of the cardiac risk factors, and developed fairly classic chest pain a few hours after a bowel resection. So the junior surgery resident saw him, even sent a troponin, which was high. But I guess it had been a really rough surgery, lasted over eight hours and he had dropped his blood pressure intra-op. So the resident didn't think the troponin was due to a heart attack, and didn't call us." He shook his head.

"To be fair, Nathan, you just said that a high troponin is often not due to a primary cardiac problem." Maybe the surgery resident had been afraid of being ridiculed.

"Yes, Sophie, but sometimes there is a primary cardiac problem. That's why you need clinical judgment. This patient was having chest pain. The ECG was abnormal. There was really no excuse."

"No, I guess not," I said quietly. "So what happened?"

"The next afternoon the patient developed heart failure, and we were finally called. For what it was worth, we were able to stent the blockage, but there had already been extensive damage done."

"That's really unfortunate," I said.

"Well, we got him stabilized with medications. We thought he was going to make it, and I think he would have, from a cardiac standpoint. But two days after that his bowel basically fell apart and he went into shock. They didn't even try to take him back for another operation, he was just palliated."

"Wow," I said.

"Yeah. Pat Tanner was the surgeon, and I heard he was really upset about it. The guy was only fifty-five. Really didn't reflect well on Tanner or his team."

Patrick Tanner had been a senior surgery resident in Kingston when I was a medical student, and had started a staff position in Toronto earlier this year. I had worked with him a few times as a student; at that stage I hadn't known enough to appreciate whether he was a competent surgeon or not, but he had cared about his patients and he had always been kind to me.

"But some complications are inevitable," I countered. "It may not have been Tanner's fault."

"Yeah, but I've heard he's had a few complications," Nathan commented.

I took a bite of ravioli and thought about this. All doctors had complications occasionally. Where was the line between a good doctor who made a mistake and a doctor who was incompetent?

For some reason I felt the need to defend Pat Tanner. "I don't think it's fair to judge Pat based on rumours. For all we know, he's had a run of hard cases, or just bad luck."

Nathan laughed. "Relax, Sophie. I'm not trying to judge anyone, just telling you what I heard."

"I just think it's hard enough to deal with the fact that a patient had a bad outcome. Having people gossip about you must make it that much worse."

Nathan's expression changed to one of sympathy. "Ryan told me about your central line incident. He said that you did the best you could in a high pressure situation."

I laughed bitterly. "That's true." Unfortunately the best I could do was to put a central line in the poor woman's carotid artery instead of in the jugular vein, where it belonged. "But Ryan did a much better job under the same circumstances."

"Ryan's a year ahead of you and doing an ICU fellowship, he's had a lot more practice putting in lines," said Nathan.

For some reason Nathan's attempts to make me feel better were making me feel worse.

"Yes, he's had more experience. But I still should have been able to do it."

"It's keeping you up at night, isn't it?" he asked me.

I had never been able to compartmentalize work the way that Nathan could. He worked hard, but when he wasn't working his thoughts didn't turn to his patients. He didn't worry about whether he had prescribed the right dose of a drug, or ordered the right test, or whether he was ordering too many tests and subjecting patients to unnecessary worry. In contrast,

I had been known to call the nursing station in the middle of dinner to ask how a patient was doing, even on nights when I wasn't on call. Nathan had sometimes been frustrated by it, and told me to trust that if a problem arose, the doctor on call would deal with it.

I toyed with my fork.

"Yeah, it keeps me up at night," I admitted. Although I realized that I hadn't had the nightmare for the past few nights. I had been so distracted by work and Chloe's situation that I had been sleeping like the dead.

Nathan reached across the table and took my hand again. It felt familiar. Reassuring. I looked up and saw him staring at me intently.

"Sophie, I know you find clinical medicine stressful," he began.

"I think everyone finds residency stressful," I countered.

"Yes. Of course," he acknowledged. "But maybe not to the same extent that you do."

I didn't say anything.

"So anyway, I was thinking that maybe you don't have to practice medicine long-term," he continued in a rush. "When I get a staff job I'll be earning real money, enough to support us both. And it will be incredibly busy. If you work as many hours as I do, we'll never see each other. Or our kids, when we have them. So maybe you should look at other options."

"What other options?" I asked cautiously.

"I don't know. Whatever you want, really. Go back to school if you want. When we have kids, stay home with them."

It was the last thing I had expected him to say and I didn't know what to think. The irony was that I had been looking for an exit strategy to get out of medicine without becoming dependent on my parents. I hardly knew whether to be flattered that he liked me enough to offer to support me or offended that he thought I would be willing to stay home and keep house for him. Maybe he just liked the idea of having a wife with thirteen years of post-secondary education picking up his dry cleaning.

But it made me rethink some of my assumptions about our relationship. It's fairly well accepted that in the majority of relationships, certainly successful ones, both parties bring roughly equal assets to the partnership. If one partner has money the other has looks or wit. I didn't flatter myself that my looks were better than average, and I had thought it was important to Nathan that his partner have a professional career similar to his own. So if Nathan truly wanted to get back together, regardless of whether I continued in medicine, it must mean that he valued me for more than the fact that I was his professional equal.

"What do you think?" he asked. I realized that I had been staring at the wall.

"I think I still need time," I answered.

He looked disappointed. "But you'll think about it?"

"I'll think about it."

***

From: ResearchEthics@torontohealthalliance.ca
To: Nathan.Fox@torontohealthalliance.ca
Cc: Sophie.Ingram@torontohealthalliance.ca
Subject: Equity in Mobility Study

Dear Dr. Fox,

Thank you for your email regarding a possible amendment to your MoPPET study protocol. We agree that there is a pressing need for further research into the socioeconomic determinants of mobility. We look forward to receiving your full proposal, and we will ensure it receives an expedited review.

Sincerely,
Ronald Allison, BSc, MSc
Chairman, Research Ethics Board, Toronto Health Alliance

Eleven

My workdays fell into a pattern. I showed up at seven AM to see the sickest patients myself, then met with the trainees to review the patients they had admitted overnight. I could usually wrap that up by ten, after which I walked home to spend a couple of hours with Chloe. I often had to coax her out of bed, and if the weather was good I tried to drag her out of the apartment for a walk. After lunch I returned to the hospital to meet with the trainees again and hear their updates on the patients. At four PM I met with Dr. Hastings to give her the updated patient list and billing information, and then I spent another two hours on the ward to try to figure out what was actually going on with the patients. I could tell that the trainees thought I was micromanaging them, and maybe I was. In truth, the majority of the patients on our list had such severe chronic medical problems that they were unlikely to get much better regardless of what we did. I thought that many would do better if we left them alone.

The youngest patient on our list also had the shortest life expectancy. Mrs. Alves was forty-two and was dying of pancreatic cancer. After the standard round of chemotherapy she had been enrolled in a clinical trial, with the hope of prolonging her life by a few months. Unfortunately she had not responded to the trial drug. Because there were no other treatment options, her oncologist had essentially made a palliative care referral and closed her file. The cancer was causing fluid to build up in her abdomen, and she had been admitted a week ago with abdominal pain. I had put a needle in and drained it, but it had reaccumulated within a few days.

Her best option was a tube that would stay in her abdomen to allow the fluid to be drained every day or two, even after she went home. Unfortunately this tube had to be inserted by the radiology department, and they were chronically overbooked. Mrs. Alves had been booked for the procedure three times, and she had been cancelled three times in favour of patients who were deemed a higher priority. Had I known that this would happen I would have sent her home a week ago, with the knowledge that when the fluid reaccumulated she would just have to come back. But she kept getting booked and cancelled.

So my morning routine now included a phone call to the radiology department to try to get Mrs. Alves on the list for the day. I could tell that the nurse who controlled their scheduling was tired of hearing from me, but she assured me that yes, Mrs. Alves was scheduled for this afternoon.

As I walked home for lunch I got a phone call from the charge nurse.

"Hello, Dr. Ingram? The non-urgent ambulance is coming for Mrs. Campbell in an hour. However, her daughter has told me that she plans to call 911 as soon as her mother gets home, because she doesn't think that her mother is stable enough to go home. She wants to talk to you."

"Okay, you can put her on the phone."

"Hello, Dr. Ingram?"

I took a deep breath and tried to keep the frustration from my voice. "Hello, Elaine. I'm so glad I got the chance to talk to you." As a medical student, I had a mentor who opened all difficult conversations with this phrase, and I had adopted it. In most cases it was a lie.

"Dr. Ingram. I have major concerns about the plan to discharge my mother today. She's clearly more confused than usual."

I couldn't imagine this poor lady being more confused than usual.

"Elaine, I saw your mother earlier today and she was at her cognitive baseline. As we've discussed, she no longer needs the services of an acute care hospital and is stable to be discharged."

"Dr. Ingram, I don't understand how you can say she's stable. She's incredibly confused."

"Elaine, she has dementia and she's unable to talk."

"Dr. Ingram, I don't think it's safe for her to leave the hospital. I think she needs at least another week."

"I'm sorry Elaine, in my opinion your mother is stable and she will be discharged today.

"I don't agree, Dr. Ingram."

"Well we'll have to agree to disagree. Your mother will be discharged this morning."

I had made it to the entrance of my apartment building when the charge nurse called again to tell me that Mrs. Campbell's feeding tube had come out of her stomach. Her daughter Elaine had reported the tube fell out when her mother rolled over in bed. I turned around and walked back to the hospital, and arrived to find Elaine at her mother's bedside. The feeding tube was designed to coil inside the stomach to prevent it from being pulled out accidentally, and the tube lying on the bed appeared to have been cleanly cut to release the coil. I had a pretty good idea who had cut it.

I left the room without a word to Elaine. Mrs. Campbell wouldn't be able to go home until we could get radiology to replace the tube, so I cancelled her discharge and ordered some IV fluids to keep her hydrated. To add insult to injury, the hospital had offered to cover the cost of a non-urgent ambulance to facilitate her discharge, and as it was too late to cancel the booking they would be stuck with the bill.

Less than half an hour later I received an email from Stacey Sullivan, titled 'URGENT'.

Hi Sophie,

I just got off the phone with Elaine Campbell. She's very upset; she tells me that her mother's feeding tube has come out, and the radiology department won't be able to replace it until early next week. Elaine is understandably concerned about this wait time. As you know, her mother is unable to take any food or pills by mouth, so she will not be receiving food or medication until this tube is replaced. I agree that this seems like a dangerous situation. Elaine also told me that she is very anxious to have her mother come home, and the delay in getting the tube reinserted is preventing her mother's discharge. I assured her that I would bring this to your attention so that you can follow-up with the radiology department.

Warm regards,

Stacey Sullivan
Office of the Ombudsperson

I tapped out a terse reply:

Dear Stacey:
Unfortunately, I have no control over scheduling in the radiology department. Perhaps you could contact them yourself.

Regards,

Dr. Ingram

When I finally made it home for lunch I found Chloe up, dressed, and in a miserable mood. She almost bit my head off when I asked her if she wanted scrambled eggs or leftover tomato soup for lunch.

"I'm not a child, you know," she said. "You don't have to come home every day to make sure I eat lunch."

"I know that, Chloe," I said. I was incredibly tired. "I'll eat by myself." I put some soup into the microwave.

My phone pinged with a text from Lucas.

"Alves's procedure cancelled for today. Hopefully Monday."

"Did they say why?" I texted back.

"More urgent case."

So when I got back to the hospital I would have to give Mrs. Alves the news that she would not be getting her tunnelled catheter, and her options were to wait until Monday or go home and come back to the ER when the swelling in her abdomen became unbearable.

Chloe took a seat across from me at the dining table. "I talked to Mom today," Chloe said. I looked at her distractedly.

"Yeah?" I asked.

"I asked her to let me have my car back, but she said no. They gave it to me, so it's *my car*, and it's just sitting in their driveway."

"Uh huh," I said. I was too upset over the fact that Mrs. Alves' tube had been cancelled for the fourth time to pay much attention to Chloe's car problem.

"It's like they don't trust me with it. It's not *fair*," she said dramatically. She saw me glance at my phone, looking for another text from Lucas. "But apparently you don't care."

"You're right, Chloe, I don't. Right now I'm dealing with the fact that I have a forty-two year-old woman with pancreatic cancer who needs a drainage catheter so that she can go home to her kids and live her final weeks in some degree of comfort. But she's been bumped four times for more urgent patients. That's not fair."

Chloe's eyes widened. "Can't you just tell them it's an emergency?"

"Well, it's not truly an emergency. She's not dying today." I didn't think she was, anyway.

"Yeah, but you're the doctor. Just tell them it needs to be done and to bump someone else."

I rolled my eyes. "It's not that simple, Chloe. Hospitals don't run that way anymore. I'd have to give them a reason."

"Why? On the psych ward, the staff did completely irrational things all the time just because 'the doctor ordered it.'"

My phone pinged again. I had received another email from

Stacey Sullivan. The subject line read 'Good News.'

> Hi Sophie,
> I have spoken to the Radiology Department and explained that you think Mrs. Campbell's feeding tube reinsertion is urgent and should be given top priority. They have agreed to fit her in this afternoon.
>
> Have a wonderful weekend,
>
> Stacey Sullivan.

I saw red. Mrs. Alves had been bumped so that Mrs. Campbell could get her G-tube reinserted this afternoon.

I stood and grabbed my jacket. "I'm sorry, Chloe, I have to run."

"Sure. Remember, you're the doctor."

I had been to the Interventional Radiology Department a few times during my ICU rotation three years ago. When an ICU patient needed a procedure, the Attending Staff almost always sent a resident or two to sweet talk Miranda, the nurse in charge of scheduling. The ICU usually had more junior residents than were needed, and I suspected this was a convenient way to ensure that procedures got done quickly and to get a resident out of the way.

When I arrived, Miranda was on the phone, and two residents stood in front of her desk waiting to speak to her. Mrs. Campbell's appointment, which had previously been Mrs. Alves's appointment, was in less than an hour, so I had to work fast.

As soon as Miranda hung up I pushed forward. I reminded myself that there was no way I would end up working in downtown Toronto long-term, so I didn't have to worry about maintaining good relationships here.

"Excuse me," I said to the waiting residents. "I'm really sorry but this is an emergency." One of the residents looked like he wanted to argue with me, so I stepped in front of him.

"Hi Miranda," I said quickly. "Dr. Ingram. We've spoken on the phone about the tunnelled catheter for Mrs. Alves. I heard that she had been bumped from her slot this afternoon. I'm sorry, but this is really unacceptable. She needs this done today."

Miranda looked aggrieved. "I just had a phone call from Stacey Sullivan in the Ombudsperson's office, and she told me that you insisted that Mrs. Campbell's feeding tube be given top priority."

I wondered if there was a hospital department that dealt with complaints against the Ombudsperson's office.

"As you know," Miranda continued. "We can only do a certain number of procedures in a day. It's a directive from the senior leadership team. So even if our staff were willing to stay, we wouldn't be able to add on another procedure for you."

"But it wouldn't be for me, Miranda, it would be for the patient," I said calmly. "I was hoping your department would want to collaborate to ensure she gets the best possible care."

I had hoped to impress Miranda with the word collaborate, but she had been in her job too long to be impressed by corporate lingo.

"And I'm telling you it's not possible to add on another procedure today."

"Okay. Then give Mrs. Alves the 2 PM spot and bump Mrs. Campbell's feeding tube."

Miranda raised an eyebrow. "Stacey Sullivan said the feeding tube was urgent."

"There was a miscommunication," I said. "Both procedures are urgent, but if you can only do one today you should do Mrs. Alves."

Miranda shrugged. "Okay. But I'll document that I've made the change on your instruction."

I nodded. "Of course." I had a moment of indecision, where I wondered if I was biased by my dislike of Mrs. Campbell's daughter. I decided that I probably was biased, but there was nothing I could do to change that, and that Mrs. Alves needed to get her tunnelled catheter.

"Was there anything else you needed?" Miranda asked. I

realized I was still standing in front of her desk.

"No. Thank you so much for your help, Miranda."

***

In a moment of weakness, I had agreed to meet with Jessica Scott, the physiotherapist Nathan had hired for the MoPPET project, at 4:30 pm on a Friday afternoon. As I didn't have an office I had suggested we meet on the ward, but it turned out she had been given an office in the administrative wing for the duration of the project. It was more like a closet than an office, with barely enough space for a desk and a chair, but it was quiet and private, and I was jealous.

It was immediately clear why Nathan had hired her. Jessica was beautiful, with chin-length blond hair and blue eyes, and her outfit of high-end yoga wear showcased an athletic figure. She had left me the chair and was perched gracefully on the desk.

"Sophie, hi!" she chirped brightly, and reached over to give me a hug. I awkwardly put an arm around her shoulders. I had always found the millennial habit of hugging a little too much.

She pulled an iPad out of her purse. "Nathan sent me the grant proposal and the Ethics application, so I think I'm up to speed," she said. "I also read the HIPPO-Falls paper. I don't really get it."

This was going to be worse than I thought. "You don't get it?" I asked warily.

"It's, like, completely ridiculous," she said. "I mean, they're trying to prevent falls by preventing patients from getting out of bed!"

I nodded, suddenly fascinated.

"But what's the end game?" Jessica continued. "They can't want patients to stay in bed for the rest of their lives. So at some point the patients will need to get out of bed, and they'll be so deconditioned they'll be at much higher risk of falling than had they just kept moving in the first place.

"Right," I said. "Well - "

"Clearly they didn't ask any Physios about HIPPO-Falls," she continued. "One of the first things they teach us in our program is that you have to use it or lose it. Which is why I'm so excited about MoPPET," she said.

"I'm glad to hear it," I said.

"But I think I'm, like, overqualified for it," she continued. "You don't need a Physio to help someone get out of bed and walk around."

Her inexperience was clear, because in our hospital, you definitely needed a Physio for that. The overworked nurses just didn't have the time.

"I could train the nurses to do it," she said brightly. "I mean, I could even train the teenage volunteers to do it." She gestured out the door to where a couple of teenage boys in blue volunteer vests pushed a cart of Styrofoam water jugs down the hall.

I laughed. "If only we could." It wasn't a bad idea, but it was logistically impossible. The entire study proposal would have to be rewritten, and I couldn't imagine the Ethics board approving a trial that involved teenage volunteers directly interacting with patients.

"You don't think it's possible?" she asked, looking deflated.

"I don't think it's possible to get Ethics approval for it," I answered.

"That's too bad, because I think it could be great," she said. "It would make a big difference to the quality of care."

All of a sudden I saw the loophole.

"We call it a Quality Improvement Project," I said. Her enthusiasm was infectious, and I had caught it. "QI projects are usually exempt from Ethics Review. The hospital already collects data on most of the relevant metrics, like lengths of stay and falls. We can just compare the data before and after the start of the project."

Jessica nodded. "Great. Do we have to run this by Dr. Fox? He's your boss, right?"

"Not exactly," I answered. "A faculty member, Dr. Hastings, is supervising both of us." I had been planning to discuss the QI direction with Nathan, but I resented Jessica's assumption that Nathan was my boss. Besides that, I didn't have the energy to deal with more bureaucracy and red tape. It would be easier to ask for forgiveness than permission. After all, I no longer had any hope of a job in academic medicine, so an unauthorized research (or Quality Improvement) project was hardly going to sink my career prospects.

"Leave it with me," I told Jessica. "I'll run it by Dr. Hastings, then contact the nursing manager and the volunteer coordinator. If I can get everyone on board we can hopefully start training sessions for the volunteers within the next couple of weeks."

"That would be awesome," Jessica said enthusiastically. "What about the equity part?"

"The equity part?" I asked.

"Yeah, Dr. Fox mentioned wanting to explore an equity angle?" she asked.

"Oh." I paused. "We will be aiming to help people who are sick stay as mobile as those who are well."

She nodded. "MoPPET for Mobility Equity. I love it."

I forced a smile.

"So, um, about Dr. Fox?" she asked.

"What about him?" I asked.

Jessica's beautiful face turned pink. "Do you know if he's single?" she asked.

"I'm not sure," I answered.

Twelve

I had plans to meet a friend for breakfast the next morning, so I was up even earlier than usual. When I stumbled into the living room I found Chloe on the couch watching TV.

"You're up early," I said, surprised. Chloe was not a morning person.

She laughed. "More like I'm up late."

"Oh." She hadn't even been to bed. "Everything okay?"

She nodded. "Justina got promoted to principal dancer. I found out yesterday."

Justina had been one of Chloe's best friends in ballet. Unlike Chloe, she had made it into the National Ballet, where she was apparently now a principal dancer.

"I didn't know you still kept in touch," I said.

"We don't. There was a press release."

"Oh," I said again. I didn't know what to say, but I could tell she was affected by this, and I considered cancelling my breakfast plans.

"Don't forget I'm making dinner tonight," she said.

"I won't forget!" I said brightly. I had forgotten. Chloe had suggested she could start to cook dinner a couple of nights per week if I gave her money for groceries, which I had happily agreed to do.

"You're up early. Rushing in to save a life?" She wasn't quite sarcastic, but her voice had an edge.

"No, breakfast with Martin."

She almost smiled at that. "Say hi to him from me."

Martin Chu was one of my oldest friends. We met in kindergarten, where we were the most serious kids in the class, and we were the top two students in our year throughout high school. Our paths diverged in university; he studied computer engineering at Waterloo while I went to Queens, but we had kept in touch and continued to meet up when we were both in Toronto.

When we returned to Toronto after university we had fallen into a routine of meeting for breakfast at Sally's Diner once a month. It was a greasy spoon in our old neighbourhood, and we had met there for breakfast most Monday mornings through our last two years of high school. At the time, my mother had thought it was a bizarre habit and figured we were secretly in love with each other but for some reason unwilling to acknowledge it. She came from a generation where people did not have platonic friendships with members of the opposite sex, but we were, and remain, just good friends. Although there was never any chemistry between us, Martin has had a huge crush on Chloe since she was in high school. He was barely able to talk to her for the first half of her grade nine year, and had become red-faced when she entered a room. My mother had hired him to tutor her in math during her second half of grade nine, and they had developed a friendship of sorts.

Martin had beaten me to the diner and snagged a corner booth. There were already two steaming cups of coffee on the table, and I fell upon mine gratefully.

"You look tired, Sophie," Martin commented.

I dumped three packets of sugar into the coffee, then added cream.

"Yeah, I've had a rough couple of weeks." Although I had seen Martin since Chloe was hospitalized I hadn't told him about it.

"Still working crazy hours?" he asked sympathetically.

I sighed. "Work's only part of the problem." I sipped the coffee and debated how much to tell him. It was still painful to talk about it, but I knew he would hear about it eventually, so I gave him the condensed version of the Chloe story.

"So how is Chloe now? Is she coping at your place?" he asked. I was a little irritated that his first concern was about how Chloe was coping with me, not how I was coping with her.

"I don't know," I answered. "Depressed, I think. She needs something to do, a job, or school, or something. Right now she seems to spend most of her time sleeping and watching reality TV."

"That doesn't sound like her."

"No. I don't know if she's depressed because she doesn't have enough to do or if she can't find anything to do because she's depressed. I think she's been a little better the past couple of days though. She's actually planning to make dinner tonight."

"With everything she's been through over the past few weeks, it's not surprising that she needs time to recover." He paused and sipped his orange juice. "What kind of work is she interested in? I might be able to help her find something."

I had no doubt that Martin would be able to help Chloe find a job, because if no job existed, he would create one. Although his lifestyle hadn't changed significantly since our high school days, Martin was rich. In his third year of university he had developed an app to teach his four-year-old niece about numbers, which he called, simply, NUMBER. It became immensely popular among the parents of the niece's kindergarten classmates, and one of them posted a link on a Facebook mom's group. Within a couple of months it went viral, and he was charging two dollars per download. Martin's follow-up program, the aptly named NUMBER TWO, was an even bigger hit. He had realized he wouldn't be able to develop programming for the higher grades quickly enough to stay ahead of copycat developers, and he ended up selling the apps to Google for millions.

Martin had then invested a significant portion of the money in tech start-ups that he thought were promising, and although he hasn't told me the details, I've heard that his money has multiplied several times since. In any case, he could have retired years ago, but he was still one of the hardest-working people I knew. Google had hired him as a consultant for the educational apps, which now included a full NUMBER line for math, and a WORD line for reading. He strongly believed that computer science and coding education were inadequate, and had started an evening coding school, named CODE, for elementary and middle school students. He taught sessions himself two nights a week, and employed computer science students from University of Toronto to teach the remaining evenings.

"That's a really kind offer, Martin, but Chloe's not really qualified to do anything in tech or computers."

"It doesn't have to be computers, I have contacts in other fields. What do you think she would like to do?"

I sighed. I was tempted to take him up on it, but I wasn't confident that Chloe would be a model employee. If Martin pulled strings and Chloe didn't follow through, he could be put in an awkward position.

"The thing is, Martin, I'm not sure Chloe could handle a job right now. I think it might be better for her to focus on small goals, like doing a bit of cooking, going for walks, that sort of thing."

He nodded. "Yeah, she should take whatever time she needs. But let me know if I can do anything to help. I could take her to lunch, or drive her to her doctor's appointments. Give her my number, tell her she can call me."

I nodded. "Thanks Martin. I'm not sure she's feeling particularly social at the moment, but I'll tell her."

The waitress brought our breakfasts, and we focused on our Eggs Benedict for several minutes. We ordered the same thing every time.

"How's your family?" I asked. "Any drama?"

Martin smiled. "Everyone's good. My parents are still asking me when I'm going to get a real job. My mother actually suggested I go to Teacher's College so I can get a proper teaching job, with job security and a pension plan."

I laughed. Martin's mother still could not believe that he had made a fortune developing an app for people's phones, or grown that fortune by investing in tech companies that didn't sell physical goods. She lived in fear that the people who had bought his app would realize they had been swindled and ask for their money back, or worse, that he was somehow engaged in criminal activity. Ironically, she was much quicker to boast of her other children's achievements, likely because they were easier to understand. Martin's sister Julia was a real estate lawyer who had opened her own practice two years ago, and I knew that Martin had quietly given her a loan to do it. His brother Simon and his wife Alice were climbing the ladder at a large accounting firm.

"So have you started the Teacher's College application?" I teased.

"Still thinking about it. Not sure I'm qualified, really. One of my coding instructors applied and said they wanted to know about volunteer work, extracurricular activities, hobbies, and a whole bunch of other stuff that seemed only tangentially related to teaching. I offered to stop paying him so that he could say he volunteered as a coding instructor but he didn't go for that. The website profiled some current students who talked about building houses in the third world." He shook his head. "These people rant about climate change, then fly halfway around the world to spend a week or two pretending to swing a hammer. They could just make a charitable donation, but that wouldn't look the same on a resume."

I laughed. "I doubt that's the kind of practical thinking they're looking for, Mr. Chu."

"No, you're right. So probably best I don't apply."

Sally's Diner solved the awkwardness of who would pay the bill. Since he made his money, Martin has insisted on paying when we go anywhere together, and it's led to some awkward arguments over restaurant bills and Uber fare. He's generous, but I know many of his friends and acquaintances take it for granted that he'll pay when they're out together. That's probably why I'm sensitive about the issue, and don't want to take advantage of him. But at Sally's Diner I could order the most expensive breakfast on the menu, along with bottomless coffee and orange juice and still come away with a bill for less than twenty dollars. I let him pay with a clear conscience.

***

I sought out Dr. Hastings mid-morning to discuss a challenging case. Mr. Wong was a 70-year-old man who had been admitted a week ago with a small intracranial hemorrhage, which translated to a bleed in his brain. Unfortunately he had developed shortness of breath overnight, and a CT scan this morning showed that he had a large blood clot in his lungs called a pulmonary embolism. The hematologist recommended that we start anticoagulation, as the pulmonary embolism could kill him and the intracranial hemorrhage had been stable for a week. The neurologist said that anticoagulation could kill him by worsening the bleeding in his brain. For completeness I had spoken to a neurosurgeon, who had said that the patient had too many medical problems to ever have neurosurgery and his only advice was to involve the palliative care team for end of life care.

My personal opinion was that we should try anticoagulation, but I explained the dilemma to Dr. Hastings and waited for her thoughts. She looked at me seriously.

"You know, Sophie, I think the important thing in this situation is to do what's best for the patient."

I waited for her to tell me which option she thought would be best for the patient, but she just looked at me expectantly.

"Don't you agree?" she prompted.

She was trying to make it easier with a yes or no question, and I knew which answer she wanted.

"Yes."

"Very good." She smiled at me. "Medicine is so much easier if you stop and ask yourself 'what is best for my patient?' I give the first year medical students a talk on this every year." She paused. "But you did med school *somewhere else*, didn't you?"

I nodded numbly.

"Well." She gave me a sympathetic look, as though anyone who had had the misfortune to do med school *somewhere else* was an object of pity. "Was there anything else?"

I saw the opportunity. "Yes, I've been thinking a lot about our MoPPET project. There's overwhelming evidence that mobilization improves patient outcomes, so I think we should change this to a Quality Improvement project. There's no doubt that mobilization is in the best interests of our patients. And we wouldn't need Research Ethics Board approval, so we could get going right away"

She blinked at me. "I think that's an excellent idea, Sophie. Will you rename it?"

"What do you mean?" I asked, confused.

"Well, the 'T' in MoPPET stood for 'Trial'. So now that it's a quality improvement project, you could consider MoPPEQIP. Mobility Preservation Program in the Elderly Quality Improvement Project."

"For now I was planning to stick with MoPPET." I had a brainwave. "It will be the Mobility Preservation Program for the Elderly Team."

Dr. Hastings nodded. "I look forward to hearing about your progress."

"Thank you, Dr. Hastings."

"I'm always happy to help."

***

I had to teach clinical skills to the first year medical students from 11 AM until 1 PM. Technically Dr. Hastings had been assigned to do it, but she had delegated it to me so that I could truly appreciate what it was like to be a Staff Physician. All I had eaten for lunch was a cupcake that I had grabbed on my way through the lobby, free as part of the campaign to promote the rebranding of the hospital to Toronto Health Teams. It had been beautifully iced, with TEAM written across the top in the hospital colours, but it had tasted of Styrofoam and sugar. I had eaten half and thrown the rest away, and by the time I made it home at the end of the day I was starving.

I walked into a disaster zone that I barely recognized as my kitchen. The sink was full of pots and bowls, the stovetop was smeared with a yellow substance, and the counter was covered in eggshells. Chloe sat at my dining table, where she appeared to be piping something into cream puffs. She was so focused on her work that she didn't seem to notice that I had come home.

"Hey Chloe," I said.

She looked up. "Hi Sophie." Her eyes were bright, and she looked like she had put on makeup. I hadn't seen her this animated since before her hospitalization.

"What are you making?" I asked warily.

"It's going to be a *croquembouche* tower," she answered. "Basically cream puffs." She wiped pastry cream off her hand and passed me her iPad. "Here's the recipe. You can make the caramel sauce."

I skimmed through the recipe.

"Chloe, this is meant to feed twenty people," I said.

"Yeah, I thought of scaling it down, but the idea is to build a tower. It wouldn't work as a half recipe. And it's meant to feed twenty as dessert, but we're having it for dinner. I figure it will last a few meals."

I nodded. As lunch had been a cupcake I had been holding out hope that dinner would include something other than pastry, but I realized that I had been overly optimistic.

Chloe gestured at a plastic bag on the floor by her feet. "I realized you don't have a cooking thermometer, so I picked one up. Temperature is really important with caramel."

"I'll do my best."

It took us almost two hours to finish the *croquembouche* tower. By the time it was done I was almost delirious with hunger, and having cream puffs for dinner seemed like an excellent idea. Chloe took a few pictures to upload to Instagram.

"It seems a shame to eat it," I said.

"But what a waste no to," Chloe replied.

And it was delicious. We sat at the table and worked our way through over a third of the *croquembouche* tower. When we were too full to eat any more we moved to the couch and put on an old romantic comedy. The movie didn't seem to have a plot, but Chloe provided some hilarious commentary that made it quite entertaining.

When my sister was in her emotional sweet spot, she was incredibly fun, with a wicked sense of humour that I had long envied. I remembered a holiday work party my father had hosted around ten years ago that had become a family legend. I was home from university, and I was asked to step in as hostess because my mother had a migraine. It was all stodgy banking types and their spouses, and although it had been pleasant enough, the party had lacked fizz. The men had talked about interest rates and the women had talked about all-inclusive resorts, and I could tell they were all looking forward to getting home so they could change into their pyjamas and turn on the TV. I had been making stilted conversation with an awkward young man when Chloe had shown up, in jeans and a sweatshirt, and announced that we were going to play Charades. My dad had tried to intervene but Chloe was persistent, and she convinced the bankers that Charades would be fun. And it was. All of a sudden it was a party, and people talked about it for months afterward. My mother had tried to organize Charades at the following year's party, but Chloe had been out of town with friends, and it had fallen flat.

Thirteen

"**M**r. Singh endorsed chest pain," said Ellis. He was giving another painfully long case presentation and my patience was thin, as I had stayed up late the night before cleaning the kitchen after Chloe's *croquembouche* tower.

"He did not endorse palpitations," Ellis continued. "He did not endorse shortness of breath. He did endorse sweating."

"Ellis, I'm going to stop you for a minute for some feedback," I interrupted. "You're describing symptoms, not trying to market a soft drink or support a political party, so you can cut out the endorsements. It would be better just to say 'Mr. Singh had chest pain but no palpitations or shortness of breath.' Okay?"

The trainees all looked stunned. No one was used to criticism anymore.

I smiled at Ellis to try to soften the blow. "Please continue, Ellis."

My phone rang, and I answered without checking the caller ID, expecting it to be Dr. Hastings or someone from work. But it was Chloe and she was clearly distressed. I nodded to Lucas to take over and stepped out into the hallway.

"Sophie. They're saying I stole a lipstick. I meant to pay for it. This is all a mistake." Her speech was fast, words coming one on top of another, and I could barely understand what she was saying. She sounded manic.

"Calm down, Chloe, and tell me where you are." I felt shaky all of a sudden, and sat down on the floor against the wall.

"I'm at the security office. This is completely unfair. I'm

being set up. They don't understand. You have to come explain."

"Which store, Chloe?"

"They're going to call the police! This is a mistake, Sophie."

"I understand, Chloe. You need to tell me where you are."

"Harrington's. On Bloor."

"Okay, Chloe, I'm on my way. Be polite but don't say too much."

I panicked. I had no idea how to approach the situation. Somehow, my advice to 'be polite but don't say too much" didn't seem particularly inspired. Could she end up with a permanent criminal record? She had sounded manic on the phone, and I wondered if I should try to explain about her mental illness. But if I did, the cops might take her back to the ER, where she could be readmitted against her will, and I didn't know if that would be better or worse than a shoplifting charge. Maybe our parents had been right, and I really hadn't done Chloe a favour by helping her get out of the hospital. I pulled myself together and slipped back into the room where my trainees were, incomprehensibly, still discussing the same patient's historical lab abnormalities.

"I have to step out to deal with an urgent family issue. Lucas, I'll let you finish up here. Please call me if any new problems come up." The team looked surprised. Maybe this would put a stop to the complaints that I micromanaged the junior trainees.

As I walked toward the elevator I Googled 'shoplifting charge Toronto' and pulled up a dizzying number of lawyers' websites. Apparently 'fraud under $5000' was an indictable offense punishable by imprisonment for up to two years. That seemed a little extreme, and I figured that lawyers tried to emphasize the worst-case scenario to scare people into hiring them. I could hardly believe that anyone went to jail for shoplifting lipstick in Canada, but I was clearly out of my depth.

I considered my options. The only lawyer friend I knew well enough to ask for help had moved to Vancouver after law school, and while she could give me some phone advice she could hardly handle the matter from there. I could cold call one of the lawyers I had Googled, but I had no idea how to pick one, and I doubted anyone would be available to help this afternoon. I thought of Nathan's cousin, Charlie, who had recently finished law school. I had only met him a couple of times, and he hadn't seemed like the sharpest crayon in the box, but I was pretty sure he had graduated. Which meant he had to have more legal knowledge than I did.

I called Nathan to ask for Charlie's number, but his phone went to voicemail. In the elevator, I tapped out a text. 'Chloe needs help. Please call me.'

It seemed like an eternity before he replied, but in reality it was probably under two minutes. I knew that Nathan functioned with his phone glued to his fingers. The reply was not helpful. "Can't talk now. Rounding with Smith. Will call later." Dr. Smith was one of the senior cardiologists, and people had been expecting him to retire since before I started my residency. He called cell phones the scourge of modern civilization, and claimed they were responsible for a decline in knowledge, work ethic, and morals. He was famous for telling his trainees, 'If your phone knows more than you do, you might as well leave us your phone and go home.' Dr. Smith would not appreciate Nathan stepping away to phone me, but I didn't care.

I sent another message: 'Chloe needs legal help. Can you call Charlie? Or send me his number?' I hated the thought of calling Charlie myself, but there was no alternative.

But Nathan didn't reply. I stood in the hospital lobby, tapping my foot and staring at my phone. I could try to track Nathan down on the ward, but that might create an awkward scene. I could call my dad for help, but he would probably call Jack Delacroix, who would point out that he was a corporate lawyer who wrote contracts and had no experience with shoplifting. Then my dad would twist his arm and convince him to do it anyway. I remembered that Jack's business card was still sitting in my wallet, and if I wanted to keep my parents out of it I could call him directly. He probably wouldn't want to get involved, but he could at least suggest a colleague. I gritted my teeth and dialled.

His voice was confident and smooth. "Jack Delacroix."

"Mr. Delacroix." My voice didn't sound like my own. "This is Sophie Ingram. Tom Ingram's daughter. I don't know if you remember me, we met - "

He cut me off. "I remember you, Dr. Ingram. To what do I owe the pleasure?"

"Sophie, please. I'm calling to ask for your help."

Even over the phone, I could sense his amusement.

"Really, Sophie? You must be desperate."

Once we got over the teasing, and I admitted that I was, in fact, desperate, he behaved like a perfect gentleman. He told me he was just leaving his office and offered to pick me up in front of the hospital in fifteen minutes.

True to his word, he pulled up fifteen minutes later in a blue Prius.

"Thank you for doing this."

"My pleasure."

The stress made me babble.

"It's just that I don't have any experience with situations like this. I don't know if we should apologize, or refuse to say anything. That's always the advice on TV, not to say anything because it could be used against you. The one time I got pulled over for speeding I wasn't sure whether to apologize sweetly and hope the cop would drop the ticket, or whether an apology could be seen as an admission of guilt."

He raised an eyebrow. "I would have thought you were too much of a feminist to trade on your looks like that."

"I said apologize, not flirt. Besides, I never claimed to be a feminist, Mr. Delacroix. Perhaps you're confusing me with my sister's lawyer."

He snorted. "No man with eyes could confuse you with Jade Tomlinson."

"Right. I'll take that as a compliment."

He smiled. "Simply an observation." There was warmth in

his dark eyes that definitely hadn't been there at Chloe's hearing.

"So I don't know whether we should bring up the mental health history or not. She sounded manic on the phone, but I'm concerned that if I bring that up, the police will send her to the ER for a mental health assessment. She told me she'd rather die than go back to the Psych ward. There's also the issue of - "

"Relax, Sophie. There will likely be charges filed, because most big stores prosecute all shoplifting cases on principle. That said, there's a good chance that if it's a first offense we can convince the prosecutor to withdraw the charges."

I sighed with relief. "I'm really hoping she can get out of this without a criminal record. I looked it up; it could make it hard for her to travel out of the country, or to get a job -"

"Worried you might be stuck supporting her indefinitely?"

"Yes. Wait, no! Well, maybe. My long-term plan didn't include Chloe living with me. But obviously if that's what she needs - "

"It's okay, Sophie. I think you're a saint for having taken her home from that hearing. After hearing that story, it was the last thing anyone expected."

I laughed. "I certainly didn't expect it. It was an impulsive decision, and I'm not usually the impulsive one."

"It was incredibly kind."

Silence fell, and I racked my brain for something intelligent to say.

"I wouldn't have taken you for a Prius owner," I managed.

"What kind of car did you expect?"

Something flashy and expensive. "I'm not sure. Maybe something less environmentally friendly?"

He laughed. "You're pretty critical for someone who needs a favour."

"It wasn't a criticism. Simply an observation."

"You wouldn't have thought I'd be concerned about the environment, and by extension, the future of humanity? You probably expected something fast and expensive."

"When you put it that way, it does sound somewhat

critical," I admitted.

"Just somewhat?"

"I'm sorry. I become critical when I'm nervous."

"I'd never have guessed." We stopped at a light, and he turned to look at me. His dark eyes were kind.

"We'll get this sorted out. It could be much worse."

"You're right," I acknowledged. I saw far worse every week. "She could have tried to hurt herself, seriously this time, and we could be heading to the ICU right now. Or she could have hurt someone else. Or one of us could have been diagnosed with cancer. Or an aggressive autoimmune disease. Or -"

"I was actually thinking that she could have stolen something more expensive than a lipstick," he interrupted.

"Oh," I said. "Yes, that's true."

A minivan drifted into our lane, forcing Jack to hit the brakes. I noted a huge yellow Baby on Board sticker in the rear window.

"People with Baby on Board stickers are usually the worst drivers," I commented. "What do they think, that you might be planning to crash into their car, but since there's a *baby* on board, you'll choose a different target?"

He nodded seriously. "That's why I got one."

I blinked. "You have a Baby on Board sticker?" I craned my neck towards the back of the car to look for the sticker, but couldn't see it in the rear window. I noticed there was no carseat.

He nodded again. "Yeah. On the bumper. I don't have a baby, but I feel safer with it in my car. And I get a break on car insurance. "

"Oh. I mean, that makes a lot of sense," I tried to backpedal. "I didn't realize there was an insurance break."

He burst out laughing. "Sophie, it's completely nonsensical. Of course I don't have a Baby on Board sticker."

Traffic was unusually light, and we made it to Harrington's, an upscale department store, in under fifteen minutes. Nathan called as we were parking. I considered letting it go to voicemail, but we had made plans to meet to work on our research project tonight, and I figured I should let him know I wouldn't make it.

"Hello Nathan," I said. My voice was chilly.

"Sophie, I'm sorry I couldn't call earlier. I just finished rounds. What's up with Chloe? Do you need me to call Charlie for you?"

"No thanks. I couldn't wait for you. I'm handling it."

Jack was looking over, unashamedly eavesdropping on my call.

"Sophie, don't be like this. I couldn't leave rounds. What's going on?"

"Like I said, I'm handling it. Don't worry about it. But I won't be able to meet you tonight."

I heard Nathan sigh with frustration. "Well can you at least explain what's going on? I'd like to help if I can."

"I'll call you later, Nathan."

We found Chloe in the security office, waving her arms and ranting at the two security guards who sat opposite her. The first guard was an overweight middle-aged man, the second a fine-boned young woman with a pixie haircut who looked as though a strong gust of wind might blow her over. I doubted this pair would be much use against a real security threat. They looked as though they were trying hard not to laugh.

"I never wanted your stupid lipstick. It's a hideous colour, too. Pastels are for old women."

The male guard chuckled at that, but Chloe didn't seem to notice.

"Can't you see that this was a setup? It was planted," Chloe continued.

"We have you on video, miss," said the female guard calmly.

"Video can be faked. You'll probably use it to try to blackmail me. You must have figured out who I am."

"Well, that's the problem, we haven't. Because I sincerely doubt that you're Coco Chanel, as you've claimed. So you can give us some ID, or we can wait for the police. I'm sure they'll figure it out.”

The older guard saw Jack and me standing in the doorway. “Friends of this young lady?” His tone was condescending.

I was paralyzed, terrified of saying the wrong thing. It was like the traffic stop all over again. I considered offering to pay double, triple for the damned tube of lipstick, but I was concerned they would see that as bribery. Maybe I would be charged too. And then my career would truly implode, and I would have no income, and Chloe and I would both be at the mercy of our parents.

My panic must have shown on my face, because Jack took the lead. He entered the room and stuck out a hand for the older guard to shake. “Hello. This is her sister, Sophie Ingram, and I’m Jack Delacroix. I’ll be her lawyer. Can you explain what’s going on?”

The guard shrugged. “We have video showing this woman putting a lipstick into her purse. Security stopped her as she was leaving the store. That’s on video too.”

“It’s a conspiracy,” Chloe cut in. “They know I’m going to be famous, so they’ve set me up so they can blackmail me when I’m rich.” The younger security guard rolled her eyes.

“Any chance we could watch the video?” Jack asked politely.

The guard shrugged, then turned the computer screen to face us and hit play.

My sister’s image was crisp and clear. We watched her pick up the lipstick, look furtively up and down the aisle, and slip it into her pocket. It wasn’t particularly well done. I think I could have done better.

“The video is a fake,” said Chloe. “Like I said, this is a conspiracy.” She turned towards the guards. “Do you know who my father is? He’s a CEO. He could buy this whole store.”

I cringed. The last thing Dad needed was for her to start throwing his name around. Fortunately, the security guards seemed to take this claim in the same spirit as the others, as the ramblings of a delusional woman.

"Chloe, you don't need to say anything," said Jack. "You've had a shock, just try to relax. You'll have plenty of opportunities to explain yourself later." It was a polite way of telling her to shut up.

The younger guard took a step towards Jack and me. "Is there any history of substance use?" she whispered. "Or psychiatric issues?"

Once again, I didn't know what to say. I hadn't even thought of substance use, but it seemed like a likely possibility.

"We're not prepared to discuss that at this time," said Jack smoothly. "But we sincerely apologize for your trouble. Of course, we will pay you for the lipstick. Is there any chance we could handle this without involving the police? We would be happy to compensate you for the inconvenience."

The older guard laughed. "Everyone wants to pay for the stuff after they're caught. If we let them get away with that, no one would pay for anything unless we caught them. The police have already been called."

Jack nodded. "I understand."

There wasn't much more to discuss while we waited for the police. Chloe continued to spout conspiracy theories, which the guards seemed to find entertaining. Jack and I sat quietly.

My phone buzzed with a text from Jack.

"Police will need ID. Try to get her licence from her purse."

Chloe had set her Kate Spade purse down on the floor beside her feet. She was waving her arms around and telling a story in which she was actually a cosmetics heiress, who 'owned all the makeup in the store.' I tried to surreptitiously pick up her purse, but she noticed right away.

"What are you doing, Sophie?" she asked.

"Just - looking for some gum. Do you mind if I borrow some?" I asked lamely. I could feel my face turning red.

But Chloe found nothing unusual in this, just nodded and continued with her story as I rummaged through her purse. I found her wallet and pulled out her license, which I slipped into my pocket while her attention was focused on one of the guards.

I found a pill bottle, which I expected to be the valproic acid; to my surprise, it was Ritalin, and it had Chloe's name on it. I dropped the pills back into her purse and helped myself to a piece of the cinnamon gum that I found at the bottom of the bag.

Ten minutes later the policewoman finally arrived. She appeared to be in her early twenties, and couldn't have been long out of police college, but she already looked bored and cynical.

"Okay, tell me what happened here. I was told there was just one suspect, not three?"

I realized in horror that she thought that Chloe, Jack and I had all been caught shoplifting.

"Just one suspect," said the older security guard. I let out a breath. He gestured at Chloe. "Jane Doe over here. Or Coco Chanel, or Princess Anastasia, depending on what you believe. This is her sister and her lawyer."

We watched the security video again. There wasn't much more to say after that, and fortunately, Chloe didn't try. The cop put the tube of lipstick in a plastic bag, wrote down the names of the security guards, then asked Chloe for her name and identification.

Chloe stuck out her lower lip mutinously. Hoping to head off an argument, and possible further charges for failing to cooperate with a police officer, I handed Chloe's license to the officer. Chloe looked at me as though I had betrayed her.

The officer took a photo of the license and handed Chloe a form.

"This is a Form 9 Appearance Notice with instructions to show up at the police station next week, and information about your court date," she told Chloe. "If you don't show up an arrest warrant will be issued, and you may be charged with failure to appear." She handed Chloe a second form. "Here's some information about your legal rights, as well as information about Legal Aid." She looked at Jack. "But I see you already have a lawyer. Questions?"

The fight seemed to have gone out of Chloe, and she shook her head meekly.

"Okay, then. You're free to go."

Chloe was quiet until we were out of the store, but as soon as we reached the sidewalk she confronted me.

"Sophie, I can't believe you gave her my license," she said angrily. She spoke so fast I could barely process her words. "And you're the one who's supposed to be smart. I never should have called you. Now they have my name, they have Mom and Dad's address, I'll have a record in the system, and my life will be ruined. And it's all your fault."

"If you hadn't been able to produce ID the cop would have taken you to jail," cut in Jack in a matter-of-fact voice. "Believe me, you're not the first person who's thought of trying to hide their identity from the police. That video gave her grounds to arrest you, and the only sensible thing to do was to cooperate. You should be grateful your sister was there."

Chloe looked so distraught that I put an arm around her shoulder and led her away from the store entrance. She was still painfully skinny, and she smelled of marijuana and cinnamon gum.

"It will be okay, Chloe," I said, with far more confidence than I felt. "Let's get you home." I pulled out my phone. "I'll call an Uber -"

"Don't be silly," Jack interrupted. "I'll drive you."

"You don't have to," I protested half-heartedly. "You've already been a huge help, I don't want to impose -"

By this time we had reached his car.

"No imposition," he said, as he clicked open the locks.

I bundled Chloe into the front seat. She looked over at Jack. "Hey, I know you!" she said. "You're the lawyer from my hearing!"

I couldn't believe that she was just putting this together now. She must really be manic. I wondered if she could be faking this, but it seemed real.

"That's right," said Jack calmly. "Sophie, where are we headed?"

"I feel like going dancing," Chloe announced. She looked

over at Jack. "Do you like to dance, Jack?"

This was awful. She was flirting with Jack Delacroix.

"Not on weeknights, Chloe," he answered kindly.

"You're just like Sophie. She never does anything fun, she's too busy working."

He didn't answer that.

"I'll go myself then," Chloe said. "Just let me out here. Sophie, can I borrow some money?"

"Chloe, you can't go dancing now," I said.

She unbuckled her seatbelt and turned to look at me. "I'm not a prisoner, Sophie," she said.

I looked at my watch. "It's only 5:30, Chloe," I said. "Nothing will be open yet. And I'm not dressed to go out. Let's go home and have dinner, and then I'll go out with you."

"Do you promise?"

"Yes, of course," I lied. "Can you put your seatbelt back on, please?"

Chloe rolled her eyes. "If you insist." She turned back toward Jack. "Would you like to join us for dinner?"

"Oh Chloe, I'm sure he has other plans for his evening -" I began.

"I don't, actually," Jack interrupted. "I would love to come for dinner."

Fourteen

When we got up to our apartment I suggested that Chloe take a shower in preparation for our night out, and fortunately she agreed. As soon as I heard the water go on, I turned to Jack.

"I'm afraid we're not prepared for guests," I said apologetically.

"Sophie, I know that," he said. "It's clear that Chloe's unwell, and I thought that maybe I could help."

"Oh," I said. "Thank you." Part of me wished he would just leave, but it was a relief to be able to discuss things with a rational adult. "You don't happen to have any sedative drugs, do you?"

I had asked it in jest, but he answered seriously. "No. Do you think that's what she needs?"

I nodded. "Yeah, I'm pretty sure she's manic. That quetiapine that she overdosed on would be perfect right now, but I doubt they renewed that prescription." I shook my head. "I found a bottle of Ritalin in her purse, prescribed by her psychiatrist, if you can believe it. That's probably contributing to this episode."

He nodded. "Okay. Do you want to take her to the hospital?"

"She wouldn't go willingly. I could call the police, but I'm not sure they would take her in. She's not herself, but it's not clear that she's a threat to anyone right now. I'm going to try to reach her psychiatrist."

It was after six o'clock, so it was unlikely that Dr. Jankovic was still in her office, but I hoped that she was part of a group, with someone on call for after-hours emergencies. But my call went directly to voicemail, and a recorded voice told me that Dr. Jankovic would be in her office Mondays, Wednesdays, and Thursdays from 8 AM to 3 PM. Patients needing care outside of those hours were advised to go to the ER. I walked to the kitchen and put on the kettle, then dumped three tablespoons of instant coffee into a large mug.

"Instant coffee is pretty awful, but would you like some?" I asked Jack. "Or something else to drink? We have orange juice and Coke in the fridge. Or there's grocery store wine, and I think Nathan may have left some beer." I paused. "If Chloe insists on going out, maybe the best thing would be to get her drunk and put her to bed. If all else fails, I may try that."

"Coke sounds great, thank you." He walked over to join me in the kitchen. I could see him examining the 'Goals for the Week' calendar we had stuck to the fridge with magnets. There was still only one goal written on it: TAKE A SHOWER. Chloe had put a huge check mark beside it.

"We'll have to log her second shower of the week," I said, trying to make a joke of it. "Although I think she may have forgotten to record a few."

"The calendar's a good idea," he said. I looked at him, expecting to see a mocking expression, but his expression was gentle, and it almost undid me.

"Would you like me to order something for dinner?" he asked. "Or go pick something up?"

"Thank you, but I'm going to see if I can convince Chloe to make dinner with me. It will give her something to do." I had been buying groceries more regularly since Chloe moved in, and I figured I could scrounge up ingredients for pasta. "It won't be anything special, in fact you may not even want to eat it, but - "

"Relax Sophie, it's fine," he said.

I heard the water go off in the bathroom and realized I needed to make a decision quickly.

"Maybe we should try to get her to a hospital," I said.

Jack had pulled out his phone. "What about a virtual walk-in clinic?" he suggested.

"That's not a bad idea," I said. "But we would have to convince her to call them. And right now she doesn't believe she needs help."

I took a large sip of my coffee in the hope that the caffeine would help focus my thoughts. I heard the hair dryer go on in the bathroom and signed with relief. Chloe could easily spend ten minutes drying her hair. Hopefully she would decide to do her makeup, too.

"I could call a virtual walk-in clinic and pretend to be Chloe, but that would be fraudulent," I said, thinking out loud.

"Yeah. It's unlikely that anyone would find out, but I don't think it's worth the risk."

I nodded. "I'll call and see if I can get some sleeping pills for myself."

In the end it was surprisingly easy. I picked a virtual walk-in service that advertised 'full spectrum medical care' with an average wait time of four and a half minutes. I filled in an online form with my demographic information, medical history, and the fax number of the pharmacy down the street. As promised, I was connected to a doctor in less than five minutes. I explained that I was having trouble sleeping.

"How long has this been a problem for you?" the doctor asked. He had a young voice, and could have passed for a high school student.

"Almost two months," I answered.

"Can you think of anything that could have triggered it?"

"My sister was hospitalized. She's a little bit better now, but I still worry about her." Might as well stick as close to the truth as possible.

"I'm sorry to hear that," he answered.

"Thank you."

"What strategies have you tried to treat your insomnia?" he asked.

I spotted the trap; he was going to try to avoid giving

me a prescription by suggesting I drink warm milk before bed. Fortunately I had learned the list of non-pharmacologic (and ineffective) strategies for insomnia in medical school. "I've tried everything," I answered. "I exercise most days, in the mornings. I go to bed at the same time each night. I make sure I don't have any screen time for at least an hour before bed. I've tried yoga and meditation in the evenings. I've tried melatonin from the health food store, but it didn't help. I've even tried therapeutic breathing. Oh, and I've given up caffeine completely."

Jack snorted at that, and I glared at him.

"Um, okay," said the doctor on the phone, sounding a little surprised by the exhaustive list I had rattled off. "It sounds like you've tried a lot of things."

"Yes," I confirmed mendaciously.

"So do you want to try sleeping pills?"

I was told that my Ativan prescription would be faxed to the pharmacy within fifteen minutes. Jack offered to pick it up so that I could stay with Chloe.

"You'll probably need my ID," I said, handing him my health card. "They may ask why you're picking up a prescription in my name."

"I'm sure it'll be fine," he said. "I'll tell them that you're my girlfriend."

I could feel my face turning red. "I hate that you'll have to lie," I said.

"Relax," he said. "It's a lie that no one can disprove. A bit like you giving up caffeine."

Chloe emerged from the bathroom shortly after Jack had left. She looked spectacular, in skinny jeans and a black halter top. Her hair was styled in loose waves, and her makeup was surprisingly tasteful. I caught a hint of a musky perfume. Given her behaviour that afternoon I had expected her outfit to be over the top, but she had shown surprising restraint. As nightclub attire went, hers was classy. I couldn't reconcile the disinhibited, delusional girl from the security office with the attractive young woman who had come into the kitchen. Maybe the Ritalin was wearing off.

"Jack just popped out to run an errand," I explained. "I thought you could help me make dinner?" I had rummaged through the kitchen and found a package of spaghetti, a jar of tomato sauce, an onion, two sad looking red peppers, and a block of cheddar cheese.

Chloe frowned at the ingredients I assembled on the counter. "This won't be great, but I think I can make it work," she said. "You can help me. Please start by chopping the onion." She grabbed a bottle of olive oil from the cupboard and dumped a third of it into a frying pan.

"Uh, that's a lot of oil, Chloe," I said.

Chloe laughed. "Relax, Sophie. There's no such thing as too much oil in Italian cooking."

I chopped up the onion and carefully added it to the frying pan. Chloe stirred it vigorously. Olive oil slopped over the sides of the pan and onto the stove. Some splashed onto Chloe's shirt, but she didn't seem to notice.

"Um, can I help you with that?" I suggested.

"No thank you Sophie," she said. "I am perfectly capable of frying onions. In fact, I don't need your help. Why don't you go take a shower while I cook dinner?"

"I'm happy to help," I said.

"Just try not to get in the way," she said. She found a bottle of red wine in the cupboard and poured herself a large glass.

Jack returned, and tried to hand me a small pill bottle without Chloe seeing. I hadn't thought about how to convince Chloe to take the Ativan once I had it. Slipping it into her food without her knowledge seemed wrong, but I wasn't sure how else to get it into her, and her behaviour in the kitchen had convinced me that she was at risk of serious trouble if she went out dancing.

As it turns out, I needn't have worried. Chloe had seen Jack hand me the pill bottle.

"Did you bring drugs?" she asked with interest. Her eyes narrowed. "You weren't planning to share them with me, were you?”

"They're not party drugs," I began.

"I can't believe you Sophie! You're trying to hide them from me! You know that if I had drugs I would share them with you!" She was really angry.

"Okay." I shrugged, then handed her two tiny blue pills. She washed them down with a big gulp of wine.

"What are they?" she asked.

"Ativan," I answered honestly.

Her brow furrowed. "I've never tried that. Isn't it, like, a sedative?"

I nodded. "But it can have paradoxical effects."

She laughed. "Paradoxical effects," she repeated. "That sounds like something you would say. But I wouldn't have thought you'd take drugs, Sophie. You're far too responsible." She said 'responsible' as though it was an insult.

I didn't answer her.

"I'm ready to go out now," Chloe announced.

"Chloe, it's not even seven o'clock. Nothing will be open for another couple hours at least," I said. "Let's have dinner first." I tried to shepherd her back towards the kitchen.

She pouted. "I want to dance now." She pushed my coffee table against the wall, clearing a two by three foot space in the middle of my living room. "Do you have a speaker system?" she asked me.

"No," I answered.

She played with her phone for a minute and salsa music filled the room. I had expected rap or pop, so the salsa was something of a relief.

Chloe looked at Jack speculatively. "Can you dance?" she asked him.

"A little," he answered.

Chloe grabbed his hand and led him onto her improvised dance floor. I had never seen her salsa dance before, but I wasn't surprised that she did it beautifully. She was a natural dancer and could make almost any partner look good. But it turned out that Jack had been modest about his dancing ability, and he actually danced quite well. They were an attractive pair. I realized I was jealous. I poured myself a glass of the wine and sat watching them. They danced for almost half an hour before Chloe said she was tired and flopped down on the couch. I brought her a large glass of water and suggested that she take a nap before going out.

"Yeah, napsh a good idea," she said. She had started to slur her words; the Ativan had worked as expected. I helped her walk to her room and put her to bed fully clothed.

I walked back out to the living room to find Jack sitting at the table drinking his Coke.

"I'm sorry you had to see that. But thank you," I said. I felt as though we had just fought a battle together.

He looked embarrassed. "I really didn't do very much," he said. "Unfortunately once the police were called, there wasn't much I could do to prevent the charges. But there's a good chance I can convince the prosecutor to drop the case." He hesitated. "Or if you would prefer a different lawyer, or a different firm, I can recommend some good people. Shoplifting isn't my field, so you might be better off with someone else."

"I'll talk to Chloe about it when she's in a better frame of mind," I said.

He nodded. "Of course."

I realized that if it were up to me I would want him to handle it. He was right that he hadn't done anything that required legal expertise, but he had shown up, driven me there, and reassured me that there was nothing more to be done. Had I gone alone I would have worried that I had said the wrong thing, or failed to say something that would have made the problem go away.

"I'm going to throw together the spaghetti if you would like to stay for dinner," I said tentatively.

He smiled. "I would like that."

I poured him some wine and set to work making spaghetti.

Jack joined me in the kitchen and gave me a funny look.

"Uh, Sophie, I hate to ask you this, but - "

My heart sank. I didn't think I could handle any more problems today.

"Are you chopping vegetables with a steak knife?" he asked.

I looked down, surprised.

"Maybe? Yeah, I think so."

He smiled. "Good thing you're not a surgeon. Move over." Before I knew what was happening he had gently nudged me out of the way and taken my place in front of the cutting board. "Please tell me you own other knives."

"I think so, yes. We have a lot of cooking supplies. It was an unexpected perk of having Chloe move in."

"Wonderful. I'll take a knife that's not serrated."

I found Chloe's knife block and pulled out one with a flat edge. "I didn't know you cooked."

"Hidden talent."

Jack was dicing bell peppers when the apartment door opened and Nathan walked in dragging a wheeled suitcase.

Fifteen

"**N**athan!" I said in disbelief.

He walked over, put his arms around me, and kissed me on the cheek.

"Hi Sophie. How was your day?" he asked. As though he had never left.

I hardly knew where to start. I stood there stirring pasta and trying to collect my thoughts.

Nathan noticed Jack standing beside me and stuck out his hand for a handshake. "Dr. Nathan Fox," he said politely. "You must be a friend of Chloe's?"

Jack nodded. "Jack Delacroix," he said, shaking Nathan's hand.

"Nice to meet you," said Nathan disinterestedly. I couldn't help but be insulted that when Nathan found a man cooking dinner in our apartment he assumed he was a friend of Chloe's and not of mine.

"Oh, Sophie, before I forget, I talked to Charlie earlier today, and he said to call him directly if Chloe needs legal help," Nathan said.

"Thanks, I'll keep it in mind," I said.

My cousin Charlie is a lawyer," Nathan explained to Jack.

Jack nodded. "Must be nice to have one in the family," he said politely.

"Well, most of them are bloodsuckers, so it's a relief to know one you can trust," Nathan said.

"That's certainly true," agreed Jack.

I turned my face away to hide a smile.

Nathan looked at Jack, then back to me. "Sophie, I was hoping we could talk tonight," he said.

I was in no mood for an emotional conversation. "As you can see, Nathan, Jack and I are making dinner," I told him. "It's not a good time." The polite thing to do would be to invite Nathan to stay and eat with us, but I had no desire to be polite.

Nathan looked confused by this. "But we were supposed to go to work on the project tonight," he pointed out. "And you told me you couldn't because of some issue with Chloe. How is she, by the way?"

"She wasn't well today. She's sleeping now," I said.

Nathan looked at Jack. "So what is he doing here?" he asked.

"Helping to make dinner," Jack answered smoothly.

Nathan shook his head, looking as though he had walked into a farce but couldn't be bothered to try to make sense of it. "Whatever. Sophie, can you please just sit down and listen to me for a minute?"

I sat down at our dining table across from Nathan. Jack stayed in the kitchen with his back to us, but the apartment was so small I knew he would hear every word.

"Sophie, I've given our situation a lot of thought, and I think it would make sense for me to move back in," Nathan said bluntly. "It's been over two months. We're both so busy that we'll hardly ever see each other if we continue to live apart. I miss you. You know that we were good together. The only way that we'll have a chance to rebuild our relationship is if I move back in."

For some reason I hadn't expected this. The suitcase should have been a clue, but I hadn't put it together.

"I'm sorry Nathan, but that won't be possible. Chloe's living with me now. Even apart from the awkwardness of that situation, this apartment is barely big enough for two people. There's no way that the three of us can live here together."

"Sophie, it feels like you've chosen Chloe over me. Why

does she get a free pass just because she's mentally ill? If I told you I had bipolar disorder would I be forgiven too?"

I had struggled so badly with this question.

"The difference, Nathan, is that you don't believe you have bipolar disorder. So if you told me that, you would be a liar."

"How do you know? Who decides that Chloe's sick but I'm a liar? Maybe I'm depressed. Maybe I had a mental break. I was under a great deal of stress, Sophie. And your sister is very attractive. Damn it, you know I've always had a thing for Chloe."

"That's interesting. I never knew."

"But I was obviously committed to you. That never changed."

I laughed. "Obviously."

Nathan scrubbed his hands through his hair in frustration. "Sophie, Chloe's taking advantage of your generosity. If you don't force the issue she may never move out."

"So you decided to force the issue yourself? By showing up here with a suitcase?" I asked.

He had the grace to blush.

"Well, I was optimistic," he said. "But I don't mind sleeping on the couch."

"Nathan, you can't live here," I said firmly. "Even if Chloe weren't staying with me, the answer would be no." I took a deep breath. "You hurt me badly, and I'm not ready to have you back in my home."

"Well, that's the other thing, Sophie," he said. "This is my home too. Regardless of our relationship status, I've lived in this apartment with you for over four years. Both of our names are on the lease. So I would like to move back in. I talked to Charlie about the situation, and he thinks I have a legal right to live here, at least until the lease is up. As I said, I'm willing to sleep on the couch. But I'm hoping we can talk through our differences, and find a way forward together."

All of a sudden, the stress became too much. I burst out laughing, loudly and uncontrollably. I felt tears running down my cheeks, and I couldn't remember when I had last laughed so hard.

Nathan looked insulted. "Sophie, I'm trying to be an adult here. I thought we were getting back together. But I was hoping that if we couldn't reconcile, we could at least live together amicably until I can find a new apartment downtown. But I guess you're not capable of that."

I had always known that Nathan had a selfish streak, but I had never seen him so petty and mean.

I made an effort to pull myself together.

"Nathan, are you fighting for our relationship or for our apartment?" I asked. I had a growing suspicion that his real motivation for coming back was the inconvenience of commuting downtown from his parents' house in the suburbs.

"Our relationship!" he said with frustration. "But obviously living together is an important part of it. And I'm willing to go to counselling, or -"

I laughed again. "Maybe we could go on one of those daytime psychotherapy shows," I suggested. "I think we have a good premise. My fiancé slept with my sister and now he wants to move in with the two of us. What do you think?"

"Sophie, I need you to take this seriously," Nathan said. His gaze fell on the bottle of Ativan I had left on the table. "Since when have you been taking Ativan?" His face softened. "Sophie, I knew you were struggling, but I didn't realize that things were so bad."

My pride wouldn't allow him to think that I needed Ativan to get over our breakup.

"It's actually for Chloe," I explained.

Nathan looked confused. "What do you mean? It has your name on it."

"Yes, but I got it for her," I said. "She was unwell, and she needed a sedative. I couldn't reach her psychiatrist, so it was just easier to get something in my name."

Nathan looked appalled. "Have you been giving her Ativan without her knowledge?" he asked.

I should have let him think the Ativan was for me.

"Of course not," I said defensively. "I told her what it was. She took it willingly." In truth, she had taken it willingly before I told her what it was, which was alarming.

"Is she even capable of consent?" Nathan asked. "Sophie, she's mentally ill. You of all people should understand that. You shouldn't be trying to treat her yourself. Some people might consider that malpractice."

Jack's voice was soft but ruthless. "That's an interesting point, Nathan. People might also ask if Chloe was capable of consenting to sex with you. Some might consider that sexual assault."

Nathan turned bright red. "That was different. She understood that. She clearly wanted it."

"The favourite defence of sexual predators everywhere," Jack commented.

I could tell Nathan was struggling to hold on to his temper. "Look, John, I need to talk to Sophie privately."

"It's Jack."

"Okay, Jack. This is between Sophie and me. I would appreciate some privacy to discuss it."

Jack smiled at Nathan, but the smile didn't reach his eyes. "I don't know, Nate," he said. Now even the tips of Nathan's ears were red. He hated to be called Nate.

"You've just accused Sophie of malpractice," continued Jack. "She may want a friend present with some legal knowledge. But I'll leave it up to Sophie." He turned to look at me.

Nathan looked at him through narrowed eyes. "What did you say your name was?"

"Jack Delacroix."

Nathan's mouth fell open. "From Reynolds Reilly?"

Jack nodded.

Nathan's entire demeanour changed. "My cousin Charlie talks about you all the time," he said. "He told me that you're the youngest person to make partner in, like twenty years." He stood up and offered Jack his hand to shake. "I'm Dr. Nathan Fox.

Cardiology Fellow. It's an honour to meet you."

Jack looked amused. "Yes, we've met. Half an hour ago, when Sophie introduced us."

"Yes, but I didn't realize who you were at the time," said Nathan. "Charlie says you're practically a legend already, and that all the associates are competing to work with you. He heard that you charge, like, seven hundred bucks an hour - "

"You should tell Charlie not to listen to rumours," said Jack. It was clear that he didn't appreciate the discussion of his fees.

"Oh, Charlie's in awe of you," Nathan continued. "He won't believe you're friends with Chloe. I know he would love to meet you." Nathan pulled out his phone. "In fact, I can see if he's free to come over now."

"I don't think that will be possible," said Jack.

"Oh, he's probably free," said Nathan, completely oblivious to Jack's tone.

"But I'm not free to meet him," said Jack.

Nathan looked up from his phone. "Oh. Well, he'll never believe that I met you in my apartment," he said.

"I think of it as Sophie's apartment," Jack said.

"Well, temporarily yes, but you must agree that the legally it's both of ours -"

"Of course," said Jack. "You should take the case to court."

Nathan looked surprised. "I should?"

"Absolutely," said Jack. "You'll probably get a court date some time next year. Some bored judge and his courtroom staff will finally get some entertainment. I'm sure they'll wonder why a cardiologist is taking his ex-girlfriend to court over the right to share a rental apartment, but you can explain that it's a matter of principle. I'll represent Sophie, and perhaps your cousin Charlie can represent you?"

Nathan's face fell. He turned back to me. "Sophie, I came here in good faith, hoping we could have a serious discussion about our future. It's clear to me that that won't be possible. I think it would be best if I leave."

I bit my lip. "Yes, I think that would be best."

As soon as the door closed behind Nathan I burst out laughing. Jack smiled.

"I hope you didn't mind my interference," he said.

"I'm not sure he would have left otherwise," I said.

"You must be hungry," Jack said. "The pasta's ready."

I realized that I was ravenous. Since Chloe had opened a bottle of wine I poured us each a glass, and we ate in silence for several minutes. The events of the evening had provided many potential topics of conversation but I didn't know where to begin, and I had the sense that Jack didn't either. There was a surreal feeling to it; if someone had told me this morning that I would be eating dinner with Jack Delacroix I would have laughed at the idea.

"Penny for your thoughts," he said.

"I was thinking how unexpected this is, eating dinner with you," I said honestly.

"Why is that?" he asked. He looked surprised, and even a little insulted. Maybe he thought I was reading too much into the situation.

"Just that it's pretty spontaneous, and I'm not known for spontaneity," I said inanely.

He nodded. "Me neither."

We finished the pasta and I carried the plates to the sink. I opened the fridge and considered the remains of the *croquembouche* tower. I decided it would not improve with age, and carried it to the coffee table. Jack stared at it, fascinated.

"What is that?" he asked.

"*Croquembouche* tower," I explained. I picked up a cream puff and took a bite. "Cream puffs. It was better yesterday, but it's still pretty good. Chloe made it."

Jack looked skeptical, but he tried it.

"That's actually delicious," he said, and took another.

Another comfortable silence fell as we worked our way through the cream puffs. Chloe had been generous with the pastry cream, and it was impossible to eat them without making a mess.

I looked up to find Jack staring at me.

"You have some custard just below your lower lip," he explained. "Right side."

I explored the area with my tongue and discovered a glob of pastry cream.

"Thanks," I said awkwardly. He had turned to look out the window.

"Thank you for dinner," he said formally. "I should get going." But he made no move to stand up, and irrationally, I didn't want him to go.

"For the apartment, what would the legal position be?" I blurted. "Our names are both on the lease. Do you think Nathan might actually have a case?"

Jack laughed. "Damned if I know, it's not my field. But I'm fairly confident that there's no way for him to challenge you legally without making himself look ridiculous. And my guess is that that's a very important consideration for him."

He had read Nathan's character accurately.

"You realize that if Nathan tells Charlie about this, there's a chance that they'll file a court case in the hope that you'll represent me and Charlie can meet you?"

He rolled his eyes. "I think I could handle cousin Charlie."

I remembered Nathan's comment about Jack's hourly rate and my heart sank. "Yes, but I couldn't afford to have you do it. Financially, I would be better off to let Nathan have the apartment and move elsewhere."

Jack looked surprised. "Sophie -"

"Don't worry, I fully intend to pay you for your work for Chloe today," I said quickly. "And if you're willing to continue with her case I want to pay your usual rates. Send the invoice to me, I don't want my parents involved. If possible, I don't even want them to know."

He looked frustrated. "Sophie, I don't expect payment for this. It's the least I can do after Samantha's unorthodox visit to your apartment. And I'd like to do this." He paused. "For Chloe."

Of course. For a minute I had thought he wanted to do me a favour, but this was, after all, about Chloe.

"Regardless, I don't want to be in your debt. So please send me an invoice."

"If it bothers you, you can give me some free medical advice."

I looked over at him, sitting on my couch with his long legs stretched out in front of him, looking completely relaxed. He had taken off his jacket and tie to dance with Chloe, and in his dress shirt and pants it was clear he kept in shape. He was probably the fittest person to have sat on that couch.

"Sure. Keep doing what you're doing."

He laughed. "Do you get paid to give people that sort of advice? Keep doing what you're doing?"

"No, because I'm a hospital-based doctor, and healthy young men don't drop into the hospital for medical advice. Most young men don't go to the doctor until they're practically dying. It's a shame, really, because my job would be a lot easier if they did. I could just pop in and say 'you look good, keep doing what you're doing."

"You think I look good?"

I felt my cheeks heat. The glass of wine had loosened my tongue.

"I didn't say that."

He laughed. "You implied it, Dr. Ingram."

In vino veritas. "I mean, it's not that you don't look good, it's just that I didn't mean to say it that way." I stopped and sighed. There was no way out of this without embarrassing myself or insulting him. "You look good. Professionally speaking."

He smiled. "Thank you." He stood. "I should go. When Chloe's feeling better, ask her whether she wants me to handle her shoplifting case. If she does, we can set up a meeting for her to sign a retainer agreement. If she prefers to use someone else I would be happy to suggest some names."

"I will. I really appreciate your help today."

"You're welcome, Sophie."

He opened the door, then turned around to look at me.

"And Sophie. About Nathan."

"What about Nathan?" I asked warily.

"I think Chloe did you a favour."

Sixteen

I had a moment of panic when I woke up the next morning, worried that if the Ativan had worn off Chloe might have gone out. I cracked open her door and was relieved to see her in bed, still asleep. I had no idea what her mental state would be when she woke up, so I sent Lucas a text to say I would be late and to start without me.

I called Dr. Jankovic's office on the dot of eight o'clock. I was pleasantly surprised when the phone was answered on the first ring.

"Good morning, my name is Sophie Ingram. I'm calling about my sister, Chloe Ingram -"

"I'm sorry, I'm going to have to stop you there. Is your sister an adult?"

"Yes." Although she doesn't always behave like one.

"And has she been deemed incapable of making medical and personal care decisions?"

"Well, no, but -"

"Then I'm afraid I can't discuss anything with you. Please ask your sister to call our office directly."

"Wait, I don't actually need to discuss anything with you, but I do need to make an appointment. For Chloe."

"Is there a reason Chloe can't call to book her own appointment?"

"Well, right now she's asleep. But it's urgent that she has an appointment as soon as possible."

"If it's an emergency you should call 911 or take her to the nearest emergency room."

"Well, I don't think it's an emergency, but I do think she needs to see Dr. Jankovic. Urgently. She's not well."

"We take the privacy of our patients very seriously, so I can't give any appointment information to you. The fact that she is seeing a psychiatrist, and the dates and times of her appointments, must remain confidential. Unless your sister has been deemed incapable, in which case we can deal with her power of attorney."

"Okay. Thank you so much for your help."

The sarcasm seemed lost on the receptionist, who remained perky. "You're very welcome. Have a wonderful day."

I resisted the urge to beat my head against the counter and went to brew some strong coffee.

Chloe stumbled into the kitchen a few minutes later. I tried to gauge her mood by her facial expression; sometimes I could tell when she was depressed, as she looked flat. Today she just looked tired.

"How are you feeling?"

"Exhausted," she answered. She walked to the fridge and pulled out a Diet Coke.

"At least have some orange juice," I suggested.

She stuck out her tongue at me.

I had meant to ease into the discussion of her behaviour yesterday, but I was so irritated by the juvenile gesture that I jumped in.

"Chloe, were you on Ritalin yesterday?"

She looked surprised, then defensive. "How did you know?"

"I saw the bottle in your purse."

"Sophie, you had no right -"

I cut her off. "Chloe, you were caught shoplifting yesterday. If I hadn't gotten your ID from your purse you could have faced other charges. So yes, I looked in your purse."

"Dr. Jankovic prescribed it," she said. "I told her about the depression, and she suggested adding Ritalin. She thinks I may also have elements of ADHD, and that could explain why I sometimes have difficulty finishing what I start.”

“Your psychiatrist gave you Ritalin?”

“Yep. I know it’s usually for ADHD, but apparently it’s also helpful for depression.”

“How much did you take?”

“I just started it a few days ago. First I just took one pill in the morning . . . ”

“How much was in each pill? And do you know if it was the regular Ritalin or extended release?” It drove me crazy when people just described their medications in terms of the number or colour of the pills. Most drugs were available in a variety of strengths, and knowing the number of pills without knowing the pill strength was not very helpful. I had been too flustered to note the dosage on the bottle yesterday.”

“I’m not sure. It was red.”

Even better. “Okay, well, you can show me the bottle later.”

She nodded. “I think it helped. I had more energy, and I didn’t need nearly as much sleep. So yesterday morning I took three, and then I took another at lunch.”

This explained so much.

“Okay, Chloe, we need to get you an appointment with Dr. Jankovic as soon as possible. I called this morning but they said you have to call yourself.”

She nodded agreeably. “Okay. I’ll call later today.”

“Could you call her now?”

“I’m still waking up, Sophie.”

“Okay. Maybe you could call after breakfast. Do you want some orange juice? An apple? Some cereal?”

She laughed. “I’m fine with Diet Coke, thanks.”

“Have you been taking the valproic acid?”

“Not exactly. I’ve been screwing myself up with drugs for almost ten years. I wanted to see who I was without them.”

I let out a long breath.

“Did you tell Dr. Jankovic about this plan for a drug holiday?”

"Well, it was complicated. I didn't lie to her, if that's what you're asking."

"But you let her think you were taking the valproic acid."

"Well, she told me she thought I should go back on it, and gave me a prescription. I never said I was going to fill the prescription."

"Chloe, you should have told her. I'm pretty sure she wouldn't have prescribed you a stimulant if she knew you weren't taking the valproic acid."

"She should have asked me," said Chloe defensively. "Doctors shouldn't just assume that people are taking medications."

This was undeniably true.

"Besides, I found a book about bipolar disorder," she continued. "It's called *Meditation over medication: Ten steps to take control of Bipolar Disorder.* It talks about natural ways to align your emotions."

"So where does Ritalin fit into that?"

Chloe bit her lip. "I didn't have the energy to try any of the steps in the book. I hoped that the Ritalin would give me a little boost to get started, and then I could get off of it. But I felt so much better with it, Sophie, you wouldn't believe it. It was like I could do anything."

I believed it. I saw the evidence yesterday.

I didn't say anything, and Chloe continued. "I don't really remember everything that happened yesterday. I remember being accused of shoplifting, and then you showed up with your hot lawyer friend..."

"Jack's not my friend, he's a work acquaintance of Dad's. He was at your hearing."

"Yep. Didn't say much, but he was very memorable. How did he get involved in this?"

"I called him after you called me. He offered to help us. By the time we showed up, the police had already been called, and there was no way to get out of the charges. You'll have to go to the police station next week to get photographed and fingerprinted. But because this was your first offense, Jack thinks there's a reasonable chance he can get the prosecutor to drop the charges in exchange for a donation to charity or something. In that case, you wouldn't have a criminal record, and he can file an application to get your fingerprint records destroyed."

She looked panicky. "And if he can't get the charges dropped? Is there a chance I'll go to jail?"

"He thought that in the worst case scenario, you'll have to pay a fine. A few thousand dollars, probably."

Her face fell.

"I can help you with the fine." I could see her relax a little, then panic again.

"Do you think this lawyer will tell Dad? Do you think he'll bill Dad for this? Can we afford to pay him ourselves?"

She had an interesting way of phrasing it. By 'could we afford to pay him ourselves', Chloe was really asking if I could afford to pay him myself. If I was willing to pay him myself. We had already established that she had no money.

"Well, we could, yes." The money would have to come from my line of credit, but I could do it. "But he said he'd handle it for free."

"Why would he do that? Do you think Mom and Dad are paying him?"

I found it interesting that Chloe and I had had the same thought. "It crossed my mind. But he says they're not. He'll want you to sign a retainer agreement so he can represent you for the shoplifting charge. I think he's telling the truth. If he were still employed by Mom and Dad for your mental health situation, that would be a major conflict of interest."

Chloe appeared to think about that. "Interesting. Maybe he's into me."

"Maybe," I answered. I didn't want to dwell on that possibility. "Anyway, Chloe, I think your priority for today should be getting an appointment with Dr. Jankovic. You need to get back on valproic acid. And you probably should stop the Ritalin, at least until you've been on the valproic acid for a while."

She rolled her eyes. "I hardly need Dr. Jankovic, you seem to know exactly what to do," she said sarcastically.

"Chloe, please call her office. You need to see her," I said.

"I will," she said.

Do you think it would be a good idea to let me hold on to the Ritalin for now?" I asked hopefully. I wished I had taken it from her purse while she was asleep.

"No," she said flatly.

"Do you have anything else planned for today?" I asked her warily.

"No."

"Okay then," I said. I was worried about what she might get up to if I went to work. I was also worried about what the trainees might get up to at the hospital if I didn't go to work. I felt like a single parent whose unruly children were running in opposite directions.

It was clear that I needed backup. I sent a text to Martin Chu: "How would you feel about taking Chloe out for lunch?"

***

Martin not only agreed to take Chloe to lunch, he offered to drive her to her doctor's appointment if she managed to get one. This was a huge weight off my shoulders and freed me to focus on work, which was actually going well. It helped that we had had a run of patients admitted with acute and treatable problems. We treated them, wrote discharge orders, and they went home to lead relatively independent lives. Even Dr. Hastings had noticed the high patient turnover, and had praised me for running the team efficiently. I hadn't had any correspondence from Stacey Sullivan in the Ombudsperson's office for over a week, which made me wonder if she was sick or on vacation.

I still hadn't heard anything about the Central Line Incident. At the very least, I had expected an email from the residency program director to set up a meeting to 'discuss the incident and offer support', which usually translated to 'make sure you don't screw up like this again.' But when I did, in fact, get a message from the program director entitled 'Offering Support' it turned out to be a mass email sent to my entire residency cohort as part of a wellness initiative, with a coupon for a free ice cream sundae.

Our MoPPET Quality Improvement project had gotten off the ground surprisingly quickly. Both the ward manager and the volunteer coordinator had given their enthusiastic approval, and the first group of student volunteers had already completed their training with Jessica Scott and started work. Jessica had used some of the grant money to buy bright blue T-shirts that said MoPPET on the front and Mobility Equity on the back. It was satisfying to see them on the wards; I could tell the patients were happy to be out of bed and the volunteers were pleased to have something to do besides deliver water jugs.

Even the medical students seemed to be improving. Ellis could now give an entire case presentation without using the word endorse. I was especially pleased with Emily's progress; she had grown from a stammering girl into a very strong senior medical student.

So I was surprised to find Emily crying in the team room in the middle of the day. It came out that the son of one of our patients had told her that she was lucky she was beautiful, because she wouldn't get far on the strength of her brain. He had then gone to the ward manager and complained that all of the doctors treating his father were incompetent, and demanded to talk to the doctor in charge. The irony was that I thought that his father had actually received good medical care. I discussed the situation with Dr. Hastings and suggested she might want to meet with him herself, but she said she trusted me to handle it. I was flattered by her confidence until I realized that she had cleverly dodged what was sure to be a difficult encounter. "Just be assertive, Sophie," she said. "You need to learn not to hide from conflict."

Emily had pulled herself together, so I took her with me. The patient was a seventy-six year old man who had been admitted about a week ago with severe pneumonia. He had finished his course of antibiotics and had actually recovered fairly well from a respiratory standpoint, but remained weak and deconditioned. At this point, he mainly needed a MoPPET mobility intervention. He smiled at me as I sat down in one of the chairs by his bedside.

His son, who occupied the other bedside chair, did not smile when I introduced myself as the acting head of the medical team. He looked about forty, with graying brown hair and a red face.

"You don't look old enough to be a doctor," he said.

"Thank you," I replied. There was a beat of silence as he waited for me to say more, to explain that I was older than I looked, to try to justify my position. I didn't.

"I'm Lawrence Graves," he finally said.

"Nice to meet you. I understand you had some questions about your father's care," I said.

"Yes. My father was perfectly well before he was taken to your hospital," he stated accusingly. "And now look at him. He's too weak to even get out of bed. And it's no surprise, given the number of students here experimenting on people."

I took a cleansing breath. It was amazing how many people claimed to have been 'perfectly well' before coming to hospital, implying that not only had we failed to cure them, we had caused their problems.

"So was your father abducted?" I asked politely.

Mr. Graves looked confused. "What?" he asked suspiciously.

"Your father. Was he abducted? Did you report it to the police?"

Mr. Graves looked at his father, who was resting calmly in bed, then looked at me as though I was crazy.

"He hasn't been abducted, he's lying right there!" he said.

"I'm just trying to understand how he came to be in hospital," I said calmly. "You said he was perfectly well until he was taken to the hospital, so I thought he might have been abducted and brought here against his will. But maybe he came to visit someone and fell ill while he was here?"

My point seemed to have gone right over his head. He peered at my ID badge. No doubt he had forgotten my name already. I held out the badge to give him a better look. He would be able to find out my name from the nursing staff easily enough, so there was no point trying to hide it.

"Dr. Ingram, this is not a joke. I have serious concerns about my father's health," he said.

"Mr. Graves, I take your concerns very seriously," I said. "And I hope you can help me to better understand your father's situation. Why did he come to the hospital?"

"Is that not in his chart?" he asked. "Do you not read the records?"

"Yes, we do," I said. "But I'm interested in hearing it from your perspective."

"I called 911 because he had a fever and was having trouble breathing," he said, as though it should have been obvious. "The paramedics came and brought him to the hospital."

"I see." I paused. "So just to be clear, he had a fever and trouble breathing before he came to the hospital?"

"Yes, that's what I said." He looked at me as though I was a particularly slow student.

I nodded. "Okay. I'm just trying to make sense of the situation, because you initially told me he was perfectly well until he came to the hospital."

"He was!" he said angrily. "He was perfectly well until he got sick!" Mr. Graves' face was turning red. I was a little concerned that he was about to suffer a medical event, and become one of the rare people who had actually been perfectly well until he came to the hospital and then fell sick while he was here.

"I understand completely," I said. "Believe it or not, we see situations like your Dad's fairly often."

"I intend to file a complaint," he informed me.

I nodded. "I understand."

I expected to hear from Stacey Sullivan soon. It would be worth it.

***

As soon as Emily and I made it back to our team office I shut the door, collapsed into a chair and laughed. She caught my eye as though asking for permission, and then dissolved into laughter herself.

When we had recovered, I debated whether to explain to Emily that what she had witnessed wasn't a typical example of my approach to conflict resolution, but she spoke first.

"Um, Dr. Ingram?" she asked.

"Yes?"

"That was amazing."

"Thank you," I answered.

Emily took a deep breath and looked at me nervously.

"Dr. Ingram, I still don't have a faculty mentor yet, and I was wondering if you would consider it?"

This was unexpected. "Oh. Emily, I'm flattered, but I'm probably not the best person to advise you right now. I'm just finishing residency, I'm not even on faculty."

Her face fell. "I understand," she said quickly. "I know how busy you are."

How to explain that an association with me was unlikely to help her career?

"I'm not busy, it's just that I'm sure you could find someone in a better position to help you."

"Yes, of course." She still looked disappointed, and I could tell she thought I was using the 'it's not you, it's me' excuse to let her down easily. I thought back to the mentor I had been assigned as a medical student, a microbiology professor in her fifties who spent far more time in the micro lab than on the ward. We had one awkward meeting during which we made small talk about my career goals and I tried not to stare at her electric blue eyeshadow. The meeting had ended with a promise to connect again in a few months, but we never had. My most vivid memory of the experience was of the awful eyeshadow.

Maybe I did have something to offer.

"Actually, Emily, I would love to be your mentor," I said. "So long as you understand that I'm not actually on faculty, and there's a good chance that I never will be. I doubt my influence will be helpful to your career. But I would be happy to share my thoughts."

Her face had lit up. "I would love that," she said. "When would we start?" She pulled out her phone and opened the calendar app. "I know you're busy this block, being on Junior Attending, but could we book a meeting time in a couple of weeks?"

"We start now," I answered. "Let's go get lunch."

Seventeen

C hloe had gone back to her previous pattern of sleeping late then spending the day moping in front of the TV. I knew that Martin had driven her to an appointment with her psychiatrist earlier in the week, but I had no idea what Dr. Jankovic's recommendations had been, or whether she was following them. I didn't have the energy to confront her about it during the week, but by Saturday morning I had had enough. I knocked on the door to her bedroom, and when she didn't answer I stepped inside and called her name.

"Go away!" she yelled from under the covers.

"Chloe, we need to talk," I said.

A hand shot out from under the covers, grabbed her aloe vera plant off the bedside table, and threw it in the direction of the door. Unfortunately for me, it was a hard throw and her blind aim was accurate. The ceramic pot hit me in the face, just underneath my right eye, and I screamed.

Chloe threw off the covers and saw me with my hands over my face.

"Oh God, Sophie, did I hit you?" she cried.

I nodded numbly.

"I'm so sorry, Sophie. I hate myself. I can't believe I did that to you. I wasn't myself. I just feel so out of control sometimes. I hate living like this."

As usual, she was twisting the situation to make it all about her. I walked over to the mirror to examine the red mark that had appeared over my right cheekbone. I suspected I would end up with a bruise. Fortunately the skin hadn't broken, so I was unlikely to have a scar.

"I don't like living like this either," I said firmly. "So. Here's the deal. You're living in my apartment. I'm basically subsidizing you financially. If you're going to continue to live here I have two conditions."

Chloe didn't say anything.

"Chloe?" I asked sharply.

"You're as bad as Mom and Dad!" she exclaimed.

"Three conditions," I amended. "First, you stop comparing me to our parents."

She gave me a ghost of a smile. "Okay."

"Two, you take the medication that Dr. Jankovic prescribes. If you think you're having side effects, you talk to her about making changes. You don't unilaterally decide to stop taking meds. And you don't take any drugs that aren't prescribed by a doctor."

There was a pause while she thought about that.

"I guess I don't have a choice, do I?" she said resentfully.

"Sure you do, Chloe. You can move out."

She must have realized that I was nearing my breaking point, because she nodded.

"Okay. I'll take the meds. What's the third thing?"

"You come with me to a barre class. I've already signed up. It starts in an hour."

I had researched barre and Pilates classes, and Barre None was supposed to be one of the best gyms in the city. They certainly charged enough, and I had paid $90 to register Chloe and myself for an hour-long class.

The studio was beautiful, with a ballet barre along the length of one wall and floor-to-ceiling mirrors opposite. A third wall was composed almost entirely of windows, and the hardwood floors gleamed in the midmorning sun. Chloe's face lit up when she walked in and I breathed a sigh of relief. I had feared that with her dancing background, she would think herself above this. But she needed to get out of the apartment and I didn't have any better ideas.

A knot of women in expensive-looking exercise gear stood talking in a corner, but there was no sign of an instructor. Chloe glanced over at the women, then walked over to the barre and began to stretch her legs. She moved through a series of warm-up exercises, graceful movements with fancy French names that I could never remember. The ladies in the corner stopped chatting to watch her.

The instructor was late, which ticked me off, given the cost of the class. I moved to a spot a few feet behind Chloe and attempted to mimic her movements.   A few minutes later the women from the corner walked over and began to follow too.

Fifteen minutes past the scheduled start time, a harassed-looking woman rushed in and took in at the scene. She had an athletic build but wore designer jeans and a sweater, and clearly hadn't come to work out. She quickly focused on Chloe, who seemed oblivious to the scrutiny.

When Chloe paused at the end of a sequence the new arrival walked up to her and tapped her shoulder.

"Excuse me," she said. "My name is Andrea, I own the gym. Unfortunately, today's teacher hasn't shown up. You dance beautifully. Would you be willing to lead the rest of this class?"

***

We left the gym with a job offer for Chloe to teach six barre classes per week, with the potential for more if things went well. Andrea had paid her $45 for teaching the class, which was ironically the same amount that I had paid to register her for it, but I hadn't pointed that out. Her face was flushed, and although she tried to downplay her excitement, I could tell she was pleased.

She pulled out her phone. "I have to tell Martin, he suggested I get a job involving dance." She tapped out a text. Her phone received an answering ping less than a minute later.

"He wants to take me out to dinner to celebrate."

"Okay," I said, surprised.

She paused. "You don't mind, do you? I mean, I know he's your friend."

I laughed. "Chloe I don't mind at all." I was grateful that she had someone to talk to, someone solid and sensible who could hopefully help her climb out of her funk.

Her phone pinged again, and she looked down. "He suggested you come too."

I considered it. Martin was always good company, and I had no other plans. But the alternative, an evening alone in my apartment with no obligations, was too appealing. "Not this time, but thank you."

***

The following day I woke up with a dark bruise under my right eye where Chloe had hit me with the plant. Fortunately I had nowhere to be, and Chloe and I spent the day together at home, making lasagna from one of Chloe's overly complex recipes and watching old movies. Chloe was full of remorse for the eye injury and unusually solicitous. She did more than her share of the kitchen clean-up and let me choose what movies to watch.

I had hoped the bruise would have improved by the time I had to go to work on Monday, but it was worse. Chloe came into the kitchen as I ate my breakfast Cheerios and bent to peer at my face. "Sophie, I'm so sorry, it still looks terrible. Let me try to cover it up."

It was the first morning that Chloe had been out of bed before I left for work, and I wondered if she had planned this. She had always been good with makeup, and after she worked on my face for ten minutes I certainly looked better.

"Can I add some eyeshadow?" she asked. "Maybe a little mascara? I think it would distract from the bruise."

I shook my head. "I have to run."

I spent the walk to work trying to think of an explanation

for the injury. The excuses of walking into a door or falling down the stairs seemed too cliché, almost code for 'I got beaten up'. I finally settled on a gym mishap; I wasn't paying attention on the treadmill and did a faceplant. Most people were too polite to ask, but it was clear they noticed. I got a midmorning text from Nathan:

"What happened to your face? People are saying we broke up because I hit you. It doesn't help that you're not wearing the ring."

I had met him at work several days ago to return the ring, in exchange for the key to our apartment.

Sophie: I appreciate your concern, Nathan.
Nathan: What happened?
Sophie: Treadmill injury.
Nathan: Can you make sure that people know that? I'm getting funny looks.
Sophie: It's painful, but I'm coping, thanks for asking.
Nathan: I'm sorry, Sophie. It's just that this makes things really awkward for me.

I had no good answer to that.

***

I had arranged a meeting with Jack and Chloe that afternoon to review the retainer agreement for Chloe's shoplifting charge. I had expected to go to his office, but he had offered to meet at the Starbucks near the hospital at five pm, with the rationale that it was on his way home. I rushed through the meeting with Dr. Hastings and arrived to find Jack already in line. I kept my sunglasses on, as I had gotten tired of people staring at my bruised face. It was better to let people speculate on whether I was recovering from plastic surgery, or had lost my usual prescription glasses, or was just weird.

'I'll buy coffee today," I said. If I remember right, you drink a venti chocolate chip frappuccino with extra whipped cream?" I paused. "Or is it a tall black?"

"Actually, today it's a tall black," he said.

I ordered a latte and reached for my wallet, but he paid before I could pull out my credit card.

"Thanks," I said.

"I see you're back on caffeine," he teased. "Your insomnia better?"

"Yes. Actually, I read a study that found that people who drink at least four cups of coffee per day live longer. Even when adjusting for other variables, like diet and exercise. No one really knows why. So I've been trying to increase my intake." This was technically true. I had read a study with those conclusions several years ago and quoted it at Nathan whenever he commented on my excessive coffee consumption.

We found a table in a corner, and I removed my sunglasses.

Jack's eyes narrowed. "What happened to your face?" he asked quietly.

"Oh, it's nothing. Minor treadmill accident, but I'm fine." I tried to change the subject. "Chloe signed the retainer agreement, she should be bringing it –"

"You're a terrible liar, Sophie." He reached up and gently brushed his thumb over the bruise. It was the lightest of touches, but it was comforting. "What really happened? Have you been icing it? I have an ice pack that stays cold for an hour, I can lend it to you if you like."

"I was on the treadmill in the gym in my building. And then I got distracted searching for a song on my phone, and I stepped off the belt -"

"What song?" he interrupted.

"What?"

"What song were you searching for?"

"Oh! Um – Let it Be." It was the first song name that popped into my head; I had been listening to it on my earbuds on my walk to work.

"Sophie, no one listens to Let it Be while running on the treadmill. It's practically a lullaby."

"It was more of a brisk walk. On an incline."

"Uh huh," he said skeptically.

"So anyway, I had Chloe read the retainer agreement . . ."

"Was it Nathan?" His voice was still quiet but there was an ugly look on his face.

"No!" I was shocked at the suggestion. For all his faults, I didn't think Nathan was capable of physical violence. "But Nathan is upset. Apparently you're not the first to ask that question. He's very concerned about his reputation."

"Good. I hope he's had a miserable day."

"I sighed. "If you must know, it was an accident. Chloe threw a potted plant and it hit me."

"Sophie." He looked appalled.

"I really don't think she meant to hit me with it. And she felt so guilty after she did it, it gave me the opportunity to lay down some ground rules."

Jack ran a hand through his hair, causing a tuft of hair to stick up near the back. I was about to reach out to smooth it down when he spoke again.

"Sophie, who do you have helping you?"

"What do you mean?" His question implied that I was failing to cope with the situation, or that I could benefit from mental health help myself. Maybe both.

"I mean with Chloe. It sounds like she has some serious problems."

"She does have a psychiatrist." One who was only available Mondays, Tuesdays, and Thursdays from 9 am to 3 pm, and who was unable to talk to me for confidentiality reasons, but still.

"I don't mean professionals, I mean family or friends. This is a lot for one person to manage."

"There aren't many people I can trust with this. Most of our friends don't even know what's going on, and I don't want to advertise our family's dysfunction."

"What about your mom? Surely she could take her out for lunch a couple of times per week. Or does she work?"

"Well, she doesn't work outside the home."

He opened his mouth then quickly closed it again.

"Oh go on, ask me if she works inside the home," I said. "I can tell it's on the tip of your tongue."

He laughed. "Never. That would be incredibly rude."

"True, but you might jump to the conclusion that she has an army of staff to run the house." I couldn't forget his conversation with Samantha at Chloe's hearing.

"Sophie, I'll say it again. I was wrong about you. Are you going to hold it against me forever?" His tone was light, but the look in his eyes suggested he was very interested in my answer.

"I'll have to think about it," I said. I suddenly felt the need to defend my mom. "She used to work, you know. My mom. She has a degree in classics and philosophy, and she was a high school teacher until I was twelve. But then my dad moved up at the bank, and his hours got worse, and it just didn't make sense for her to keep working . . ." I trailed off. I realized that I had never thought about how my mom might have felt about giving up her job. "Anyway. I think Chloe and I kept her busy."

"I can believe that," he said.

"Anyway, I appreciate your handling the shoplifting," I said, in an effort to change the subject. "And handling Nathan. If you hadn't been there I might have given in and let him move back in."

He smiled. "Don't sell yourself short. You demonstrated some pretty solid advocacy skills at Chloe's capacity hearing. It helped that you didn't introduce yourself as a doctor, and showed up with toothpaste on your shirt. The diabetes insipidus stuff kind of came out of nowhere. Is she doing any better from that standpoint?"

I had almost forgotten about the diabetes insipidus. "Oh yeah, she's off the lithium. But I'm pretty sure that she was just drinking all that water to mess with the staff at the hospital. It would be pretty unusual for lithium to cause that in a couple weeks, it usually takes months to years.”

He looked surprised. “So you were bluffing?”

“Not really. The point was, it *could* have been a side effect from the lithium. Edwards was probably right, but he really should have checked her labs. I was just trying to create reasonable doubt.”

“Well you sounded damned impressive, and you were far more effective than your sister’s lawyer. Did you ever consider a legal career?”

I laughed. “Many times in the past few months. But I really don’t want to pay another three years of tuition. And I doubt I could pull off the toothpaste stunt more than once.”

Jack laughed at that. He was surprisingly easy to talk to.

“I’ve also considered moving to a small town where I could just practice medicine, without pretending to do research or teach. But there’s so much uncertainty with Chloe right now, it’s not a good time to make plans to leave the city.”

He nodded. His gaze fell on my left hand, which was wrapped around my coffee cup. “You’re not wearing your engagement ring,” he commented.

I shook my head. “As I said, the engagement’s off. But Nathan had applied for a competitive fellowship, and he was worried that a broken engagement would be held against him, so I agreed to keep wearing the ring at work.” I rolled my eyes. “I doubt anyone would have cared. But he got his fellowship, so I gave the ring back.”

“I think that was a good decision,” he said.

The conversation was becoming uncomfortable, so I fell back on Chloe’s strategy of turning a question back on the questioner. “Have you ever been married?” I asked.

A strange expression flashed across his face, then disappeared so quickly I wondered if I had imagined it.

“No,” he answered. “No, I -”

Chloe showed up then, cutting off what might have turned into a very interesting sentence. She looked spectacular, in a silky blue top and jeans, and she greeted us with a big smile.

"I see you've started without me. It's okay, I don't need a drink."

Jack stood up. "Let me get you something."

"Really, I'm fine."

Jack shrugged and sat back down. I could tell Chloe was surprised that he hadn't insisted.

Eighteen

T he time had come for Mrs. Campbell to go home, only three weeks after I had first tried to discharge her. The new feeding tube was in, and she had been stable to go for a week. I had attempted to discharge her three days ago, but when the transport paramedics showed up Elaine had told them that there had been a mistake. She had claimed that her mother was far too sick to go home, and that she would need nursing home placement. So the paramedics had left, and sent another bill to the hospital for an ambulance trip that was never taken.

The afternoon after the second ambulance left I had sat down with Elaine to discuss a nursing home application and she had said no, there was no way she would ever put her mother in a home.

So today I had shown up in Mrs. Campbell's room half an hour before the ambulance was booked to arrive, ready to deal with any last minute concerns about movie premieres, sick pets, or medical problems. Elaine was already there.

"Dr. Ingram, did you know that the new James Bond movie opens in three days? It's only reasonable to delay the discharge until opening day, so -"

"No." I interrupted.

She tried again. "Stacey Sullivan in the Ombudsperson's office told me that I have a right to advocate for my mom, and I shouldn't consent to a plan unless I'm confident that it's in her best interest," she told me.

I mentally cursed the absent Stacey Sullivan.

"I agree," I began. "But living in the hospital indefinitely is not an option that we are offering, nor is it in her best interest. So your options are to take your mother home today, as planned, or to apply to a nursing home. Today. If you don't think you're capable of making a choice, we will look for someone else to make decisions on your mother's behalf. Another relative, maybe, or even the Public Guardian and Trustee." I smiled at her. "Sometimes making decisions can be a burden, you might be relieved to let someone else do it."

Elaine bristled. "I'm the only person with the right to make decisions for my mother."

I looked her in the eye. "So what's the plan?"

My expression must have made it clear that I had had enough, because she backed down.

"She'll come home today."

The paramedics arrived, and transferred Mrs. Campbell onto a stretcher. She let out a little moan as they strapped her in. I wondered if she had any understanding of how hard her daughter had fought to keep her from coming home.

As they wheeled her out of the room, I overheard Elaine chattering to the paramedics.

"I'm so relieved she's coming home today," she told them. "I always think doctors keep people in the hospital far too long."

***

I floated back to the nursing station on a wave of adrenaline and relief. As a medical student, if someone had told me that one of the most difficult tasks I would face as a doctor would be to discharge a patient like Mrs. Campbell I wouldn't have believed it. It was a hollow triumph, and I recognized that something was wrong when kicking a demented old lady out of the hospital felt like the greatest achievement of my week. Either the system was broken or I was.

I pushed the thought aside and checked my email. At the top of my inbox was a message from the hospital's Chief of Medicine.

Dear Sophie:

I would like to set up a meeting to review how your year is going, and to discuss some concerns. Would Thursday at 4 PM in my office be convenient?"

Sincerely,

Stuart

'Stuart' was actually Dr. Stuart Jones, and he was near the top of the hospital's physician hierarchy, even above Dr. Hastings. He probably had three or four degrees after his name, and I wasn't sure what to think of the fact that he hadn't tacked them all on to his email signature. Regardless, his influence was such that when he suggested a meeting, it was convenient. I wished he had specified what the concerns were; I figured it was most likely related to the Central Line Incident, but figured it could also refer to the fact that I had relabelled a research trial as a Quality Improvement project to bypass the need for Ethics review. I had been less than diplomatic over the past few months, and I could think of several patients and their relatives who could have filed complaints. He had been courteous enough to give me almost a full week's notice of the meeting, which meant I would have plenty of time to stew over the possibilities.

I was still trying to process this when Nathan marched up to me, with Jessica Scott following closely behind him. It was the first time I'd seen him since the night he had tried to move back into our apartment, and he looked irate.

"Sophie, we need to talk about MoPPET," he said. "Jessica told me that you completely changed the project without telling me."

Jessica sent me an apologetic look.

"Nathan, it's not completely changed," I began.

"Well you'll have to explain what's going on, because Jessica says that you've started the project with *youth volunteers*! And unless the approval came through without my knowledge, you're doing this without Ethics approval. Or am I missing something?"

Nathan wasn't quite yelling but his voice was loud, and everyone else at the nursing station had suddenly fallen silent.

"Nathan, maybe we should discuss this elsewhere," I suggested. I stood up and tried to think where we could move the conversation. There was a good chance that the medical students would be in the team room, and Jessica Scott's tiny office was at the opposite end of the hospital.

"Sophie, I don't care where we discuss this, but we're going to discuss it now!" I had rarely seen him so angry in public.

"You're right, Nathan," I said, trying to be conciliatory. "Let's go to the cafeteria?" That would be only marginally better than the nursing station, but there was a chance we could find a quiet area.

"We'll go to Dr. Hastings' office," Nathan said decisively. "She needs to hear this too." He turned and began to walk in the direction of her office. Jessica and I followed.

"Actually, Nathan -" I started to tell him that Dr. Hastings was aware of the changes to the project, but he cut me off.

"Did you do this to punish me, Sophie?" he asked as we marched down the hall.

"Of course not, Nathan," I protested. "I thought that a Quality Improvement project was actually a better fit. And we don't need Ethics for it, so we could get going right away."

"But Sophie, when we want to publish we'll be limited to QI journals, which hardly anyone reads. And we had a real chance of a high impact publication. Especially if we approached things from an equity angle."

"My first priority wasn't publication, it was to improve patient care," I argued.

"Yes, but we would have had much broader reach as a trial," he countered.

"If it ever got off the ground. It might have died in the Research Ethics Board and never seen the light of day. If this succeeds, someone could always pursue a trial down the road."

Nathan shook his head in frustration, and I started to question my own motivation. He was right that I should have told him. Maybe I had been trying to punish him.

Nathan knocked impatiently on Dr. Hastings's door, then walked in before she had a chance to answer. I followed behind, embarrassed to be barging in unannounced but happy to get the argument out of the hallway. Jessica hovered nervously in the doorway.

Dr. Hastings looked surprised but not unhappy to see us.

"Nathan, Sophie," she greeted us. "Please sit down."

As there was only one chair facing her desk there was no way we could both sit. Nathan gestured for me to take it but I remained standing.

"Dr. Hastings, we need to talk about the MoPPET project," he began.

She nodded. "Yes, I'm interested to hear how that's progressing. I think the changes you've made are really brilliant. I assume they were your idea?"

Nathan looked stunned. "I'm sorry?"

"You know, turning it into a Quality Improvement project and involving the volunteers. It's a great use of volunteer energy and talent."

Nathan opened his mouth then closed it again.

"One of my friends is chairing next year's American Internal Medicine conference in Chicago," she continued, seemingly oblivious to Nathan's shock. "I mentioned your project to him, and he thinks it has real potential as an oral presentation. He suggested you submit an abstract. The deadline's in a month, but you could use preliminary data." She paused. "Of course, that's assuming you would be interested."

The American Internal Medicine conference was a very big and very prestigious conference, attended by physicians and residents from all over the continent. Very few people were invited to give oral presentations of their research, so this would look terrific on a CV.

Nathan finally recovered his composure and nodded

enthusiastically at Dr. Hastings. "Yes. Absolutely. I would be very interested. Please let your friend know that I'll be submitting an abstract. And thank you, Dr. Hastings. I really appreciate your guidance and support with this project. We couldn't have done it without you."

She smiled. "It's my job, Nathan, and I'm always happy to help."

***

Nathan took off as soon as we left the office, with no apology or discussion. I figured he was probably rushing to start work on the abstract. Jessica and I walked to the cafeteria to eat lunch and debrief.

"I'm really sorry, Sophie," she apologized. "I thought he knew."

"It's not your fault," I told her. "He's right that I should have told him."

She shook her head. "I can't believe he took the credit for it. It wasn't his idea at all, it was yours."

"It was ours," I corrected. "You had the idea to involve the volunteers."

"I'm going to tell Dr. Hastings," she said decisively. "You deserve to submit the abstract and do the oral presentation."

I was touched by her support. During the short time that we had worked together I had grown to like and respect Jessica Scott. I realized that the one silver lining to the day's events was that she had seen Nathan's true colours, and it was clear that she was no longer romantically interested in him. She deserved better.

"You don't have to tell anyone," I said. "Let Nathan have it. I can't imagine standing in front of an auditorium full of people and talking about a MoPPET trial – sorry, Quality Improvement project – with a straight face."

She looked conflicted. "Really? Nathan told me how

important this kind of stuff is for academic promotion."

I laughed. "Trust me, Jessica, there's no chance that I'll end up in academic medicine."

Nineteen

Jack called Chloe the next day with good news. He had met with the prosecutor and explained her mental health situation, and the prosecutor had agreed to drop the charges in exchange for a thousand dollar donation to the Toronto Mental Health Association. It seemed like a small price to pay to avoid a criminal record, and I happily wrote a check on her behalf. Chloe was overjoyed. A week had passed since the plant-throwing incident, and she seemed to be doing better. She told me she was taking the valproic acid regularly, and I had no reason to doubt it. She had taught a few barre classes which seemed to have gone well, and she had cooked dinner twice. She still spent most of her time on the couch watching reality TV, but I figured that change had to happen gradually.

I was on call the following weekend, which meant I had to go in in the mornings to round on the newly admitted patients and hear about any critical issues that had arisen during the night. Patients' relatives are more likely to visit on weekends, and I had learned that it was best to round early, and get in and out before the relatives with questions had made it out of bed. So I hit the ward with Lucas and Emily at seven AM. Mr. Warner of the self-diagnosed spider-bite arthritis had been readmitted, which was hardly surprising, as he still refused to treat his autoimmune condition with anything other than morphine and hypoallergenic laundry soap. Lucas asked how to approach patients whose delusions were compromising their treatment. I thought about giving him Dr. Hastings's line about doing what was best for the patient, but I decided to tell him the truth, which was that I had no idea.

I got out of the hospital in time to make it to one of the barre classes Chloe taught. I still had to pay $45 to take the class, which was the exact amount that she got paid to teach it.

Mid-afternoon I got a text from Jack.

Jack: What would you think about giving a four-year-old a quarter-tab of adult Tylenol?

Sophie: I'm guessing this is not a hypothetical question.

Jack: Unfortunately not.

There were so many questions I wanted to ask about why he was trying to drug a four-year-old. The *Toronto Times* piece hadn't mentioned a wife or a kid, and I had assumed he was single.

Sophie: It's probably fine. I would weigh the child and Google the dose.

Jack: That really inspires confidence, Dr. Ingram.

Sophie: I don't do pediatrics. But I Googled for you. 10-15 mg/kg. Do you need help with the math?

He didn't reply to that, but fifteen minutes later another text came through:

Jack: What would you do if the child refused to take the Tylenol?

Sophie: Hide it in food? Crush it in puree? That's what we do for patients with no teeth.

Jack: Forgot to buy puree this week.

Sophie: Yogurt?

Jack: I don't eat yogurt either.

I wondered if that meant he was currently single and wanted to ask, but couldn't think of a way to work it into this text exchange.

Sophie: I've heard they make liquid Tylenol specifically for children. I think it's called Children's Tylenol.

Jack: And you claim not to know pediatrics . . .

Sophie: If you're calling in your medical favour I could drop off some Children's Tylenol.

Jack: Please.

Chloe was having a good day and was stretched out on the sofa, watching a cooking show. From what I could see, a bunch of pretentious people were sitting at a fancy restaurant preaching about methane emissions in agriculture.

"I'm heading out to run an errand," I told her. "Is there anything you need before I go?"

She shook her head. "No, I'm good."

"Okay. You have my phone number if you need anything."

She rolled her eyes. "Yes, Mom."

Jack sent me an address in midtown, not far from my parents' neighbourhood. I stopped at a drugstore and bought Children's Tylenol and Advil, along with an ear thermometer, a two litre bottle of ginger ale, a couple bottles of red Gatorade, and three KitKat bars. The subway was busy, and within two stops the straps of the plastic bags were cutting into my hands and I regretted buying the drinks.

Jack lived in an upscale building near the Mount Pleasant Cemetery. I gave my name to the security guard by the entrance and waited while he called Jack for permission to send me up. I wondered how often Jack had female visitors. I guessed fairly often, but I bet I was the first to come bearing ginger ale and an ear thermometer.

Jack opened the door wearing well-worn blue jeans and a University of Toronto Law T-shirt with holes near the hem. He looked exhausted.

"Hi, Sophie. Thank you for coming."

The condo was beautiful, with large windows facing out over a park. The furniture was modern, similar to Ikea in style but clearly much higher end. The TV was on in the living room, and I could hear what sounded like a kids' cartoon program.

I handed over my shopping bags, which he unpacked onto

his kitchen counter. He raised an eyebrow at the KitKats.

"Energy bars," I explained.

Jack laughed at that. "This is great. Thank you."

"It's no problem," I said.

We stood in the entrance to his kitchen, staring awkwardly at each other.

"Stay for dinner?" he asked. "I'll order something."

"Oh!" I said, surprised. "I don't know. I mean, I should get back to Chloe."

I could feel my cheeks getting warm. For some reason I turned into a stammering idiot in his presence.

But now he looked embarrassed himself.

"Oh, you're right," he said quickly. "I wouldn't want to expose you to whatever bug Austin's got."

"What?" I asked. "Oh no, I'm not worried about that, I see sick people at work all the time and I'm hardly ever sick myself - "

"Who's there, Uncle Jack?"

So he had a nephew. A young boy rose from the couch and walked to join us in the kitchen. He was a good-looking child, with curly dark hair and bright blue eyes that currently looked glazed with fever. I guessed he was around four or five.

Jack made introductions. "Austin, this is my friend Sophie. She's brought you some medicine and some drinks."

Austin gazed at me seriously. "It's nice to meet you, Sophie. Do you like trains?"

"Sure," I answered. "I came here on a subway train."

Austin looked suitably impressed. "Did you come over to watch *Thomas?*"

Jack must have caught my confused expression. "*Thomas and Friends* is a show about trains," he explained to me.

Austin nodded enthusiastically. "Mom doesn't let me watch it at home. So I only watch it at Uncle Jack's."

That sounded a little strange to me, as I couldn't see what harm could come from a show about trains that was clearly meant for kids. Then again, I didn't have kids.

Jack winked at me. "Not educational enough," he

explained.

"If you're friends with Uncle Jack you can probably watch it here too," Austin said, as though offering a special treat.

"Austin, I think Sophie has to go," said Jack.

Austin's face fell. "But she *likes trains*, Uncle Jack," he protested.

It was probably irrational, but I was flattered that this child wanted my company.

"Actually, I can stay for a while," I said.

***

The thermometer confirmed Jack's suspicion that Austin had a fever, and we dosed him with Children's Tylenol, Gatorade, a peanut butter sandwich and a KitKat bar. Apart from the fever and occasional cough he seemed okay, and I figured he had one of the viral respiratory illnesses that are so common in childhood. He lasted through two episodes of *Thomas* before falling asleep on my shoulder. Jack carried him to bed.

"Austin's a cute kid. He seems to really like you," I commented when Jack came back to the living room.

Jack laughed. "He really likes watching *Thomas and Friends*."

"Do you have him for the whole weekend?"

Jack looked aggrieved. "Yes."

"Don't pretend you're happy about it," I said sarcastically.

"What?" he asked. "Oh. I love Austin, I'm happy to have him, it's just not the best weekend. I was planning to work this weekend, but my brother called me yesterday afternoon in a panic. I guess he and my sister-in-law got their wires crossed. He had a business trip, and she forgot to tell him that she was supposed to go away on some sort of team-building retreat for work." He rolled his eyes. "They go to an outdoor education centre and sit around the campfire and sing Kumbaya or something."

"That sounds . . . interesting?" I hazarded.

He raised an eyebrow. "It sounds awful. My firm does something like that every couple of years. I went once as an associate and vowed never again. Unfortunately there's only so many times I can pretend to be sick on the retreat weekend before people start to suspect something. I may have to go next year." He shook his head. "And despite having the *legitimate* excuse of needing to look after her child, my sister-in-law chose to go on a team-building retreat this weekend."

"It's a curious choice," I agreed. "On the plus side, you get to spend time with your nephew, and your brother and sister-in-law will owe you a favour."

"Oh, believe me, I've thought of that. But I have no doubt I'll be blamed for the fact he got sick."

"Well if he got sick today he must have been exposed to something a few days ago," I pointed out. "So it's hardly your fault. Not that it's really anyone's fault, just part of life. Hopefully it will build up his immune system or something."

Jack grinned. "I wish you could explain that to my sister-in-law," he joked.

"Oh, I'm sure you can hold your own," I said.

He shook his head. "You haven't met my sister-in-law. She doesn't try to argue logic, she goes for the moral high ground. Half the time when I talk to her I can't tell if she's being sincere or passive aggressive. She's sincerely passive aggressive."

"That's the worst," I agreed.

He nodded. "The first time I met her she told me that she had great respect for the moral courage it must take to do my job."

"What? What does that even mean?" I asked, confused.

"That's what I said. So she explained that it must take courage to work in a profession that adds no value to society and is solely concerned with making money."

"That's ridiculous," I said, outraged on his behalf. "I'm sure you help a lot of people. You've been hugely helpful with Chloe's shoplifting charge."

"Yeah, but that was a one-off," he admitted. "I do spend a lot of time trying to help rich corporations get richer."

He looked surprisingly relatable, sitting on the couch in jeans and a T-shirt, questioning the worth of his job. I felt angry at his unknown sister-in-law.

"Still, someone needs to advise corporations on transactions, to ensure everyone plays fair, and no one gets cheated. Rightly or wrongly, we have a capitalist society, and people like you play an essential role in it. If you didn't do it, someone else would. If the corporations are willing to pay you well for your time, all the better." I paused for breath. "And I'm sure you didn't go into it for the money."

He laughed. "Actually, I did."

"Oh." I suspected many people in professional careers were motivated by the money but this was the first time I had heard someone admit it. I waited expectantly, hoping he would elaborate.

"I was almost engaged once," he said abruptly.

"Oh," I said again. This was an unexpected conversational turn. "I can understand being almost married, but how can you be almost engaged?"

"I bought a girl a ring, but she broke up with me before I could propose," he answered.

"I'm sorry," I said.

"I'm not," he said. "I was at the time, though. We were twenty-one. You don't have much perspective at that age."

I nodded. "That's young."

"We'd been together since we were fifteen," he said, a little defensively. "We had planned it all out, we would both go to U of T for undergrad and Teacher's College and then we'd move home to teach. I was worried about whether we'd both be able to find jobs, as we're from a pretty small town."

"So what happened?" I asked.

He sighed. "We were in our third year of undergrad, sharing an apartment. One day I came home from class and her stuff was gone.. She had left me a note, explaining that she couldn't see herself teaching in a small town. She had met someone else, and she was moving in with him. She hoped we could still be friends."

"After six years?" I asked, outraged. "She didn't have the guts to say it to your face?"

He shrugged. "Not her finest hour. Not mine either, as I blocked her number but followed her on Facebook for a few months. It turned out her new boyfriend was about ten years older than us, and very well-off. Her Facebook page was full of pictures of the fancy house, the sportscar, the boat. A very different life than she would have had teaching in a small town with me."

"She sounds incredibly shallow," I commented.

"Kristin didn't have much growing up," he explained. "And she was pretty insecure. In hindsight, I hadn't made enough time for her. It turned out that she was really struggling academically, and she probably would have failed the year if she hadn't dropped out. I had no idea, and that's my fault. I had to keep good grades to keep a scholarship, and I was on the track team, so I spent most of my time in the library and on the track." He paused and shook his head. "But I still can't believe I didn't notice she was dating someone else."

I could sympathize with that. I could also guess where this story was going.

"Was the new guy a lawyer?"

He smiled. "Bingo. I think most of his money was actually inherited, but at the time I assumed he had earned it practicing law. And I decided that I was going to be better than he was. Richer. More successful. I had this fantasy of going up against him in a high profile court case and making him look dumb." He rolled his eyes. "I was pretty naive, but as I said, I was only twenty-one."

"Why is that naive?" It sounded pretty understandable to me.

"Well, for one thing, he does labour law, which rarely goes to trial. And those dramatic courtroom scenes you see on

TV hardly ever happen in real life. But fortunately, I liked law school. I was lucky enough to get an internship at Reynolds Reilly after my first year, and then a job offer when I graduated. And yeah, the money's nice, but it's not really the main focus anymore."

"So no regrets?" I asked.

He laughed. "Well, there are moments when I question my life choices. When a case isn't going well, or I'm putting in crazy hours to make a deadline. Or working with an articling student who thinks that he's God's gift, and the firm would fall apart without him." He paused and thought for a minute. "It feels like we're asked to do impossible things on a regular basis. Often my job is to explain to the client that what they want can't be done, and to make them believe that no one else could do it either. But every now and then we achieve something that should have been impossible, and well, that's a rush. I feel like I'm doing what I'm meant to do."

Even though I was in a different profession, I knew exactly what he was talking about.

"I guess something good came out of the breakup," I commented.

"We wouldn't have lasted," he said. "I've heard she lives pretty close to me, but I haven't seen her in years. Apparently they're still together and have two kids."

He stared out the window, and I could tell he was thinking about how differently his life could have turned out if he had made different choices. Or more accurately, if Kristin had made a different choice.

I tried to lighten the mood. "I hope you told the law school interviewers that you wanted to be a lawyer to make more money than the man your girlfriend left you for?"

He raised an eyebrow. "I explained that I wanted to be a voice for those who couldn't advocate for themselves. The law is a noble calling, Sophie."

"Of course," I agreed. You should use that line on your sister-in-law. What does she do that's so valuable?"

He laughed. "I'd rather not talk about my sister-in-law." He sighed and looked down at his phone. "But I should call my brother and let him know Austin has a bug, then I'll order some dinner. Are you okay with pizza?"

"Yes." I remembered his comment about all the work he had to do that weekend. "But I should probably go. I know you have work to do."

"The work will still be there tomorrow," he said practically. "And I have to eat."

I nodded. "Okay."

He handed me the remote. "I'll just be a minute. Put on whatever you like."

"Do you have a preference?" I asked.

"Anything but *Thomas the Train*."

I nodded. I hated having to choose what to watch with people I didn't know very well. If I chose something that I really wanted to see, like a romantic comedy or a British period drama, Jack would probably pretend to like it while secretly thinking I have awful taste.

When he returned to the couch, I was flipping through the Netflix menu for the third time.

"Do legal dramas drive you crazy because they're so implausible?" I asked him. "Nathan can't watch medical shows, he gets so angry at the inaccuracies. He yells at the TV when they do something ridiculous, like a CT scan to rule out a concussion. Which they seem to do all the time."

"Is that not a thing?" Jack asked.

"No, a concussion is usually diagnosed based on the history and physical exam," I explained. "The CT is usually done to rule out a bleed, or skull fracture. So anyway, we didn't watch medical shows. But I kind of like them. They're not realistic, but they're entertaining." I sighed and looked at the Netflix menu. "The problem is there's too much choice."

He grinned. "Worried that I'll think less of you if you choose *Bachelor in Space*?"

"I don't think that comes out until next year," I joked

weakly. But the truth in his jest must have shown on my face, because he took the remote from me and turned off the TV.

"You should know that there's very little chance of that," he said, suddenly serious.

"Of *Bachelor in Space*? You might be surprised."

"That I would think less of you."

Twenty

After we finished the pizza Jack and I sat side by side on the couch, eating KitKat bars and drinking ginger ale. For something that appeared to have been designed by a Swede, his couch was surprisingly comfortable.

"So," he asked. "How are things going with Chloe?"

I really didn't want to talk about Chloe. She had consumed my life for the past several weeks, and I was sick of it.

"If we have to, but I'd rather talk about anything else."

"Okay," he agreed. There was a beat of silence while we searched for anything else to discuss. He finally landed on: "Do you see much of Nathan at work?"

"Not really, we're on different wards," I explained. "I've had to work on a research project with him, but now that it looks like it might be successful I think he'll take it back over. Which would be fine with me."

"That wouldn't be fair." Jack looked offended on my behalf.

"It hardly matters, to be honest. Nathan wants an academic career, and I don't, and even if I did, I have no hope of getting an academic job in this city, so -"

"Why not? Surely you're just as capable as Nathan."

"I botched a routine procedure and caused a young woman to have a stroke," I said bluntly. "The night after I found Nathan and Chloe together. Now the Chief of Medicine wants to meet with me. This Thursday." It was actually a relief to talk about it. "I don't know if I'm facing an internal review at the hospital, or a lawsuit, but whatever it is won't be good. Besides that, everyone knows about it. I'll forever be known as the girl who screwed up the central line."

He was quiet for a minute. I shrank away from him a little, worried that if I hadn't destroyed his respect for me, I had significantly damaged it.

When he finally spoke, his voice was gentle.

"I guess you're the first person to ever make a mistake at that hospital?"

"No, but -"

"And you have a pattern of repeated mistakes?" he continued.

"No. But -"

"Then they should be supporting you!" he said, sounding almost angry now. "Mistakes happen. If we crucified everyone who made a mistake, it would only encourage people to cover them up. The fact that you've sweated over this means you'll do everything possible to reduce the risk of making the same mistake again.

I laughed bitterly. "I'm not sure I'll ever do a central line again."

"That would be a shame."

I remembered Lucy's story about Jack firing an associate. "So you would never fire someone for making a mistake?" I asked.

His dark eyebrows furrowed as he thought about it.

"Well there is a limit. I had to let a secretary go for gross incompetence. But if someone who was hard-working and generally good at their job made an honest mistake and owned up to it? I hope I would support them. Other than the secretary, the only person I've fired was an associate who tried to cover up a mistake by blaming a paralegal. Dishonesty is unforgivable."

He was staring at me intently, and the tension between us was so thick it was uncomfortable. I asked the first question that popped into my head. "Have you really gone through five secretaries in three months?"

He looked pained. "Four months now. And Mary is still

with me. For better or for worse."

"I'd like to hear that story."

"There's not much to tell, really. I had a competent legal secretary who went on maternity leave for a year."

I nodded. "That's the problem with employing women of child-bearing age."

He looked at me suspiciously. "No comment. Anyway, Alexis went on maternity leave and I hired Rachel for the year. She was great. It was like she could read my mind, she knew what I needed even before I did."

I felt irrationally jealous of Rachel.

"So then Alexis came back," he continued. "And I had to let Rachel go, and one of the senior partners hired her."

I nodded again. "You should have insisted on a finder's fee."

"I thought of that too!" he joked. "The worst part was that Alexis wasn't even back for two weeks before she decided that she couldn't stand being apart from her kid. She quit to be a stay at home mom, and she didn't give notice, either, so I had to deal with temps while we recruited for the job."

"And the next?" I asked.

"Trina. She was the one I fired. She was practically illiterate. Her writing read like a teenager's text message, with strange abbreviations and virtually no punctuation. She spelled 'you' as a single letter, 'u', even in business correspondence. She claimed to have worked for a big Montreal firm, but it was a lie. Apparently her mother wrote her a fake letter of reference." He shook his head. "I'm confident she didn't write it herself, because it actually had paragraphs and punctuation."

I laughed. "And next?"

"Next was Julie, who had great references and seemed perfectly normal at her interview. But then she started dressing really strangely. Stuff that wasn't really office appropriate, it got embarrassing." He turned a little red.

"Well you know, a lot of women can barely dress themselves." I said it without thinking and immediately wished

I hadn't.   His comments at Chloe's hearing were really best forgotten, and it was juvenile of me to keep bringing them up, but for some reason I couldn't help myself.

Silence fell for a minute. "Sophie, I was having a bad day." He paused. "You are one of the best dressed women I know."

I snorted. "I can't believe that." I thought of Samantha Albright, and of all the beautifully dressed women I had seen passing through the lobby of his office building.

He looked uncomfortable now, like he would rather be discussing anything other than my clothing choices, and he wouldn't meet my eye. "I'm serious. Your clothes just seem . . ." he trailed off and seemed to be searching for words. "They fit you well."

"Damned with faint praise," I said lightly. "You know, I'm beginning to doubt the rumours about you."

"What rumours?"

"That you date a different celebrity every week. You're not smooth enough."

"What?"   Jack's eyebrows rose so high they almost disappeared into his hairline.

"Unless I'm just so different from the women you usually date that the best line you can come up with is 'your clothes seem to fit you well,' I said.

"Sophie, what are you talking about?"

"Just that it's not a particularly flattering thing to say," I said.

"No, the rumours? What do you mean?" He looked genuinely dismayed. He stood and began to pace the room.

"Well, you must know that there's a lot of interest in your love life," I said.

"Interest from whom?"

"Most of the single women in your firm," I said. Along with some of the married women in your firm, the female security guards in your office building, and the Starbucks baristas.

He shook his head, still looking stunned. "What are they

saying?"

I hesitated, searching for the best way to phrase it. "That the reason you've never shown any interest in the women in your office is that you only date supermodels and actresses. Also, that in all the time you've worked at Reynolds Reilly, you've never had a long-term relationship."

"Well yeah, of course I don't want to start anything with anyone at work. That's a fast road to a human resources complaint. Or a lawsuit." He shook his head. "Who's been talking about this?"

"Apparently most of the women in your office."

"Including the other partners?"

"I'm not sure," I hedged. "I don't really know that much about it."

"Well, where did you hear about it?"

"A friend of mine knows a paralegal," I said.

"At our firm?"

I looked down. "A different firm," I answered. "But she's friends with some people from your firm."

"People talk about this at other firms?"

"Well probably not many."

He shook his head again. "I don't understand," he said.

"Well, there were some tabloid photos of you at an event with Lily Lawson," I pointed out.

"Our mothers are friends!" he exclaimed. "They grew up in the same small town. I met Lily a few times growing up. A few years ago, she broke up with a boyfriend right before the Toronto International Film Festival. She wanted to show that she had moved on, and she asked if I'd go to a few events with her. I don't know why she asked me, really, except that I was in the city and I've known her forever. It was actually really boring. A few of the celebrities were lovely, but a lot of them seemed to make a point of telling insider stories about people and places I knew nothing about. After the festival Lily went back to LA and I haven't seen her since. I think she's back with the ex now."

He really had no idea how women perceived him. I

wondered if it stemmed from being dumped by his high school sweetheart, the insecure Kristin, or if he had always been oblivious. I knew exactly why Lily Lawson had asked him to take her to TIFF, and it was the same reason that his third (or fourth?) secretary had started to wear inappropriate clothing to work.

He continued to pace the room. "Don't tell me that all this talk has grown out of a few pictures on a gossip site?"

"Well, apparently you took dates to two of the firm's holiday parties. Different women both times, both knockouts."

"I've worked there for nine years! So I've taken dates to two parties, it's not like I have a different date every year," he protested. "I don't understand how these rumours even start. Is there more?"

"Not really," I paused. "Well actually, apparently you had your secretary send flowers to a woman a couple of years ago."

He looked confused. "I wouldn't usually involve a secretary in something like that," he said.

"Maybe they're mistaken," I said.

"No, I remember! A neighbour's husband died, and I couldn't make the funeral. I had Alexis send flowers and a sympathy card. He paused. "Surely people don't think I send flowers and *condolences* to women I date?

I laughed. "Sorry for your loss, but I don't want to see you anymore?"

He chuckled. "Or I'm sorry that the evening didn't meet your expectations?"

"That would hardly fit the narrative," I said.

"Nothing about this narrative fits." He shook his head. "I hope the people spreading these stories weren't hired for their logical reasoning abilities."

"And then there's the *Toronto Times* article," I said. "*Jack Delacroix closes the deal.*"

He shook his head. "*Toronto Times* is a glorified tabloid," he scoffed. "I'm surprised you even saw that."

"I Googled your name after Chloe's capacity hearing," I admitted. "I was hoping to learn that you were one parole violation away from going back to prison, or embroiled in a bitter divorce battle and about to lose most of your assets to your ex. Instead I learned that you'd won a bunch of awards through high school and university and have had a wildly successful legal career."

He laughed, and it made him look younger. In his jeans and university T-shirt he could have passed for an undergraduate, and he seemed like a completely different person than the lawyer I had met at Chloe's hearing.

"Were you disappointed?" he asked.

"At the time, yes. I'm coming to terms with it now."

He sat back down on the couch, closer than he had been before. I couldn't tell if that was deliberate or not. I leaned forward to set my drink back on the coffee table, and my arm brushed his, and all of a sudden his arm was around my shoulders and he kissed me. He was cautious at first, as though I were a fragile object worthy of great care.

He pulled back after a minute to look me in the eye.

"Is this okay?" he asked in a gravelly voice.

"Yes," I said,

"I've been wanting to do this since you walked in the door," he confessed.

The kiss changed after that, and it was clear that he had been holding back before. Now he abandoned restraint. I felt like I couldn't get close enough, and I sensed he felt the same. Time slowed down and my heart sped up.

His phone rang. We ignored the first call, and after four or five rings it mercifully stopped, but after a brief pause the ringing began again. The mood was ruined, and we reluctantly broke apart.

Jack picked up his phone and cursed.

"It's my sister-in-law," he explained. "Probably freaked out because Austin has a fever. I should talk to her." His expression conveyed both an apology for the interruption and a promise that once he was off the phone we would pick up where we had left off.

"Of course," I said. He walked over towards the kitchen and paced back and forth. I overheard phrases like 'low-grade fever' and 'really not very sick.' His expression was frustrated but his voice was calm and patient. Soothing. I couldn't imagine how Austin's mother could doubt that he had the situation under control. I closed my eyes and let Jack's words wash over me.

***

The next thing I knew his voice was in my ear, and fractionally less calm. "I'm so sorry, Sophie, but you have to wake up."

I dragged myself out of the deepest sleep I had enjoyed in months. After a moment of disorientation I realized that I was on the Swedish couch, cocooned in a blue plaid duvet that smelled faintly like Jack. I remembered meeting Austin, eating pizza, and then our interrupted kiss. I realized I must have fallen asleep while Jack was on the phone, and I sat up quickly.

"I'm so sorry, what time is it? I should get home," I said blearily.

"Seven AM," he answered.

It seemed that I had slept the entire night on his couch. For an instant I wondered if things had progressed beyond kissing, but the memory of the kiss was so vivid I was sure I would remember if things had gone farther. The pillow I had slept on matched the plaid of the duvet, and hadn't been there last night. Jack must have tucked me up with a pillow and duvet; I couldn't believe I hadn't woken up.

"Sophie, I'm sorry, but my sister-in-law's on her way up," he said apologetically. "I really thought I calmed her down last night, but she called five minutes ago to say she was in the parking lot. She'll be here any minute."

My brain was still half-asleep and I struggled to process this. I noticed that Jack was wearing the same T-shirt as yesterday, but he had changed into frayed gray sweatpants. He hadn't shaved, and a tuft of hair was sticking up behind his right ear. Clearly the sister-in-law had taken him by surprise.

"You have three options," he said quickly. "What I recommend is that you stay here and I introduce you as a friend who came for dinner and ended up crashing on my couch."

That sounded like a terrible idea.

"Alternately you could wait in my bedroom until she leaves," he continued. "Or you could leave right now and take the stairs. I'm pretty sure she'll come up the elevator." He looked embarrassed to be suggesting it. "I know that would be demeaning, and there's no reason for you to do it, but -"

I opened my mouth to say the stairs, obviously the stairs, but at that moment there was a knock on the door, and that option was off the table.

"Bedroom," I said decisively. Jack led me to a door at the end of the hallway.

His bedroom was furnished in the same minimalist style as the rest of the condo, a king bed covered in familiar blue plaid sheets with a single pillow at the head. There was no duvet or bedcover; he must have given me the duvet and pillow off his bed. An abstract painting hung above the bed, with bright blues and greens that made me think of the ocean in a storm. The room was fairly neat, with the exception of yesterday's jeans, which had been left in a puddle by the bed with boxers still inside them.

I heard muffled voices in the hallway. I moved closer to the door to hear them better.

"I could barely sleep last night, I was so worried, so I left the retreat early this morning. I need to know exactly what happened yesterday," said a woman. Jack's sister-in-law.

"Stacey, as I said, he was fine in the morning, then he developed a low-grade fever -"

"Did you check his temperature?" she asked.

"Yes," Jack said. "It was 38.2, so I gave him some Tylenol. He said he wasn't in pain. He hasn't been vomiting. He drank about a litre of Gatorade and ate a peanut butter sandwich.”

I noticed he didn’t mention the KitKat bar.

“Did you check on him in the night?” she asked anxiously. “Wake him up to make sure he’s not confused? He could be delirious.”

“Stacey, if I were sick and someone woke me up in the middle of the night I’m pretty sure I would be confused,” Jack said. His patience was clearly wearing thin. “He needs to sleep. I checked on him from the doorway before you got here, he was breathing easily, looked comfortable. I looked it up; apparently little kids get viruses like this all the time. It will probably build up his immune system, or something.”

“Oh, so now you’re a medical expert?” she said critically. “Jack, I don’t think you’re in a position to talk. You have no idea what it’s like to be a parent.”

“You’re right, Stacey,” he said. “But I do know that I talked to Theo yesterday afternoon and gave him the exact same facts I just gave you, and he didn’t rush here in a panic.”

It was obviously the wrong thing to say.

Stacey’s voice rose in pitch. “Well you have no idea what it’s like to be a *mother*!”

Jack sighed. “Just go wake him up, Stacey,” he said wearily. “You can judge for yourself, and take him home, or take him to the hospital, whatever you want.”

And then the doorknob turned a few feet away from me, and Jack said “No, the other door,” in a panicked voice, and I found myself face to face with his sister-in-law.

***

She was petite, a full head shorter than me, with curly red hair, green eyes and delicate features. Despite the early hour she was well put-together, in a deep red blouse, brown dress pants and a brown leather jacket. She reminded me of a little doll, and at the moment she looked like a doll that had been shocked speechless. I was shocked too, and couldn’t think of a thing to say to explain my presence in Jack's bedroom.

Jack recovered first, and performed introductions.

"Sophie, my sister-in-law Stacey," he said calmly. I extended my hand and we shook awkwardly. I was glad that she didn't attempt a hug.

"Stacey, this is Sophie Ingram," he continued. "She came for dinner and stayed over last night." Stacey's eyes widened when she heard my name.

"Sophie!" she exclaimed. This time she did come in for a hug. "It's so nice to see you!"

She spoke familiarly, as though we knew each other, but I was confident I had never seen her before in my life.

Jack looked confused. "Do you two know each other?"

"No," I answered.

"Yes," Stacey said at the same time. She trilled a laugh. "I mean, this is our first time meeting in person, but we correspond all the time at work."

All of a sudden her first name registered, and I had an awful suspicion I knew who she was.

"Are you . . ." I began, then trailed off, afraid to put it in words.

"Yes!" She said with a big smile. "I'm Stacey Sullivan."

"You must have kept your maiden name," I said inanely. This shouldn't have been worthy of comment in the 21st century, but for some reason it was the first thought that popped into my head. "I assumed Stacey Delacroix, that's why I didn't put it together."

She nodded. "Yep. All of my professional work has been done as Sullivan, so I didn't want to change it. I imagine you'll be in a similar situation, right? I mean, you won't change your name to Fox?"

Hospital gossip really was the worst. I had never met this woman in person, and I don't even think we had friends in common, but she still somehow knew that Nathan and I were engaged. Apparently, though, she had missed the update that the engagement was off.

"Of course she won't," Jack looked irritated. "She's not going to marry Nathan."

"Oh," said Stacey. There was a momentary pause while she looked expectantly at me, hoping I would elaborate.

"That's true," I said succinctly. "Anyway, I was just leaving." Unfortunately Stacey was between me and the front door, and she made no move to get out of the way.

"Speaking of names, your name came up at the team building retreat this weekend," Stacey said to me.

"That's nice," I said. I didn't want to know in what context.

"Some of the senior leadership people have heard about your MoPPET project," she continued. Jack raised an eyebrow at that. "It was used as an example of the innovation we can achieve with teamwork."

"Right," I said. I made a show of checking my watch. "Anyway, I'm sure you want to check on Austin, and I need to get going, I have to round at the hospital this morning." I would be late to meet the residents, but at the moment that was the least of my concerns.

"Yes, of course," said Stacey, looking flustered. "Jack, where *is* Austin?"

"Next door," he answered. He opened the door and they walked in together.

I fled. In less than a minute I had grabbed my purse from beside the couch and slipped on my sneakers. I had walked half a block before I realized I had forgotten my jacket. The fall air was crisp, and I broke into a jog. There was no way I was going back for it.

A bouquet of flowers arrived later that afternoon. There was a handwritten card, and I recognized Jack's scrawl. He must have gone to the florist's in person.

Sophie:
You forgot your jacket. I'm ~~holding it hostage~~ keeping it safe

until you come back for it. Dinner Friday?
JD.

I felt a rush of excitement, until I remembered that Chloe and I were planning to go to the Leafs game with Martin on Friday night. I tapped out a text:

Sophie: Flowers are beautiful, thank you. I'm busy Friday. Another time?

The reply came back almost immediately.

Jack: "Saturday?"
Sophie: "Saturday works."
Jack: "I'll expect to hear all about the MoPPET project."
Sophie: "That's classified. How is Austin?"
Jack: "He's fine. He's building up his immune system."

<h1 style="text-align:center">Twenty-one</h1>

Under other circumstances, the promise of dinner with Jack would have brightened my entire week, but I was too consumed with worry about my meeting with Dr. Jones to give it much thought. My nightmares had returned, and I relived the Central Line Incident in my dreams almost every night. I alternated between wishing Thursday would never come and wishing it was over.

Despite my contradictory hopes, Thursday morning came as scheduled, and I awoke to a thunderstorm. When I stumbled into the living room I found Chloe watching the morning news.

"Can you believe this?" she asked, gesturing at the TV. "The number of armed carjackings in the city has almost doubled this year compared to last." She shook her head scornfully. "And the police don't seem to care. Tough on shoplifting, soft on gun crime."

I nodded at her vaguely. In truth, I didn't have any interest or energy for that issue. I realized that it had been weeks since I had worried about gun crime, or climate change, or the possibility that the caramel colour in my cola was carcinogenic. My real problems had eclipsed my theoretical ones.

As I reached the hospital I got a text from Jack, stating simply: "Good luck today." It was the first I had heard from him since we had made our date for Saturday, and I was touched that he remembered my meeting.

Dr. Jones fit the physician stereotype perfectly. Late middle-aged with wire-rimmed glasses, he dressed with care but without ostentation. He was a kidney specialist; early in his career he had invented some new dialysis technique and became moderately famous in the medical community. He had a reputation as a straight shooter and as someone who didn't suffer fools.

"Sophie. Thank you for coming in. Please have a seat."

I liked his office. There were the usual diplomas on the wall, and two comfortable chairs in front of his desk. A neat stack of papers sat off to the side. Beside his medical degree was a framed copy of Kipling's *If*.

I smiled at him nervously. "Thank you Dr. Jones."

"Please call me Stuart. We're colleagues now."

"Yes sir." There was no way in hell that I would call Dr. Jones by his first name.

He caught me staring at the Kipling poem.

"Are you familiar with the poem?" he asked.

"Yes. My mother was an English teacher," I added.

"Some people think it's sanctimonious," he said.

"I see that. But I think it's inspiring," I said. "And I suspect you do too, or it wouldn't be hanging on your wall."

He smiled, causing his eyes to crinkle at the corners. "You're right, Sophie," he said.

I nodded. "But I suspect you didn't request a meeting to discuss poetry?" Two months ago I would not have been so direct, but I was tired of the suspense, and I was ready to know the worst. I thought he was unlikely to tell me about a lawsuit, as I would have been served papers for that directly. I expected to be told the hospital was reviewing the Central Line Incident, and if I was very unlucky, that they were going to report it to the College of Physicians and Surgeons. As Jack had pointed out, other doctors had made mistakes and continued to practice medicine, and I realized that I really wanted to continue to practice medicine. I wanted to fight for patients like Mrs. Alves, and mentor students like Emily, and occasionally experience the rush that comes from accomplishing something that should have been impossible.

"How are you enjoying your time as a fifth year resident?"

Dr. Jones asked.

What could I say to that? I love doing the work of an Attending Staff for far less pay and even less respect? I racked my brain for a diplomatic answer.

"It's certainly been a learning experience."

He smiled. "Yes, I think I learned more in my first year of practice than I did throughout my residency."

I nodded. I didn't think it would help to point out that although I was qualified to practice independently, I was, in fact, still a resident.

He looked me in the eye. "Dr. Ingram, one of the medical students has filed a complaint that you used demeaning language when he was giving a case presentation."

I stared at him in shock for what felt like an eternity but was probably actually about thirty seconds. I couldn't believe that I hadn't been summoned to discuss the Central Line Incident, or that one of the students had cared enough to complain about me.

I finally gathered my wits. "I'm surprised to hear that, sir, and I can't think of when that could have happened. Can you give me any more details?"

"As you know, university policy prevents me from disclosing the name of the student who complained. But it was related to a comment about endorsements. Apparently you told him that he was describing a patient's symptoms, not a soft drink or a political party, and he should cut out the endorsements."

I was actually a little impressed that Ellis had remembered my comments so accurately.

"Well, Sophie? Do you recall this conversation?

"Yes sir, I did say that."

"I see. Did you give him any suggestions as to what he could say instead?"

"Yes, I gave him some examples of better phrases to use."

"I see. And do you recall using demeaning language? I assume you didn't call him names?"

I bit back a laugh. "No sir."

"So to summarize, you gave a student some constructive criticism on how to improve his case presentations?"

Put like that, it really seemed quite reasonable. "Yes sir."

"Do you consider that part of your job description as a senior resident?"

I paused for a minute, wary of a trap.

"Yes, I think that giving feedback to junior learners is an important part of my job." I considered adding a comment about the importance of mentorship but thought that would be taking things too far.

"I think you're absolutely right, Sophie. Far too many staff physicians shy away from giving trainees meaningful feedback for fear that it will lead to complaints. As a result, the trainees fail to reach their full potential because no one tells them how to improve."

I nodded. "Yes sir."

"Good. Now, there was a second matter."

My heart sank. It was cruel of him to set me up this way, and let me think I was off the hook. I braced myself for a discussion of the Central Line Incident.

He cleared his throat. "A week ago, I received a call from the daughter of Winnie Campbell. She was concerned that you were trying to discharge her mother before she was medically stable. I'd like to hear your side of the story."

"Well sir, Mrs. Campbell is an 87-year-old lady with advanced dementia. At baseline, she's unable to communicate, and she's fed through a feeding tube. She was admitted with pneumonia, which we treated. I had several discussions with her daughter about discharge options, including applying to long-term care, but her daughter insisted that she would never 'put her mother in a home.' So, as she no longer needed acute care, I discharged her."

I studied his face to see how he was taking this, but I couldn't read his expression.

"And her daughter didn't agree with this plan?"

"I think her daughter was hoping that there was more we could do for her mother. But as you know, sir, there's no effective treatment for dementia, especially in the advanced stages. And Mrs. Campbell was at least as good as she was prior to admission. We cut back on her sedatives, so I think she may actually have been a little better."

"I see. Elaine also said that you told the radiology department to give her mother's appointment time to another patient?"

"That's technically true, but the spot had belonged to the other patient in the first place. The other patient had metastatic cancer and needed a tunnelled catheter so that she could go home for end-of-life care. Her procedure had already been cancelled four times."

Dr. Jones nodded. I still had no idea what he was thinking.

"Were there any other concerns raised about Mrs. Campbell's discharge?" he asked.

I racked my brain trying to think of what else he might have heard. Surely Elaine could not have complained about her sick dog, or the timing of the discharge relative to the James Bond movie premiere.

"I can't think of anything."

"Her daughter mentioned something about a James Bond movie? I believe her exact words were that 'attending the movie on opening day is essential to my mother's psychosocial and spiritual well-being.' Did you discharge her regardless?"

I swallowed. I felt like I had fallen down a rabbit hole into an unfamiliar world. Dr. Jones had a true poker face, and I still couldn't tell what he thought of the situation.

"Yes sir, I did." I didn't mention that her daughter had, as promised, brought her back to the ER several hours later, where she had been readmitted under a different doctor with the popular diagnosis of 'failure to cope.' Apparently Elaine had requested a different physician because she didn't have a good rapport with me. But Dr. Jones probably knew that.

"How did you do it?" The corner of his mouth lifted, just a

fraction of an inch, but I was encouraged.

"Well, sir, I just wrote a discharge order. And she left."

"Good for you." He was clearly smiling now.

I let out a breath.

"I looked after Mrs. Campbell two years ago," he continued. "She was difficult to discharge. I had to assist the residents."

"How did you do it?" I blurted.

"I shouldn't go into details," he said. "Probably the same way you did." We shared a look of understanding.

"This isn't an easy job, Sophie, and it gets harder every year. There are more and more people trying to tell us how to do the job, and it can be hard to stand up to pressure. But it seems like you've been handling it well. I've also heard good things about your research project. MoPPET, was it?"

"Yes, sir. It's a Quality Improvement project, actually."

"Of course. Interesting name. I look forward to seeing the results."

He stood up, signalling that our interview was over.

I stood on trembling legs, a little shell-shocked.

"Thank you sir."

"Please call me Stuart."

***

On my way back to the ward I ran into Lucy Zhang.

"Sophie, I was just thinking about you," she said. "Do you have a second?" I didn't, really, as I was late to meet a bunch of students, but she seemed to think it was important. I let her lead me to a quiet corner of the hallway.

"I was down on the rehab ward the other day," she began.

"A rehab patient fell and broke a hip?" I asked.

Lucy frowned. "Why does everyone assume that we never follow up on our patients after surgery?" She asked. "For all you knew, I could have been following up on post-operative patients. The ortho stereotypes get really old."

She had a point.

"You're right, Lucy. I'm sorry," I apologized.

She nodded. "It's okay. Anyway, I was down on the rehab ward because someone fell and broke a hip," she said. I bit my lip to keep myself from smiling.

"And I'm pretty sure my patient's roommate was your patient. The one who had a stroke. You know, from two months ago."

I sighed. As though I could forget. "Lucy, I've spent the past two months trying not to think about it."

"But she was walking, Sophie," she said. "With a specialized high walker, and two people helping her, but she was moving her weak leg. Taking steps. That's progress, right?"

That certainly was progress. For the first couple of weeks following the stroke, she hadn't even been able to lift her left leg off the bed. Maybe she would do better than anyone had expected.

"Thanks Lucy," I said.

***

When I was a medical student, a senior resident once told me that the rehab ward was the place where hope went to die. At the time I thought he was incredibly cynical, but I've since realized he was right. Unfortunately, most of the patients who are sent to the hospital's rehab ward have very little potential for rehabilitation. There are exceptions, usually high functioning people who suffer an acute injury or illness and are motivated to get back on their feet. But the majority have suffered a gradual but relentless decline, and are too burdened by an accretion of years and medical problems to ever get better. Often they follow a one-step forward, two-steps back pattern, where a small gain is followed by another problem, like a urinary tract infection or a fall, and they end up weaker than when they started. For many patients the major purpose of rehab was to give them and their families time to adjust to a new reality.

I had no excuse to delay the visit, so at the end of the day I took the elevator down to the rehab ward. A whiteboard by the nursing station displayed the Riddle of the Day: "If you speak my name, you will break me." I knew the answer was supposed to be silence, but it could equally well have referred to any of the ten patients sitting in front of the nursing station in geriatric wheelchairs. They all looked feeble and fragile, as though a strong breath of air could blow them to the floor. An ancient CD player was playing YMCA by the Village People, and a couple of nurses were trying to encourage the patients to sing and move their arms to the music. A few of the patients appeared to be swaying to the music, but most just looked confused. I was vastly relieved not to see Mrs. Gerard in the wheelchair line-up. At least she was spared the indignity of participating in an activity for dementia patients who were on average fifty years older than she was.

I knocked before entering her room, and a man's voice called "Come in." I recognized Mrs. Gerard and her husband immediately. She was sitting in a chair beside the bed, and appeared to be trying to knit. She had secured the needle between her left hand and her thigh, and her right hand moved nimbly around it. Her husband sat beside her, holding the ball of wool. They smiled at me politely. The left side of Mrs. Gerard's face was looser than the right, and her smile was a little lopsided. I would never forget them, but I could tell they didn't remember me. I had no idea if my name would be familiar or not.

I stiffened my spine.

"Hello," I said. "My name is Dr. Ingram. Sophie. I met you on the night you were admitted."

I could see recognition dawn on her face. Her husband took her weak hand between his.

"I was the doctor who attempted the central line that caused the complication," I continued. "I wanted to tell you how sorry I am for what happened."

***

As it turned out, the Gerards didn't blame anyone for the stroke, but accepted that it was just bad luck. They did, however, recognize my name. Apparently Ryan Wells had spent a lot of time with them during their initial days in the ICU, and he had credited me with recognizing how sick she was and acting quickly to get her on strong antibiotics. They were under the impression that without my intervention her outcome might have been much worse, and they thanked me profusely. I listened awkwardly, feeling an odd mixture of guilt and relief, and fought the urge to confess that I had made a mistake. To say that someone else would likely have done better. Ryan Wells's spin on the events of that night was so generous it bordered on fiction. But maybe I had judged myself too harshly.

Twenty-two

The Toronto Maple Leafs were playing Montreal on Friday night. It was the first home game against Montreal of the season, which made it the hottest ticket in town. Martin told us that a friend had given him tickets he couldn't use.

"I didn't even know you liked hockey," I said when he suggested we go.

"I don't, really," he confessed. "But I know that you do, and Chloe loves it. It will give her something to look forward to."

"You don't have to do this," I protested. "You've already helped a lot, taking her out to lunch, cooking with her. I feel like we're taking advantage of your kindness."

He smiled. "Sophie, this isn't exactly a sacrifice for me. I like spending time with you."

It turned out that Martin's friend had given him tickets to some of the best seats in the house. We were four rows up from the ice, close enough to see the players' facial expressions as they warmed up. Any closer and our view would have been obstructed by the boards.

"This is amazing!" said Chloe, as she sat down. "I've never been this close to the ice before. Your friend has awesome seats."

Martin smiled, clearly pleased with her reaction. "I thought about renting a box, but I thought this would be better."

"You were right," said Chloe. "We've been in a box once, with our dad, and we could barely hear the cheering. We might as well have been watching it on TV."

"Which of your friends is lucky enough to own these tickets?" I asked. "It seems strange to have a set of three."

"I don't think you've met him," Martin said evasively. I had a strong suspicion that Martin had just bought the tickets himself.

Chloe had convinced Martin to buy us Maple Leaf headbands from a booth near the entrance. She managed to look cute wearing a four-inch high blue foam Maple Leaf attached to a headband, but I was pretty sure I just looked silly. The headband scratched the back of my left ear, but when I tried to take it off Chloe protested. Martin had conveniently forgotten to buy one for himself.

The Leafs started strong, as they often did, then fizzled in the second period. Chloe threw herself into the game, cheering when they made a good play, groaning when they gave up the puck, and jumping up and down when they scored a goal. In the second period the Leafs appeared to score a goal that was disallowed because the shooter had been offside. The game was paused for video review.

Chloe stood up and joined the loud chorus of fans booing the referee's decision. Martin leaned over towards me in an effort to be heard over the cheering crowd.

"What's happening? Why aren't they counting that goal?"

The boos were incredibly loud. I leaned over so that my mouth was almost touching Martin's ear.

"I think the ref called it offside. They'll review it and then make an announcement."

"What does offside mean?" He yelled back into my ear.

I laughed. It wasn't incredibly complicated, and had we been at home on the couch watching the game on TV I could have summarized it pretty easily. But this was louder than a nightclub.

I leaned in close to his ear again "An offensive player can't cross the blue line before the puck. If he does, he's offside and the play is stopped."

"Why didn't they stop the play before they scored a goal?"

I laughed again. That was a million dollar question to which I did not have the answer.

"Linesman wasn't fast enough, I guess."

Chloe looked over at us. "What's so funny? They just disallowed our goal."

During the second intermission Martin and I left our seats to buy some popcorn and drinks.

"Tell me the truth, are you enjoying this?" I asked him.

He smiled. "Very much. I have to say, half the fun is watching your sister jump up and down and yell at the ref. Does she always throw herself into it?"

"Into hockey? Pretty much, yeah. You'd never guess to look at her, would you?" I said.

"No, you certainly wouldn't," he answered.

The concession area was packed. Martin and I joined a long line for the snack bar.

"Sophie!" I turned when I heard my name. It was Samantha Albright, weaving her way through the crowd. Jack Delacroix was holding her hand. He did not look happy to see me.

"Hello Samantha," I said, as coolly as I could without being rude. "Jack."

"Hello, Sophie," he said. He pulled his hand awkwardly away from Samantha's.

They didn't seem to be in any rush to move on, so I reluctantly made introductions.

"This is my friend Martin Chu," I said. "Martin, Samantha Albright and Jack Delacroix. They're lawyers who have done some work for my parents."

Samantha looked at Martin appraisingly. I could tell she was trying to decide where he fit in the social hierarchy. He didn't dress that much differently than he had in high school, and he had come to the game in jeans and sneakers. But his clothes were of higher quality than they had been in high school, and he carried himself with a confidence that he had lacked as a teenager.

"Nice to meet you, Martin," said Samantha.

"Are you enjoying the game?" I asked them.

"Very much," said Samantha. "We're here with some clients. Our firm has a box. So much nicer than regular seats. Really luxurious, you should come see it."

I forced a smile. "Thanks. We're pretty pleased with our regular seats, actually. We're four rows up from the ice." I hated myself for stooping to her level, bragging about our seats, but Samantha Albright clearly brought out the worst in me. Especially after she had been holding Jack's hand.

"You must have a great view," said Jack politely.

"One of the perks of your dad's job, I guess?" asked Samantha.

"Well, actually -"

Martin cut me off. "Her dad gets great seats, yeah."

Samantha laughed. "And by extension, so do Sophie and her friends."

Martin nodded. "We certainly do." I wasn't sure why he wanted Samantha to think that my dad was responsible for our tickets, but I wasn't about to contradict him.

"So, Martin," continued Samantha. "Are you a doctor like Sophie?"

He laughed. "No. To my parents' eternal disappointment."

"So what do you do?"

Jack looked uncomfortable with her questioning. "Samantha, you sound like you're cross-examining him."

Martin smiled easily. "It's all right. It's not a secret. I'm a teacher, actually."

I did my best to hide my surprise. I supposed that was technically true, he taught kids to code, but he was also a programmer and an entrepreneur. It was subtle, but I saw the corners of Samantha's lips rise in a small smile of satisfaction. I could tell she was thrilled he wasn't another doctor, or a lawyer, or a bank executive.

"I've always thought that teaching was such a *worthwhile* career," said Samantha. "Much more valuable to society than us lawyers. Right Jack?"

"Absolutely," said Jack, without taking his eyes from

Martin and me.

"Well, I guess we should be going," said Samantha. "We have full food and drink service in our box, so we're not actually waiting for snacks. Just wanted a walk to stretch our legs."

"Of course," I said.

"It was so nice to meet you, Martin," she gushed.

"Likewise," Martin answered.

Jack nodded at me. "It was nice to see you, Sophie. You look well."

"Thanks." I was still processing the fact that he was there with Samantha, trying to parse whether they were together in a personal or solely a professional capacity, and I couldn't think of a better reply.

I realized I was still wearing the foam Maple Leaf headband.

"Wow, what a piece of work," said Martin, after they had walked away to continue stretching their legs. "Was she one of the lawyers at the hearing?"

I nodded. "Yep. And he was the other." I had given him the broad strokes outline of Chloe's capacity hearing but none of the details.

"I'm pretty sure I've met him before, at some charity thing," said Martin. "I think he's a big deal at his firm. Are they together?"

"A couple, you mean?" I asked. "I have no idea." I tried to pretend that this was of no significance to me, but I couldn't stop the questions from pouring out. "I didn't think so, but maybe? Did they look like they were together?"

He laughed. "I'm a terrible judge of these things," he said. "And it's really none of my business." He paused. "It's just interesting, because I remember when I met him the first time, I thought he was pretty decent. I'm surprised that he would go for someone like her."

"A lot of men will overlook a lot of flaws in a beautiful woman," I said. He must have sensed the bitterness in my tone, because he quickly changed the subject.

"Anyway, this line is finally moving. Have you decided what you want to eat?"

"Actually Martin, I think I'm going to head to the washroom. Do you mind? I'll meet you back at the seats?"

He nodded. "Of course."

I ran into Samantha again as I stood at the sink washing my hands. I hoped to make it out without speaking to her, but it wasn't my lucky night.

"Hi Sophie," she said with a smile.

I nodded at her. "Samantha. I'm a little surprised to see you here, I would have thought that your private box would have a private washroom."

She frowned slightly. "No, it doesn't," she said. "We have private catering, though."

I smiled. "Yes, you mentioned. How nice."

"Anyway, I was sorry to hear about your sister's shoplifting trouble," she said. She said shoplifting in a loud whisper, as though she was trying to be discreet, but she ended up attracting the attention of the other three women standing at the sink. "She was so lucky Jack was able to get that resolved."

I gritted my teeth. "Yes. How did you hear about that?"

"Oh, there are no secrets within a law firm," she laughed.

"I'm not sure that's something to advertise," I said.

She laughed again. "Oh, everyone's very professional." Apart from Samantha herself, who was discussing a case in a bathroom at Scotiabank Arena. "But Jack took time off from a big case to work on that, so word got around. And he pulled two senior associates to help him research shoplifting case law for a couple of days. Your sister got the best possible defense. I guess it helps to have a father with money."

"Yes. I highly recommend it." I dried my hands and walked out.

The next morning I got a text from Jack stating that a work issue had come up and he had to cancel our dinner plans. I replied saying I understood, and I did; I had cancelled many social plans myself because I just couldn't get out of the hospital in time. I tried not to read into the fact that he used the word cancel, and not reschedule. An hour later a package arrived containing my jacket and another handwritten note from Jack. It read simply:

"*I misread the situation. I apologize.*"

Twenty-three

It should have been a good week. My team of residents and students knew my style and my expectations, and we worked together like a well-oiled machine. I had made it through meetings with Dr. Jones and the Gerards, and I no longer feared the consequences of the Central Line Incident. As far as I could tell Chloe was doing well, and seemed to be enjoying teaching her barre classes. But for some reason I was tired and irritable, and the week was a slog. I felt irrationally let down by Jack, and I wasted hours trying to understand the meaning of his note. I wasn't sure what situation he could have misread. I wondered if he had started a relationship with Samantha, and thought that a cryptic note was the best way to let me down. Or maybe he had never been interested in me and thought I had misread the situation. But when I thought of the kiss, and the flowers with that charming note, I convinced myself that he had been interested and something had changed.

By Thursday evening I was physically exhausted and bruised in spirit. Chloe was out when I got home, and while I normally would have been happy that she was doing something other than watching TV, I would have appreciated her company. I had gotten an email from Stacey Sullivan that afternoon and it had made me think of Jack. I wondered if Stacey had said something to him about me, and then I remembered that he seemed to like her even less than I did.

I had just put a frozen pizza in the oven when Chloe walked in, humming, and set several shopping bags on the dining table.

"Hey, Sophie," she smiled. "Wait until you see the stuff I

bought. Just a couple of new outfits, and the nicest pair of shoes. The shoes were on sale, too."

I blinked. "Chloe, how much did you spend?" And where had she gotten the money?

She shrugged. "I don't know. Not more than a couple of thousand, I don't think."

"A couple of thousand?" I was stunned.

"Well yes, but they're investment pieces. Classics, they won't go out of style. I've decided to look for a second job, as I'm only teaching six barre classes per week, and it's so important to look professional at interviews."

At one time I would have been ecstatic to hear her talk about job hunting, but today the words washed over me.

"Where did you get the money?"

She looked defensive. "I don't think that's really your business, Sophie."

"I think it is. You've been living with me for almost two months, and I haven't asked for any rent. I buy your food. I pay your cellphone bill. I made a thousand dollar donation to a mental health charity to get you off a shoplifting charge. So if you're going to spend a couple of thousand dollars on clothes, I think it damn well is my business."

Chloe looked confused. "Only a thousand dollars?"

"What do you mean?"

"The charitable donation. I thought it was more."

I rolled my eyes. "Given that the lipstick that you took was worth less than thirty dollars it was enough. You must not have been paying attention."

"No, really. They emailed me a tax receipt."

I wanted to comment on the futility of a tax receipt for someone who had almost no income, but I held my tongue. I wished I could have had the tax receipt in my name, as I had put up the money for the donation.

Chloe pulled out her phone and scrolled through her email.

"There," she said triumphantly, handing me the phone.

"Ten thousand dollars." She smiled. "You must not have been paying attention."

I stared in disbelief at the tax receipt. She was right. She had received a receipt for a ten thousand dollar donation. I forwarded the email to myself and handed her back her phone.

The only explanation I could think of was that my parents had hired Jack to look out for Chloe, and when money was needed to make her legal problems go away, they let me pay a token amount and made up the difference themselves. I had foolishly believed that Jack had helped us because he liked me, but it now seemed clear that he had tried to get close to me to keep tabs on Chloe. I wondered if my parents knew that Jack was pretending to be interested in me, and whether it had been their idea, driven by the hope that he might help me move on from Nathan. Either way, it was an unforgivable deception.

Jack's decision to cancel our dinner date coincided with an improvement in Chloe's situation; either my parents had told him to end it, or his conscience had intervened, and he had realized that it was cruel to lead me on. I hadn't thought that my heart could break again so quickly, but it had. And once again, Chloe was indirectly responsible.

I debated whether to explain this to Chloe, but decided it wasn't the time. I still needed to sort out how she had managed to pay for her shopping spree.

"You still haven't explained how you paid for the clothes," I said. "Please tell me you didn't sign up for another credit card."

"No," Chloe shook her head happily. "I used Martin's credit card."

My heart sank. I had asked Martin to take Chloe for lunch a few times, as a favour, and she had stolen his credit card. I sighed. I would have to pay him back.

"Give it to me," I said. I pulled out my phone to call Martin. I wondered if he had figured out that his card was missing. I dreaded making the call, but it had to be done.

Chloe laughed. "Give you what?"

"Martin's credit card. We have to give it back. I'm going to call him right now to explain."

"Wait – you think I *stole* Martin's credit card?" She looked confused and hurt.

"Chloe, you just told me you bought clothes with it!" I exclaimed.

"Sophie, we went shopping together. He bought this stuff for me. We bought a lot of stuff for him too. It was a lot of fun. And it's not a lot of money for him."

I paused and took a deep breath. This was a much better explanation than theft, although her statement that it wasn't a lot of money for Martin still irritated me. I always made an effort not to take advantage of his wealth, and my sister's casual acceptance of a fortune in clothes seemed wrong. "Honestly?" I asked her. "He bought all this stuff for you?"

"Yes, honestly. I would never steal from him! I can't believe you would think that of me," she said angrily. Her face was turning red. I hadn't seen her this upset since the awful day she was caught shoplifting.

"Well, you did try to shoplift a lipstick," I said in an attempt to defend myself.

"From a *store*!" she shouted angrily. "And I was sick at the time, Sophie. Manic. But Martin is a *friend*. Don't you see how that's different?"

I realized that I had misjudged the situation. "I'm sorry Chloe, I made a mistake," I said.

"Yeah, well, I'm sick of everyone expecting the worst of me. Just because I've made a few mistakes, while I've been *mentally ill*, everyone expects the worst. You're as bad as Mom and Dad. Worse, actually."

This was incredibly hurtful. I thought I had been patient in the face of great provocation.

"Chloe, I don't think that's fair," I began.

"Of course you would say that! Everyone thinks I'm the unreasonable one. You don't understand what my life is like. I don't think you've even tried. There's no way I'm ever going to get healthy while I'm living with someone who blames me for everything."

"Well you're welcome to move out whenever you like," I said, goaded beyond endurance.

"I think that would be best. It will take me a few days to make other arrangements, so you'll have to put up with me for a little while longer. But I'll be gone as soon as I have somewhere to go."

I nodded. "Okay."

She thrust a shopping bag at me. "Here. I thought this would look good on you, so we bought it. It was final sale, and it's not my colour, so you might as well keep it. Or give it away, or throw it out, I really don't care." She walked to her room and slammed the door.

The shopping bag held a cashmere sweater in a warm shade of plum, and I couldn't stop myself from trying it on. It fit perfectly, and the cashmere was soft on my bare arms. I walked over to the mirror in the entryway and saw that Chloe had chosen well. The colour brought out my best features, and I looked like a better version of myself.

****

I didn't see Chloe before I left for work the next morning, which was a relief, because I didn't have the energy for another argument. I had mixed feelings about her decision to move out; I was concerned about where she would go and how she would manage, but I also knew that the status quo could not continue. I felt like she was taking me for granted, and my patience had run out.

I had organized to work as a locum for the weekend, in a small town called Carlisle an hour and a half east of Toronto. I would be on call from Saturday morning until Sunday evening, but I had been told that unlike being on call at a downtown hospital, I could expect to get a fair bit of sleep in the call room. It would be my first time working outside of my residency program, and I was nervous. I had planned to drive up early Saturday morning, but I decided to book a room in a motel in Carlisle for Friday night. Chloe and I needed a break from each other.

My parents were driving to the cottage tomorrow for a week's vacation, and my mother had offered to lend me her car while they were away. I had planned to Uber to their house to get it, but my mother insisted on picking me up on Friday evening. She would drive us back to the house and let me take the car.

I was still angry about the fact that my parents had hired Jack to befriend me in order to babysit Chloe, and I considered refusing the loan of the car to make a point, but I realized that would be foolish. I needed a car to get to Carlisle, and I had no desire to organize a last minute rental.

My mother had never been intimidated by city driving, and she navigated the rush hour traffic with ease.

"Thanks for picking me up," I said.

She smiled. "Happy to do it."

We drove in silence for a few minutes.

"Chloe seems to be doing well," said my mother while we were stopped at a red light.

"Where did you hear that?" I asked cautiously. I wondered if she would confess that Jack had been spying. I thought of asking if she and my dad had formally hired him to keep an eye on us or if it was a quid pro quo, with the expectation that my dad would continue to send bank business to his firm.

"Your father and I had lunch with Chloe on Wednesday. We met downtown, near your father's office."

This was the first I had heard about this, and I was surprised. The last I had heard, Chloe still hadn't forgiven my parents for their stance at the hearing.

"I see," I said.

"She looked well, much better than she did in the hospital," my mom commented.
"She seemed more positive, too. The barre classes were a brilliant idea."

I suspected that this was as close as my mother would get to an admission that she and my father had been wrong to push for Chloe to stay in the hospital.

"Yeah, she's done okay," I commented. I didn't bring up our most recent fight, or the fact that Chloe had vowed to move out.

"Did you discuss having her move back in with you?" I asked.

"No. And to be honest, I'm not sure how I would feel about that. I worry that we've been enabling her by letting her live at home, buying her a car, supporting her financially. Giving her that ultimatum was the hardest thing we've done as parents, but I think it's been good for her. I think she knows that she can't push you around the same way."

"Maybe," I said noncommittally.

We drove in silence for a few blocks.

"If you send me a list of what needs to be cancelled for the wedding, I can take care of it," my mother offered.

"Oh," I said surprised. I had thought my mother was still hoping that Nathan and I would get back together.

"You do still want to cancel the wedding?" she asked.

"Yes. Yes, definitely," I confirmed.

"Okay. Just send me a list," she said.

"Thank you," I said.

"You look surprised," said my mother.

"I am," I admitted. "I thought you were hoping I'd reconsider."

"I was concerned you were rushing the decision," she explained. "And I know that even a good person can make a mistake, or have a momentary lapse in judgment. These things aren't black and white."

I nodded but didn't say anything. It seemed black and white to me.

"But it's been over two months, and I suspect it's about more than one incident," she continued.

We were stopped at a red light, and my mother was staring

at me. I nodded again.

"Chloe told me that he suggested you give up work. Be a stay-at-home wife." She rolled her eyes. "It's the most ridiculous idea. There's no way you would be happy doing that."

"You did. Were you unhappy?" I asked.

"What?" My mother looked surprised. "Oh, Sophie, that was entirely different. I gave up teaching after fifteen years, on my own terms, not because your father thought I should or because I thought I couldn't hack it. I liked teaching, but somehow over the years it evolved from a noble calling to a bureaucratic nightmare."

She must have caught my expression, because she said: "You might think you're there already, but believe me, you're not. I've heard you talk about the patients you treat. You throw your heart into it. And if Nathan suggested you would be happier if you gave it up and stayed home to keep house, he really doesn't know you."

It seemed like my mother could forgive Nathan's infidelity but not his suggestion that I be a stay-at-home wife.

"I had some trouble at work. I made a mistake," I admitted. It was the first time I'd discussed it with my mom. I think I had hoped that if I didn't tell anyone about it, the problem would go away. "I made a mistake on a procedure and a patient had a stroke. So I was having a tough time, and I think Nathan was just trying to support me." This was a generous interpretation of his motives; it may have been part of it, but I think the truth was that he wanted to get back together and was willing to say anything to get me to agree. But ironically, now that my mother had turned against Nathan I felt the need to defend him.

"I suppose Nathan's never made a mistake?" My mother sounded a lot like Jack.

"I'm sure he has, but probably not like this." Although I doubted he would have told me if he had.

"And if he had, would you have suggested he quit?

I had never looked at it that way. "Probably not."

"Sophie, if Nathan wanted to support you he should have believed in you."

***

I had a lot to think about on the drive to Carlisle. It was a relief to get out of the city, and I hoped that some physical distance would help turn my thoughts away from Chloe, Nathan and Jack. Especially Jack.

The first patient I saw was an elderly lady with a straightforward case of pneumonia. I had admitted hundreds of patients with pneumonia during my residency, and I could do the orders in my sleep. I admitted her and moved on.

I moved on and dealt with a diabetic patient with a critically high blood sugar. As I was finishing up my notes, I got called because the first patient, the lady who I thought had a straightforward case of pneumonia, now had a low blood pressure. I tried more fluids, but her blood pressure didn't improve. She needed a central line and vasopressors to bring up her blood pressure. I considered asking if one of the ER doctors could do it, but I wasn't sure how to explain why I couldn't.

So I explained the procedure to the patient and had her sign a consent form. She was incredibly anxious and so was I. My hands shook as I set up the equipment and positioned the sterile drape.

"You're going to feel ultrasound gel on your neck, it's really cold," I warned her. She was trembling, and it was causing the sterile drape to move up and down.

I kept talking to try to calm her down.

"I went to see the new James Bond movie last night," I told her. When I arrived at the motel I had been too keyed up to sleep, so I had found the movie theatre. "I had been wanting to see it for a while. It's about time they gave the role to a woman."

She didn't reply, and I didn't expect her to, but the trembling stopped and I could tell she had relaxed. I kept up a monologue of meaningless chatter, hoping to distract her and myself.

I placed the ultrasound on her neck and immediately got beautiful images of her jugular vein, right where it was supposed to be. And all of a sudden I relaxed too. I had done this before and I could do this today.

"This is the freezing, you'll feel a sting and a burn," I explained. I heard a faint "okay" from under the drape. And I kept talking through the rest of the procedure, which went as smoothly as anyone could have hoped. I secured the line with a suture and removed the drape.

"All done," I announced.

She looked surprised. "That wasn't nearly as bad as I thought."

I was thinking the same thing.

I immediately thought of Jack, and wanted to send him a text to let him know that I had successfully placed a central line. Then I remembered that my parents had probably been paying him to serve as my psychotherapist, and he wasn't actually interested in my career. I thought of texting Chloe, which was strange because I hadn't told her about the Central Line Incident, but then I remembered our fight. In the end I sent a message to Lucy.

"Just put in a central line. Went well."

Her reply came back minutes later: "Never any doubt!"

The real excitement started in the afternoon. The ER was starting to fill up when the paramedics brought in a fifty-six year old man with chest pain. His ECG suggested he was having a bad heart attack. The ER doctor drew some bloodwork, gave him some aspirin, and referred him to me.

He looked miserable, sweaty and breathless, and it was clear that he was going to need thrombolytic therapy to break up the clot blocking his artery. I had never prescribed it. In fact, I had never even seen it given. In Toronto, when a patient had a heart attack an interventional cardiologist did a procedure to stent the blockage. But out here, there were no interventional cardiologists. Hell, this Saturday there wasn't even a cardiologist. The Emergency doctor had moved on to her next emergency. So I was it. I asked the nurse if there were any protocols for thrombolysis, and she found me an order set. I checked the appropriate boxes and watched the nurse hang the IV bag.

Within ten minutes of receiving the thrombolytic therapy he was feeling much better, and his repeat ECG showed improvement. At the moment he was stable, but he would still need to be transferred out for an angiogram to make sure that the blockage had fully cleared.

I put through a call to CritiCall, to try to get him transferred to Toronto, which was the closest major centre. After I gave the operator my name and asked to be connected to the on-call cardiologist, I was told to hold for Dr. Fox.

During the two minutes it took for Nathan to respond to the page I thought about the likelihood that he would be on-call. Only the final year residents answered CritiCalls, and there were nine others in his year. So a one in ten chance. Just my luck.

"Dr. Fox," he said confidently.

"It's Sophie Ingram. I'm working in Carlisle this weekend, and I have a fifty-six year old man with a heart attack. His chest pain started two hours ago while raking leaves, and his ECG showed inferior ST elevations. We thrombolysed him, and - "

"Does he have any cardiac risk factors?" Nathan cut in.

"He's a former smoker. No other known risk factors but he hasn't seen a doctor in years," I answered.

"Did you consider other possible causes of his chest pain?" Nathan asked. His tone was condescending, as though he had already decided that I had done a suboptimal job. I couldn't tell if this was his usual attitude to community doctors who called him for help or if this was just a convenient opportunity to criticize me.

"The history and ECG were both consistent with a heart attack," I explained. "After we gave him the thrombolytics his pain improved."

"Do you have a troponin back yet?" he asked.

"No, not yet," I admitted. "That may take another hour."

"Well, I can't justify accepting this patient in transfer when we're not even sure that he's having a heart attack," he said pompously.

"Nathan," I said quietly. "You're better than this."

Suddenly Nathan's tone of voice changed. It was as though my words had flipped a switch and changed him from Nathan the physician to Nathan the person. I had long envied his ability to compartmentalize his personal and professional lives, to make medical decisions that weren't clouded by emotion and then go home and forget about work. It was why he was a good doctor. It was also why he would never be a great one.

Now he was trying to convince himself that he was a good man.

"Sophie, I was wrong. I treated you disrespectfully and I regret it." He paused. I was so surprised that I didn't say anything. "You can't imagine how much I regret it," he continued. "If I could go back and do things differently I would."

I couldn't imagine what the CritiCall operator would make of this. It was probably the first time she had heard an academic physician give an abject apology for belittling someone who was trying to make a referral. I knew that his apology was about far more than our current argument, and it was the most sincere apology I had heard him make since the beginning of the debacle with Chloe. I realized the guts it must have taken for him to say this with an audience, even if it was just a CritiCall operator.

"Thank you for that, Dr. Fox," I replied. "I think we can both move on now."

"But Sophie, I want you to know, if there's anything I can do - "

"I'd really appreciate it if you accepted this patient in transfer, Dr. Fox," I cut in. "I'll send along my notes in the transfer package.

"Of course Sophie," he said. He paused. "Take care of yourself."

There was a beat of silence on the line before the CritiCall operator cut in to close what was undoubtedly one of the strangest phone calls she had ever facilitated.

"Thank you, doctors," she said. "We will organize emergency transport. Are we done?"

"Yes," Nathan and I said simultaneously. And we were.

Twenty-four

Overall, the weekend was a success, and on Sunday afternoon I got an email from the Carlisle Hospital Chief of Medicine to say that the staff had enjoyed working with me. They hoped I would pick up more locum work and consider applying for a permanent position there when I finished my residency. I knew they were fairly desperate for doctors, but I was still flattered. When I returned to my apartment late Sunday night I was in a much better mood than I had been when I had left on Friday. I didn't see Chloe, but I remembered that she had been the one to push me to try locums outside of the city. If nothing else, I owed her for that. I fell into bed and sleep came quickly.

The next morning I found a note from Chloe scrawled across the fridge calendar in purple dry erase marker. "*Sophie – I've made a big decision and gone away for a while. Don't worry about me. Love, Chloe.*" She hadn't bothered to erase 'Take a Shower', her first and only entry on the calendar, but had written her note around it.

I panicked. Chloe hadn't put a date on her note, and I realized that it could have been written anytime since Friday morning, when I had last used the fridge. For that matter, I couldn't remember whether I had even used the fridge on Friday, and the note could date back to Thursday night. It was horribly vague, and could mean anything from 'I've gone to stay with a friend' to 'I've decided to join a cult.' It didn't really seem like a suicide note, and 'gone away for awhile' implied that she would be coming back. But with Chloe, I never knew.

I tried to call Chloe, but wasn't surprised when her phone went straight to voicemail. A quick search of her room showed that her designer suitcase was still in the closet. I called my mother, then my father, but neither answered. They had chosen this, of all weeks, to go to the cottage, and there was a good chance that they were boating and hadn't taken their phones. My father works insane hours most weeks, but he makes it very clear to his colleagues that when he is on vacation, he is unavailable. I left frantic messages for both of them, and then debated what to do next. I considered calling 911, but decided against it. I doubted the police would be too concerned about an adult who had left a note to say she was going away for a while, and then had, in fact, gone away.

I sent Dr. Hastings a text message to say that I was sick and wouldn't be able to come in. It was the first time I had called in sick since I had had a bad case of flu in my first year of residency. Unlike my parents, she called me back immediately. I could tell she wasn't happy about this, and she even asked if I could review cases with the residents by phone, but I explained that I felt too unwell to focus properly, and in the interests of safe patient care, she would have to do it. I knew that she didn't spend much time in the trenches, and under different circumstances I would have loved to be a fly on the wall when she reviewed with the residents. But today I really was unable to focus.

I wondered if Chloe had decided that living with my parents was preferable to living with me, and had run back to our parents' house. I drove my mother's car over and let myself in. It was pristine, spotless, with no signs that Hurricane Chloe had touched down.

On the way back to my apartment I thought of Martin, who had had lunch with Chloe just last week and might have some insight about her mental state. I was also prepared to beg him to use his considerable resources to pull strings and help me look for her. But his phone went to voicemail too.

I didn't have contact information for Chloe's other friends, and I was running out of ideas. I unlocked my phone, planning to scroll through my contacts in search of someone who might know Chloe's whereabouts, and saw that I had received a text from Jack. "Sophie, we need to talk. Let me know if I can call or come by later today." Hope flared; there was a chance he was in touch with my parents or with Chloe. I took a deep breath and called him.

His phone went to voicemail, and I didn't bother to leave a message. I got a text reply thirty seconds later, stating simply: "In meeting. Call later? Or coffee tonight?"

"Chloe is missing," I texted.

"What do you mean?"

"I haven't seen her since Thursday night. I was away for the weekend, and this morning I found a strange note from her."

He called me less than a minute later.

"What's going on, Sophie?"

I told him about our fight, then coming home after a weekend away to find this awful, ambiguous note.

"It's okay, Sophie. I'm sure she's fine. She's probably gone to stay with friends. We'll find her. Can you read me the note?"

I read it out to him.

"Okay. Don't panic. 'Gone for a while' implies she's coming back.

"You would think. But she's not always rational."

"I assume your parents don't know where she is?"

"I can't reach them. They're at the cottage, I've left messages."

"When did your parents leave? Could Chloe have gone with them? Or left to join them?"

"I hadn't thought of that. The cottage has never really been her thing, but it's possible, I guess."

"Okay. So there's a good chance she's at the cottage, or on her way up there. Sophie, I'll be right over. I want you to have something to eat. I'll be there within twenty minutes and we can talk about what to do next."

I already felt a little better.

True to his word, he was there within twenty minutes, carrying coffee and pastries. It was clear he had come from work, as he was dressed in a designer navy suit over a cream silk shirt. He looked so confident and capable, and I was so tired and anxious, it was all I could do not to throw myself at him and cry on his shoulder.

"Have you had anything to eat yet?"

"No."

"Okay, first thing then, I brought macarons, and I think you should eat one."

When I had had a few bites of a pistachio macaron he asked to see the note, so I directed him to the fridge door.

"Okay, this could really mean anything. There's no need to panic yet."

I laughed. I was almost hysterical. "I'm glad you think so. Because I was thinking we should call the hospitals, maybe the police -"

"Hey." He closed the distance between us and put a hand on my shoulder. "Slow down. I know you're imagining the worst-case scenario. It's how you're wired. I am too. It's why we're good at our jobs. But ninety-nine times in a hundred, the worst-case scenario doesn't happen. Have faith, sweetheart."

In spite of everything, I was really enjoying the feeling of his hand on my shoulder, and I was seconds away from resting my head on his chest when we were interrupted by a loud knock on the apartment door. I ran to answer it, hoping that it was Chloe and she had forgotten her key.

But it was Samantha Albright, and she looked incensed. Before I could say anything, she pushed past me and headed straight for Jack.

"You need to get back to the office right away," Samantha said. "The deal is going to fall apart. Johnson is livid that you left and is threatening to walk. Tony tried to step in, but he couldn't answer half the questions. He convinced everyone to take a coffee break and meet back in an hour. There's a chance we can save this if you come back now."

"No," said Jack simply.

"Jack, you don't understand. He's not bluffing. We'll lose this deal."

"I don't give a damn about the deal," Jack said quietly.

Samantha threw up her hands. "Then I don't understand," she said angrily. "The biggest deal I've ever worked on, and you walk out on it because Sophie calls? Has her precious sister stolen something else?"

"Samantha, I apologize for walking out. I'll apologize to Johnson and to everyone involved when I'm back in the office. But that won't be today. And you need to leave." He paused. "How did you even know where I was?"

"When you stepped out of the meeting to make your call, one of the secretaries heard the name Sophie. As I was the only one who knew where Sophie lives, I was sent here to look for you. Mary has gone to check your condo."

He looked puzzled. "How did Mary get involved in this?"

"Jack, the whole firm knows about this. Jack Delacroix walked out on a deal. It doesn't look good for you. For any of us."

He nodded. "I see. Well, Samantha, thank you for coming. You can head back to the office now and tell everyone that you've found me and advised me of the situation."

Samantha looked like wanted to argue further, but Jack's expression was uncompromising. She stood and moved towards the door.

As she reached the front hallway the door opened and Chloe burst into the apartment, followed closely by Martin Chu who was dragging a large suitcase on wheels. Chloe stopped when she saw Samantha in the front hallway and stared, bewildered.

"What are you doing here?" she asked bluntly. "I thought Sophie told you to stay away from our apartment."

Samantha rolled her eyes. "I was looking for Jack," she said. "But don't worry, I'm leaving."

Chloe nodded. "Good." She spotted me standing next to the dining table and ran towards me. She looked happier than I had seen her in months.

"Sophie, you'll never guess! We went to Vegas and got married!"

Twenty-five

"I'm sorry? Who did you marry?" I didn't understand. I hoped Chloe hadn't married a complete stranger, and I couldn't figure out how Martin had gotten involved in this fiasco.

"We got married!" She held out her left hand, to show me an enormous diamond ring. I noticed that Martin was wearing a sheepish look.

"To each other?" I couldn't keep the shock out of my voice.

Chloe looked insulted. "Of course to each other, silly. Who else?"

"Wow, that's a surprise. I didn't even know you guys were dating," I said.

"It's a recent thing," said Chloe. "But when you know, you know. I was telling Martin that I had always dreamed of eloping to Vegas. So romantic. So we decided to seize the day."

"Yes, very romantic," I said, for lack of anything else to say. And cliché. And a little trashy. I kept those other thoughts to myself.

"Martin chartered a private plane. I've never been on a private plane before, Sophie, it's so much nicer, you can't imagine. You should really try it sometime. And then we got married in the Elvis chapel." She laughed. "We didn't pack anything, but the shopping in Vegas is *amazing*. We bought a lot more stuff, but had it sent straight to Martin's condo."

"Wow," I said. "That's amazing."

Chloe nodded. "So I'm moving into Martin's condo, obviously. We've been talking about buying a house. So my housing problem is solved."

I flushed at that, sensitive about the fact that I had asked her to move out. I looked at Martin, worried that he would think that she had married him for a place to live. But Martin was gazing at her like a man who had won the lottery.

"Excuse me," came a loud voice from the front hall. I had forgotten that Samantha was still there. "Was this your emergency, Jack? Please tell me you didn't abandon the biggest deal of the year because this crazy bitch eloped?"

Martin turned toward her. "What did you say?" In the two decades I had known him, I had never seen him look so angry.

"I called her crazy. You must know that she is. You're in for a rude awakening if you don't. She recently spent a month in the psych ward, where she pretended to be a princess." Samantha laughed.

"If I'm not mistaken, you learned about her health history in your role as her parents' lawyer," Martin said. He spoke calmly, but there was no mistaking the steel in his voice. "And you attended a hearing that was understood to be confidential. You clearly have trouble with the concept of confidentiality, so let me explain something to you. If you speak about her, write about her, post on social media about her, if you so much as mention her name, I will see you disbarred."

Samantha laughed again. "I'm not sure how long she'll be your wife. Her parents will probably try to get the marriage annulled, on the grounds that she wasn't capable of consenting to it."

Chloe looked at Martin anxiously. "Could they do that?"

Martin turned to look at Chloe, and his expression softened. "No. I mean, they could try, but they wouldn't succeed. I know some excellent lawyers. In the unlikely event that your parents want to waste their time on this, we'll drag out the court fight until they run out of money. Or until they see how happy we are together and give up the fight." He kissed the top of her head. "I wouldn't jump to the conclusion that your parents will be unhappy. Surprised, yes, but I've always gotten along with them. I think they were hoping that Sophie and I would get together at one point." He winked at me, and I blushed. This was a side of Martin I had never seen.

Samantha couldn't let it go. "Her parents won't run out of money," she said scornfully. "Her Dad's a bloody CEO! But you must know that. I assume you married her for the money she's likely to inherit. You'll probably have to wait years."

Martin stared at her, as though she was a piece of gum he had scraped off his shoe. "I don't understand why you're here," he said to her. "As this is really none of your business. But I'll give you some advice." He looked at her Vuitton purse. "I may not spend money on overpriced accessories, but you shouldn't assume that I don't have money to spend on other things." He smiled at Samantha, but it was not a pleasant smile. I barely recognized him. "And I'm confident that I have more than enough money to ruin you." He took a breath. "I married Chloe because I love her. I would do anything for her. Don't ever forget that."

Samantha looked at him, confused. Seeing that she was on the brink of opening her mouth again, Jack walked towards her and whispered in her ear. She flushed as red as a tomato.

"Uh, I'm sorry," she said weakly.

Martin nodded. "I trust you can find your own way to the door." Samantha turned and left. I wanted to clap.

Chloe broke the silence that followed Samantha's departure.

"Guess what else?" she said.

"What else?" I asked.

She laughed. "You're supposed to guess."

"I can't guess, Chloe, you'll just have to tell me."

"I'm going to work with Martin. I'm going to teach."

"You're going to teach *coding*?" I asked. I doubted Chloe knew any more about coding than I did. Which was absolutely nothing.

"Of course not, I know nothing about coding," she said with a laugh. "I'm going to teach dance."

"Dance?" I asked.

"Yep. I think I'll be really good at it," she said confidently.

"How does dance fit into the coding class?" I had a vision of Chloe pirouetting around rows of computers.

"It will be a separate class. We'll offer combination sessions. An hour of coding followed by an hour of dance. It won't be just ballet, either, I'll incorporate some hip hop, jazz, maybe even some yoga. There will be mostly classical music, to appeal to the parents, with some pop thrown in to appeal to the kids. And if it's popular, I'll start training more dance instructors for other branches."

It was a good idea, actually. A ton of parents were concerned that their kids spent too much time in front of screens and not enough time moving. A one-stop program that offered both coding and some physical activity would be really popular. Martin's waitlists would grow even longer.

"That's a great idea, Chloe," I said. "Congratulations."

She nodded. "Thanks. We're going to call it DANCE CODE."

I smiled. "It's brilliant."

Chloe smiled back. "Thanks. I think it will be a good project for me. I'm going to go pack up my stuff." She left for her room. Martin and I were left staring awkwardly at each other.

An elopement was exactly the sort of thing I would have expected from my sister, but the last thing I would have expected from Martin. I hoped that Chloe hadn't somehow tricked him into it.

"Um, congratulations?" I said uncertainly.

He smiled. "Thank you, Sophie." I debated whether to say more.

"I never would have guessed you would elope," I laughed awkwardly. "Chloe yes, but it just seems so out of character for you."

"Maybe you don't know me as well as you think."

"Maybe not." I realized that was true. He had seemed like a completely different person when he had taken on Samantha in defense of my sister. "You know that she may not be stable on the valproic acid long-term, right? She's likely to have another manic break, or depressive episode -"

Martin cut me off. "Sophie, I know that.   And I could be paralyzed in a car crash tomorrow. I can't predict the future." He smiled. "But I went into this with my eyes open."

Although I realized that warning Martin about Chloe's challenges after he had married her was akin to closing the barn door after the horses had bolted, I couldn't stop myself from saying everything I would have said if he had asked for my advice before the elopement. I felt guilty that I had played a role in bringing them together, and I worried things would end badly.

"It's just hard to imagine the stress and the uncertainty until you're living with it," I continued. "And it's really hard to find good mental health care. I know you could afford private care, but our system probably wouldn't allow it. The Canadian dream, huh? Universally mediocre health care for all." I laughed weakly. It was funny and tragic at the same time. "It sometimes feels like you're never off duty, you know?"

I realized that Martin was no longer smiling. "Chloe will never be a duty, Sophie," he said emphatically. "I'm happier when I'm with her than I've ever been before in my life. I'm not going to stand here and listen to you disparage her. I'll go help her pack." He turned and walked out. I heard the door to Chloe's bedroom close.

I sat down at the table and mindlessly ate a macaron. Jack walked over and sat down next to me. He had been sitting in a corner of the apartment and reading something on his phone while I talked to Martin. Giving us as much privacy as was possible in my shoebox apartment without hiding in a bedroom or bathroom.

"This may not be the best time for this, but I'm sorry, Sophie," he said gently.

"Why did you do it?"

He looked confused. "Do what?"

"Lie to me. I know my parents were paying you to watch

out for us. I can understand why they did it, but it's insulting. I'm an adult. And I trusted you when you said my father wasn't involved."

"What? Sophie, I never lied about that. The day after that damned hearing I sent your father a letter stating that I could no longer represent him on this issue. I was very clear. He wasn't happy, but he understood. You can ask him."

Now I was confused. "So why were you helping us? And who made the ten thousand dollar charitable donation?"

His cheeks went pink. "How did you find out about that?"

"I saw the tax receipt. I knew I only paid a thousand, so I guessed my parents had made up the difference. At first I thought my parents were paying you to keep an eye on us, like Samantha did with the photos. But you insisted that wasn't the case, and I believed you. I thought that you were helping us out of the goodness of your heart, and we had avoided a shoplifting charge by making a comically small charitable donation. You must have thought we were pretty naïve. And I still don't understand where the money came from."

He looked uncomfortable. "Sophie. It was my fault that the prosecutor requested ten grand. The truth is, I didn't approach him properly. I should have opened with the fact that your parents kicked Chloe out of their house because of her mental illness. But I didn't, so when he saw the address on her driver's license he came up with an amount that he thought was appropriate given her financial situation. I didn't want you to suffer for my mistake. You were doing a good thing, trying to help your sister, and the money was going to a good cause. So I made up the difference."

"And by made up the difference, you mean you let me pay ten percent while you paid ninety? I'm not a charity case, Jack." I reached for my phone. "I'll e-transfer you the money right away. I paused, remembering that the e-transfer limit on my account was two thousand dollars. Transferring the money in instalments over five days would diminish the gesture. "Actually I'll write you a cheque." If I could find my chequebook.

"Sophie, please. You don't have to do that."

"I think I do." I paused as I remembered what Samantha had told me. "And did you really pull two senior associates to research shoplifting case law for two days? Let me know the cost of their hours, too." The money would have to come from my line of credit, but I would pay it.

"Sophie, I don't want your money." He seemed almost angry.

"I don't understand."

He looked at me. "Don't you?"

"No. I really don't understand any of this. And if you weren't working for my parents, what were you apologizing for? If what you say is true, you've been nothing but generous to Chloe and me. Since the day of the hearing, I mean. I'm clearly missing something here."

His face was turning red.

"I don't remember apologizing," he began.

"After Martin left, you said you were sorry."

"Oh. I was trying to be sympathetic. But the truth is, I'm not sorry."

I was still confused. "About what? This isn't exactly a bad outcome for me. I mean, I'm surprised that they eloped. But I'm already getting used to the idea, and I think this may turn out to be a good thing for Chloe. I've been pretty upfront with Martin about her situation, so as he said, he went into it with his eyes open. And if she has more psychiatric problems, and there are concerns about her capacity to make decisions, he can deal with it. It won't be my responsibility anymore."

He looked surprised, and still sympathetic. And hopeful? "I don't know how you can forgive them so easily. I know you and Martin were together. Especially after what happened with Nathan, this must be incredibly painful, and you handled it very well." His smile was hesitant, almost shy. "You've handled everything very well."

Suddenly everything clicked. "You thought I was dating Martin?"

"I saw you at the Leafs game. I had noticed you and Chloe even before Sam and I ran into you in the snack line. You were very visible with your Maple Leaf hats." He smiled at the memory. "Anyway, I saw you with Martin. You were whispering in his ear."

"I was explaining the offside rule. It was loud."

He snorted. "It took you a hell of a long time to explain the offside rule."

"I might have had to explain icing too. Martin's never been into hockey, he just took us because Chloe's a huge fan. He'd take Chloe anywhere she wanted to go. Jack, I've been friends with Martin since elementary school, and he's been in love with Chloe for almost that long. There was a period of several months when he could barely speak in her presence, he just sort of turned red and stammered. It was a bit of a joke at our house. When he regained the ability to speak, he tutored her in math for a while. Mostly I think he just did her homework for her. And he and I were friends, and we stayed in touch, and whenever I saw him he asked about her."

I paused. Jack didn't say anything; he just sat there and stared at me.

I offered him the box of macarons. "Eat something?"

"Unbelievable," he muttered. His voice was husky and so low I could barely hear him.

"What?"

Jack put his arms around me and lifted me to my feet, pulling my face into his chest.

"Unbelievable that any man acquainted with you would pay any attention to your sister." And then he lifted my chin and kissed me.

***

Because Chloe and Martin were still packing her stuff, we left them to it and drove to Jack's condo. I already knew the way to the bedroom, and today I found myself there by choice. It felt exciting and comfortable at the same time, like simultaneously starting a great adventure and coming home.

"I can't believe you thought I was with Martin," I said, sometime later. "To be fair, there was a time when my mother encouraged me in that direction." I laughed. "But there was never any spark."

"I hope not," he said.

"Although I thought that you were interested in Chloe for a while," I admitted.

He sat up straight. "What?" He looked so appalled that I burst out laughing.

"Men usually are," I said. "And you made it perfectly clear that you took on the shoplifting case as a favour to Chloe, not to me."

He laughed. "Sophie, it's true that I didn't want you as a client. Dating a client's sister is awkward enough, but dating a client is far worse. And I knew I wanted to date you. I wished I didn't, because it was damned inconvenient, but it was a force beyond my control."

"Oh," I said. I was silent for a moment, working through what he had said. "You found it inconvenient?"

"Sophie, I found my attraction to you inconvenient. Falling in love with you was inconvenient. But I found you irresistible.

"Could a relationship with me cause problems for you? With the Law Society, I mean?"

He shook his head. "It's not ideal, but I'm not worried. I've looked into it. You may be interested to know that of all the provinces, Ontario has some of the most permissive laws for lawyers dating their clients. But even though it's technically allowed, it wouldn't look great. So I wanted it to be clear that Chloe was the client, not you."

So this was why he had emphasized that he was helping Chloe with the shoplifting, and had wanted the donation to come from Chloe's account. "When did you look into this?"

He looked embarrassed. "After you came to confront us about the photos Sam took of your apartment."

"You were interested then?" I asked, surprised.

His face flushed. "Yeah. I blew off a lunch meeting to drink coffee with you, and it wasn't just because I was concerned you would complain about Sam's photography. Then I spent a week trying to think of an excuse to get in touch with you, and I had made up my mind to ask your dad for your number when you called about Chloe's shoplifting." He paused. "Actually, I've been interested in you since your performance at that ridiculous hearing."

I shook my head, barely able to believe it.

"Why do you look so surprised?" he asked.

"I don't know," I said. "I think it's because you've got your life together, and you're successful, and when you're not being insulting you're incredibly kind. And, you know . . ." I trailed off, searching for the words to describe his looks. He was smiling now.

"No, I don't know," he teased. "You'll have to explain it to me."

"You look good," I said simply. "And men like you aren't usually all that keen to date me. Chloe, yes. But not me."

"You underrate yourself," he said fiercely. "Sophie, your sister is very beautiful. And I hope she and Martin will be very happy together. But I find you much more interesting." He smiled and kissed the tip of my nose.

"Just interesting?" I asked.

"Also intelligent. Witty. Compassionate. Incredibly beautiful and infinitely desirable," he continued. "But you must know that."

I smiled. "I think you should show me again," I said, and he did.

Epilogue

From: Erika.Hastings@torontohealthteams.ca
To: Sophie.Ingram@torontohealthteams.ca
Subject: Clinical Fellowship

Dear Dr. Ingram:

Congratulations! Given your exemplary performance throughout your residency training we would like to offer you a position as a Clinical Research Fellow for the upcoming year.

We recognize that your MoPPET Quality Improvement project has been a tremendous success, and would like to see you expand it throughout the rest of the hospital. We hope that you will take this on as your Fellowship project.

We encourage all of our clinical associates to pursue a Master's degree, which is now a requirement for academic promotion. We suggest you consider a Master's in Quality Improvement.

Funding has been secured, and we are pleased to offer a five percent raise over your salary as a resident.

We believe you have a bright future in academic medicine.

Sincerely,

Erika Hastings, BSc (Hons), MD, PhD, FRCPC
Division Head, General Internal Medicine

***

From: Stacey.Sullivan@torontohealthteams.ca
To: Sophie.Ingram@torontohealthteams.ca
Re: Organic diet/detergents

Hi Sophie!

It was so nice to see you at dinner last week. Austin talks about you often.

I realized that we never closed the loop about Mr. Warner and his request for organic food. Now that he has been admitted again, he has sent me some literature about the benefits of an organic diet, which I have attached for your review. He has also sent me a list of acceptable organic laundry detergents. If you prefer, we could meet in person to discuss this.

Warm regards,
Stacey Sullivan, BA, MA
Office of the Ombudsperson, Toronto Health Teams.
Committed to equity and excellence

www.ingramcontent.com/pod-product-compliance
Lightning Source LLC
Chambersburg PA
CBHW071602150726
48000CB00004B/1566